DIARY OF A SURFER VILLAGER

Books 6-10

(a collection of UNOFFICIAL Minecraft books)

By,

Be sure to check out my other books, including:

Published by Eclectic Esquire Media, LLC
P.O. Box 235094
Encinitas, CA 92023-5094
www.drblockbooks.com

Table of Contents

Book 6

AN UNOFFICIAL MINECRAFT BOOK

DIARY OF A

Surfer Villager

BOOK 6

DR. BLOCK

Day 31

Yesterday was a very emotional one. After Notch appeared and decreed there would be a series of three surf contests, the lieutenant of the Ender King teleported me, Emma, and Mr. Blaze back to Zombie Bane.

In Zombie Bane, Emma and I were reunited with our parents. Everyone was crying. Even Mr. Blaze shed a few tears as he watched the joyful reunion.

After I explained how Mr. Blaze had put the vision of hope into our parents' heads to believe we were still alive, our parents thanked him for helping get them through the worst days of their lives.

My family and Emma's family went over to Biff's house. Biff's parents apologized for the evilness of Clayton. They asked us if it were true that Notch had agreed to Herobrine's idea about the surf contest rather than war.

"You could say that," I had said, "but you could also say that Notch does whatever he wants and he would have stopped the war anyway, even if Herobrine had no ideas."

Biff's parents said there were rumors circulating in Zombie Bane that Herobrine and Notch weren't telling everything. Some said Herobrine and Notch were part of one religious duality.

Biff's parents said some more stuff, but I tuned out after I heard the word "duality." I mean, I realize that I should pay attention to important stuff like the manifestation of the Great Creator and his relationship with Herobrine, but my brain just shuts off when I hear fancy words like that.

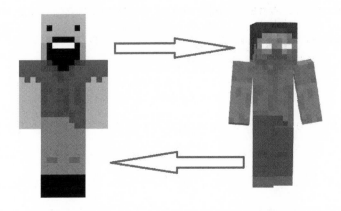

I just knew that Notch was in charge and that surfing was going to decide the dispute between the Dretskys and the Ender King. It was very awesome, humbling, and frightening at the same time.

Biff's parents decided to have a barbecue to celebrate our safe return and the avoidance of war. We ate pork chops and steak and chicken and watermelons and apples and carrots. Mr. Blaze even brought out a few dried chorus fruits that he saved for special occasions. We each ate a chorus fruit and teleported a short distance. It was pretty fun, but once you had teleported with an enderman, chorus fruit was a poor substitute.

As the sun began to set, we all returned home, fearing the appearance of zombies and the other mobs of the night. When I got home, my mom pulled out a gigantic apple pie and gave the entire thing to me.

"I'm so happy you're alive, Jimmy," she said as a slight mist of tears appeared in the center of her eyes. "I don't know what I would've done if you hadn't returned."

"I'm glad I'm back too, Mom," I said with a mouthful of apple pie. "I'm just glad Emma was there in the Nether. Without her, I'm not sure I would've ever escaped, and we'd be in the middle of a gigantic war between the Ender Army and Capitol City."

My mom smiled at me and patted my head and said, "I have to admit, when you first started to do all that surfing stuff I thought it was pretty stupid and reckless. But now, even Notch thinks it's cool. I guess I think it's pretty cool too."

I smiled at my mom as I finished the rest of the apple pie.

As a result of eating so much food at Biff's house and now a gigantic apple pie, I was slowly slipping into a food coma. I went upstairs, brushed my teeth, and went to sleep.

Now, I have just woken up in the morning and wrote that stuff you just read in my diary because I thought it was important and I didn't have time to write it yesterday.

Anyway, so I woke up and stretched, brushed my teeth, fixed my hair, and put on my robe. I was excited to get back to the Surf 'n Snack to see how things have gone in my absence and to find out how many emeralds I had earned.

I also wanted to get back in the water. It had been several days since I'd been surfing and already I was feeling sad and depressed. Surfing always did away with those feelings in me.

After a big breakfast and *another* apple pie (my mom obviously missed me), I walked to Emma's house to pick her up on the way to the Surf 'n Snack.

"Emma, what's up?" I said as I approached the fence surrounding her yard. She was outside messing around with some redstone and various switches.

"Hey, Jimmy, I'm just trying to come up with a more efficient mechanism to generate waves."

Oh, that Emma, always thinking about science.

"You know ... hurrr ... before Clayton sent me to the Nether, I surfed his wave pool. It was pretty awesome. He had three different types of waves."

Emma looked up, her eyes wide. "What types of waves?"

"Well, he had a long barreling A-frame wave, like we have, and he also had a really mushy, soft wave that you can learn on. Then, he had a really long, point-break style wave that didn't have a barrel, but you could do a lot of maneuvers on."

Emma shook her head. "How are we supposed to practice for that contest in Capitol City if we only have one type of wave?"

I shrugged. "I don't know, should we build another wave pool somewhere?"

"That would be ideal, but how could we build a wave pool with three different waves without being able to manipulate the floor of the ocean? We would have to swim and move rocks around."

I shrugged again. I liked shrugging. It kept my shoulders loose and ready for paddling out into the water. "Maybe the Ender King will have some ideas?"

"I guess so."

I suddenly remembered the fourth member of our surf team. "By the way, have you seen Laird around?"

She shook her head. "I haven't seen him in a week."

I rubbed my chin in thought. "Yeah, the last time I saw him was at the Capitol City wave pool a couple days ago." I was somewhat concerned. There was no way to contact Laird via some miraculous technology, like sending sound over the air in an analog or digital format, which is what I've heard some players call a "telephone." So, we were kind of at the mercy of Laird just showing up.

"Maybe the Ender King will have some ideas about how to track him down?" said Emma.

I smiled, but it probably looked like I was in pain. It was one of those unhappy smiles people make when they don't know what else to do. "I hope so. If not, we will have to find someone else to be on the team."

Emma stood up. "I'm sure it will all work out. Let's go surfing!"

I smiled again; this time for real. "Yes, let's!"

* * *

As Emma and I walked to the Surf 'n Snack, we passed by the library. We noticed that there were several police officers standing outside the library, each holding iron swords.

I nudged Emma and said, "I guess the books are dangerous now, right?"

Emma smirked in pain at my pathetic joke and walked up to one of the police officers. "What's going on Officer ... um?"

"It's Officer Wyatt, little girl," he said gruffly.

"Well, hurrr, Officer Wyatt, why are you standing outside the library?"

The police officer looked at her and said, "We're making sure that no criminals use the DOTS."

"What's the DOTS?" asked Emma.

"It stands for the Dretsky Overworld Transportation System. After Notch prevented Clayton from enslaving villagers, Clayton converted his slave and resource transportation system to a public transportation system to help villagers travel through the Overworld more easily."

I shook my head. I couldn't believe this. Someone as evil and horrible as Clayton, whom Notch punishes, still ends up making money from his old slavery infrastructure. This was crazy. And, he converted it in a single day!

"That's stupid!" I yelled. "It's not fair!"

The police officer shrugged. "I just do what I'm told."

"How much does it cost to use the DOTS?" asked Emma.

"I'm not sure, but I've heard people say it's only a few emeralds to go between here and Captiol City and the trip only takes like thirty seconds," said Officer Wyatt.

Even though I hated Clayton, I had to admit that he was able to make lemonade out of lemons. Of course, I don't really know what a lemon is since I've never seen one, but I've heard players use that expression: "When life gives you lemons, make lemonade."

Anyway, I actually wanted to use the transportation system the see where else it went besides Capitol City.

"So, if we want to use the DOTS, we just head inside the library and someone will tell us what to do?" I asked.

The officer nodded his head.

I looked over at Emma. "Come on, let's check it out. I bet it's wicked"

"Wicked?!? Is that your catchphrase now?" asked Emma.

"I don't have a catchphrase. I just heard some of the other kids using it and I thought it sounded ... hurrr .... well ... wicked."

Emma shook her head. "It sounds ... hurrr ... I don't know ... like something a school-aged wizard in England might say."

"Where's England?"

"Oh, I met a girl player a few weeks ago who said she was from there. It's some dimension where the players live. They call it a 'country' or a 'kingdom' or something."

11

"The world where the players come from sounds weird," I said. "Except for the real waves."

We walked into the library and saw a big sign pointing toward the entrance to the basement which said, "DOTS This Way."

We walked down the basement stairs where only two days earlier we had nearly been killed by one of Clayton's Zombie Pigman allies. I was feeling uncomfortable, but I forced myself to continue.

We walked up to the villager standing in front of the nether portals. I asked, "Where do all these portals go?"

The villager smirked at me like I was totally ignorant. "Hurrr, they go to the Nether, obviously."

"Yeah, I know, I spent some time there myself, but where can you go after you get to the Nether?"

The villager sighed and handed me a piece of paper. "Here's a map. You figure it out."

Rude.

Emma and I walked away from the annoying villager clerk and studied the map. It appeared as though there were several locations within Capitol City to which we could travel, including Clayton's Surf Park, the Capitol City library, the Capitol City government buildings, and the museum district. There were also several other villages to which one could travel, including Creeper Junction.

There were even a few portals that opened in the middle of the wilderness, probably where Clayton had captured animals for meat and obtained raw materials to craft into products for sale, but now they transported people to enjoy the beautiful vistas offered by the pristine, unspoiled areas of the Overworld.

I looked over at Emma and said, "I have to admit, this is pretty awesome. Think of how much time DOTS will save people."

Emma nodded her agreement. "I wish I'd thought of this. It's so obvious and simple yet no one had done it before."

I was totally jealous of Clayton. "Yeah, but now everyone's going to do it. Knowing how greedy villagers are, I bet there are several DOTS competitors already in the planning stages."

"I'm sure there are," said Emma, "but Clayton has the advantage of already having alliances with all the Nether mobs. Anyone else who wants to set up permanent nether portals is going to have to probably pay a fee to the mobs in order to avoid having them destroy the portals or attack their customers."

I shrugged. "I suppose," I said. But, the geopolitics of trade and transit between realms was not of interest to me at the moment. "But, whatever. Let's go surfing."

* * *

As we walked from town toward the Surf 'n Snack, I looked out at the ocean and smiled. It always made me happy to look at the water. Now that I could actually go surfing, it made me even happier.

Before we got to the Surf 'n Snack, we passed Biff's SUP school. Biff was there checking on everything and getting ready to open. We waved to Biff and he waved back. He put down the SUP he was carrying and came over to us.

"Hey guys, I just want to apologize again for how evil my cousin Clayton is. I knew he was greedy and all, but I had no idea he would enslave villagers."

"It's not your fault," said Emma. "I know that if you had known what he was up to, you would've told us."

Biff smiled, relieved.

"Yeah, man," I said. "I know you've been a bully in the past, but your heart's in the right place. Especially when you saved me from that evil squid."

I could see Biff standing a little taller now. He realized that we didn't hold him accountable for what Clayton had done.

"Thanks guys, that means a lot to me," he said softly, wiping a tear away from his eye.

I rubbed my chin a bit and then said, "Do you think Claire was involved with Clayton's evil plans? We saw her standing next to her father and Clayton just before Herobrine appeared at Capitol City and announced his idea about the surf contest."

Biff shook his head. "I can't imagine she would be, but then again I didn't think Clayton was a slaver. I'm sure she'll be at the surf contest. Maybe you could talk to her."

"I suppose I could," I said.

Emma gave me an evil look and said, "I don't know if we should talk to her. She's a Dretsky after all. I'm sure her loyalty to her family is stronger than anything else."

"I don't know," I said. "Maybe she's more loyal to her friends? Whoever they are."

Emma smiled at that statement. She knew I was referring to my loyalty to her and her loyalty to me, which had allowed us to escape from the Nether together.

"Okay, Biff, we'll see you later. Good luck today with business," I said.

Biff waved at us as we walked on.

We didn't get very far before I stepped into something squishy and ... hurrr .. stinky. I looked down and saw that I had stepped in a pile of something brown and disgusting.

I shook as much of the goop off my foot as possible. "What is that nasty stuff?"

Biff saw what had happened and said, "I think it's llama poop."

I freaked. I ran to the water and furiously washed my foot until all the turd was gone. Then, I realized there was some on my hand, and I freaked again until I washed it all off. Finally clean, I returned to the shore and asked Biff, "Llamas?!? Since when do llama's live in Zombie Bane?"

Biff shrugged. "I saw one walking around here when I first arrived. It was weird though. It looked like it was someone's pet – it was wearing a fancy saddle – but there was no one here. I ignored it and kept working and a few seconds later, it was gone. I guess it ... hurrr .. left that present for you."

Biff and Emma both laughed at me. I crossed my arms and pouted. "Wait until *you* step in a llama patty. Then you'll see who ... hurrr ... laughs."

"Oh, chill out, Jimmy," said Emma. "It washed right off. Come on, let's go surfing." I was still upset, but knew that surfing would make me feel better.

A few minutes later we arrived at the Surf 'n Snack. Our employees, Michael and Geronimo, whom Emma had hired shortly before she was kidnapped, were already on site.

"Hi, Jimmy and Emma, we're all ready to open," said Geronimo.

I smiled. "Great. Emma and I want to go surfing for a half an hour before you guys open, can one of you turn on the wave machine after we paddle out?"

Geronimo gave me a mock military salute and said, "Sure thing, boss."

Emma and I changed into our bathing suits, grabbed a couple surfboards, and then paddled out. Michael turned on the wave machine.

I let Emma catch the first wave. She dropped in, made a deep bottom turn and then hit the lip really

One young villager named Yash, paddled over to me. "Say, Jimmy, is it true that you met Herobrine and actually talked to Notch?"

I smiled. "Yes, it is true."

The kid's eyes got wide and his mouth fell wide open. "I didn't believe it. I thought people were just making that stuff up. That's amazing."

"I agree, it is amazing. I still think I'm in the middle of some sort of dream."

Yash kept gawking at me, like I was some superhero or famous celebrity. "Wow, man, I can't wait until the surf contest."

"Yeah, it's going to be tight, sick, awesome, and wicked all rolled into one!"

"Wicked?" asked Yash, rolling his eyes. "Hurrr ... anyway ... are you going to sell tickets to it?"

"I hadn't thought about that. I don't think I will. This is a historic event. Maybe if we have future contests I'll sell tickets to them, but I think that everyone should be able to see this contest for free."

The kid smiled. "Awesome. I don't really have very much money and I wasn't sure I would be able to afford a ticket."

I laughed. "Just get here early. I have a feeling there's going to be quite a few people here on the day of the contest. But, don't forget, the first contest is in Capitol City. The Zombie Bane contest isn't for two weeks."

"I know, but I can't afford to travel there, so I'm making plans for the second contest you'll be holding at the Surf 'n Snack."

"Just wanted to make sure we were talking about the same thing."

"We were. Thanks, Jimmy."

"Anytime, kid," I said as I whipped around the nose of my board and paddled into a wave.

* * *

That evening, after we closed the Surf 'n Snack, I walked Emma to her house.

"So, the Ender King is supposed to be here tomorrow?" asked Emma.

"Yes, that's what he said anyway. I hope he shows up."

"I'm sure he will. I know he doesn't think this contest is a very good idea, but he isn't going to cross

Notch, and he certainly doesn't want to let Clayton win by default," said Emma.

"I totally agree. I can't wait to see what his surfing style is like," I said with a grin. "Should be interesting."

Emma laughed and then got a really serious expression on her face. She pointed down the street and said, "I just saw a zombie spawn. It's getting dark. You had better get home."

I looked over my shoulder and saw the stupid zombie lurching towards me.

I sighed. "Why did Notch make zombies anyway? It seems so weird."

"Why don't you ask him the next time you see him," said Emma with a grin.

I grinned back. "I'll do that. I'll do that."

Day 32

I woke up earlier than normal because of a loud banging on the front door to my house. I could hear my father stumble out of bed and walk to the front door. It was still so early that even he hadn't gotten up yet. The first rays of the sun were just beginning to crease the nighttime sky.

I heard my dad unlock the door and then heard the creek of the hinges as he opened it. Then I heard him gasp and scream, "Don't look me in the eyes! Don't look me in the eyes!"

It could only be one person: the Ender King.

I quickly got out of bed, tossed on a robe, and ran down the stairs. "It's okay dad. It's the Ender King."

By now my mom had come out of the bedroom and was also shielding her eyes from the purple rectangles glowing in the Ender King's pitch black head.

"Endy, what up, my man?" I said, putting my hand out for a bro grip.

The Ender King was not amused and ignored my outstretched hand. "Jimmy Slade, I have come to participate in the surf contest as required by Notch. I would appreciate it if you'd stop calling me 'Endy.' You can call me your Highness, his Royal Majesty, or just King."

There was no way I was gonna call this guy your Highness or your Majesty. "Okay then, King, what up man?"

The King raised one of his slender black arms and slapped his head with his tiny black hand. "I will tell you what is up, Jimmy Slade. I have arrived with my wife and daughter. My servants are setting up a makeshift, palatial structure near the center of town in one of the vacant lots near the library. After you've had breakfast, retrieve Emma Watson and meet me there so that we may discuss our strategy for the surf contest."

"Sure thing, King. But, why so formal? I thought we were getting a good rapport going while you were preparing to attack Capitol City."

The King leaned down and put his mouth next to my ear so that he could whisper his response without my parents hearing it. "Jimmy, never forget that I am a royalty. Just because I have treated you well, does not mean that we are friends or that you can treat me with disrespect."

The Ender King then leaned backwards and stood ramrod straight, looming above me.

I swallowed hard. Sweat was forming on my forehead. The Ender King was a nice guy, but he was from a level of society I could only dream about. Maybe if I were a billionaire like Clayton, I'd understand what it's like to have people fawning all over you and listening to your every word, but I was just a common villager, who'd done one amazing thing by inventing surfing. Other than that, I was just a regular schmo. "Yes, your Majesty," I said in all seriousness. "Emma and I should be around in the next two hours."

The Ender King smiled. "Thank you. I shall tell my servants to expect you then."

And with that, the Ender King vanished into thin air as he teleported away.

I went back inside and went upstairs. I put on my bathing suit and my robe before returning downstairs. I ate a quick breakfast of scrambled eggs and apple pie.

"I'm going to go get Emma and then go see the Ender King," I told my parents.

My mom was concerned. "I don't know if you should be spending much time with an enderman. You know what they say about them."

I rolled my eyes. "What do they say about them, Mom?"

She put her hand to her robe and clenched it tightly around her neck. "They say that if you look in their eyes too long you'll go crazy."

"I heard that if you look in their eyes they attack you. They can't help it. It is in their nature," said my dad, also worried.

I laughed. "Those are just stories by people who've never met endermen. The Ender King is cool. He's a bit arrogant and rude sometimes, but his heart is in the right place."

"Well, hurrr, I guess you've spent a lot of time with him already and he basically saved your life," said my dad. "I guess he can't be all bad."

I laughed again. "All he had to do was save my life for you to think it was okay for me to hang out with him?"

My mom pointed her finger at me and said, "Don't be rude, Jimmy. We've never met endermen before. This is all new to us. We don't know if the stereotypes are true or not."

I realized I was being a jerk. Old people are always set in their ways. "It's okay, Mom. I'm sorry."

I walked over to my mom and gave her a hug. I shook my dad's hand and said, "Well, I'm off to practice for the contest. I'll be home before it gets dark." And I walked out the door.

* * *

I knocked on the front door of Emma's house about five minutes later. Her mom answered and let me in to the kitchen. I told her the Ender King was here and he had summoned me and Emma.

Emma's mother had the same concerned look on her face as my mother had. Emma's father came in and also expressed his concern. I told them what I had told my parents. At that moment Emma came down the stairs. She had on a brown robe with a light pink fringe on the end of the arm sleeves.

"Where did you get that crazy robe?" I asked.

Emma's parents looked at her robe and said, "Young lady, I don't know if you should be showing off with that decorative robe. People will think you're getting airs."

Emma shook her head. "I just want to have something a little different than everybody for a change. I realize we live in a conformist society, but even a little thing makes me feel different and unique."

"Kind of like my rainbow colored robe that Claire gave me," I said smiling.

Emma gave me the evil eye. Every time I mentioned Claire in a favorable light Emma wasn't happy.

Under Emma's withering gaze, I suddenly felt very hot. I reached up and pulled on my collar to get some fresh air into my robe. "Anyway, the Ender King wants to talk to us. Let's go."

"You kids be careful," said Emma's father.

Emma and I were already in the front yard and I waved back at him and Mrs. Watson and said, "Don't worry, Mr. Watson, everything will be fine." In order to emphasize my words, I started skipping. Emma laughed and started skipping too.

It took us about 10 minutes to skip and walk – try skipping for ten minutes straight; not possible – from Emma's house to the location where the Ender King and his entourage were staying.

You couldn't miss the place. It was about one hundred blocks tall and several hundred blocks deep. It looked like a solid block with tiny slits for windows. There were twenty ender soldiers standing around guarding it. Villagers were walking by covering their eyes and looking away, fearful of meeting the supposedly devastating purple gaze. The ender soldiers sat or stood implacably silent.

It was then that I noticed a llama hitched to a tree near the building. It looked like it was well groomed, like a fancy pet. I nudged Emma with my elbow. "Do you think that is the llama Biff was talking about?"

Emma squinted her eyes. "I suppose it could be. I wonder why it is here?

That mystery would have to wait for another time. Emma and I walked up to the enderman standing in front of the door. "The Ender King sent for us," I said.

The enderman looked down and asked in a deep slow voice, "Names?"

"Emma Watson."

"And, Jimmy Slade," I said. "What's your name?"

The enderman looked at me with his blank expression. *Had I been rude to ask?* He took his time deciding whether to respond to my question and finally said, "John. General John."

"A general in the Ender Army?" I asked.

John nodded.

"I don't remember seeing you at the siege of Capitol City."

"I was guarding the End. In case the Dretsky's sent forces there," said General John seriously.

"Really?" I said. "Cool."

"Enough of this nonsense," said the general as he opened a book and consulted its contents. Apparently he located our names in there because he stepped aside and opened the door for us. We walked inside and down an undecorated, narrow stone hallway. When we got to the end of the hall there was a door.

I looked at Emma and shrugged. "I guess we go in here."

I reached out to turn the handle and push the door open. I wasn't prepared for what I was to see on the other side.

We walked into a gigantic, luxurious, opulent chamber. Several ender women wearing fancy dresses were standing next to another ender woman who was seated on a throne. I assumed these women were the Ender Queen and her servants. The Ender King stood in a corner of the chamber speaking with several endermen.

I leaned over to Emma and whispered, "Should I say something? Should we announce our presence?"

Emma shrugged. She looked somewhat uncomfortable.

At that moment a young ender girl about as tall as us and wearing a fancy dress embroidered with chorus flowers trotted over to us and gave us each a hug and said, "You must be Jimmy and Emma. My dad has told me so much about you."

At that moment the Ender King looked over and saw that his daughter, the Ender Princess, was hugging us.

"Tina, back away from them."

The Ender Princess hugged us tightly, squeezed and then let go and stepped away a few paces. She looked over at her father and said, "Daddy, don't be so overprotective. It's Jimmy and Emma. You told me they were good people ... for villagers."

For villagers?

The Ender King's expression softened and he walked over and gave his daughter a hug. "I'm sorry, daughter. It's just that when we're outside of our normal realm of the End, you never know what could happen."

"Well, nothing ever happens at home, so it might be nice if something interesting happened while we were here," said the Ender Princess.

The Ender King sighed and shook his head. "You would not say that if you knew what *could* happen."

While he had been talking like a Debbie-downer, the Ender Queen had walked over and was standing in front of us. "It is nice to meet you, Jimmy and Emma," she said in a kindly voice. "My husband has told me so much about you."

"Thank you, your Majesty," said Emma, curtseying slightly.

"Yeah, thanks Queen. Only the parts where I save the world from a destructive war are true," I said, smiling at my joke and winking at the Queen.

The Ender King shot me a angry look. "You will address her as your Majesty," he demanded.

"Well, I call you 'King' so I thought it would be okay to call her 'Queen.' Don't have a cow, man."

The King slapped his head and then said to his wife and daughter, "Please excuse us, we need to plan for this ridiculous surf contest. Then, I will teleport everyone over to the surfing practice area. I'll be home for dinner."

The Queen and the Ender Princess smiled and gave the Ender King a hug and then left the room.

"I'm sorry, Jimmy and Emma," said the Ender King, "but we will have to have several ender soldiers with me while we practice. I don't want to risk any problems."

I shrugged. "That's cool. But hey, have you seen Laird around anywhere? He is the fourth member of our team, after all."

"I have not, nor have I met this person. However, we can send a few of my endermen around to find him. They will teleport to all the villages and should locate him shortly. When they find him, they will teleport him back to the surfing practice area."

I smiled. "That's awesome. Let's go."

Before he left, the Ender King gave instructions to his men to locate Laird. He also instructed several others to teleport to the Surf 'n Snack and establish a security perimeter. Then he wrapped his arms around us and we teleported.

* * *

Upon arrival at the Surf 'n Snack, there was already a long line of kids waiting to get in. Our employees were about ten minutes away from opening the place to the crowd.

The Ender King looked at me and Emma. "We can't practice if all these kids are in the water. You'll have to shut the Surf 'n Snack down."

"No way, King, I've got to keep the money flowing in. It's all about gettin' paid, yo!" I said.

The Ender King, as he always did when he got upset with me, swelled to triple his size and said, "We have to win the surf contest, Jimmy, not 'get paid.' I think this surf contest is a stupid idea – may Notch forgive me – but I don't want to lose to Clayton Dretsky. Either you shut down the Surf 'n Snack or I'm going to find some other people to be on the team."

I looked over at Emma and said, "What do you think?"

She crinkled her eyes in thought and then scratched her head before saying, "Didn't you tell me Clayton's wave park has three different types of waves?"

"Yeah, a mushy one, an A-frame like we've got, and a long, point-break style wave."

Emma nodded her head. "I thought so. How can we practice for a contest in Clayton's wave pool if we only have one type of wave?"

I was deflated. Not like an old, disgusting balloon, all sticky and stretchy, but just sad. "You're right. I hadn't thought about that." I looked over at the King. "How are we going to practice for the different types of waves?"

The King, still triple his normal size glanced around and then said, "We'll just build another surf park."

"How can we do that? It will take days to build the place and we don't even know where we could put it," I yelled, almost hysterical.

"Jimmy, have faith in me. When I was angry at you and my head was high in the sky, I looked around and saw the perfect location. It's far enough away that we don't have to deal with crowds of tourists and big enough that we can probably figure out a way to construct all 3 different types of waves. My ender soldiers will help. We just need Emma to tell us what to do."

I had to admit, it was a brilliant idea. We would be able to practice as much as we wanted, Clayton would probably think we're only practicing on our wave, and I could still get paid stacks of emeralds by kids wanting to surf. It was a perfect solution.

"I guess it's ideas like this that made you the King," I said.

The King shook his head. "Actually, I'm king because of my numerous victories in one-on-one mortal combat against other pretenders to the throne."

I searched the Ender King's face to see if he was making a joke. But his flat expression, which seemed to be almost unchanging no matter what situation he found himself in, gave me no clues. I decided not to say anything.

"Well ... hurrr ... let's go build surf park," I said.

* * *

I didn't really have much to do during the construction of the surf park.

Emma told the Ender King's soldiers how to move the rocks around on the bottom of the large portion of ocean the Ender King spotted. She also told them how much redstone and wood she would need to construct the wave-making machines. With the endermen's teleporting abilities and Emma's experience building a wave machine, the new, three-wave set up was done by late afternoon. In the meanwhile, the Ender King's soldiers had located Laird.

"This is amazing," said Laird, watching the endermen work. "I can't wait to try this place out."

"Yeah, it's pretty awesome," I said. "And after the contest, I can open a second wave pool for more experienced surfers."

"You can have a whole chain of surf parks pretty soon," said Laird. "It's too bad you can't surf in the ocean without having these contraptions make the waves. There's nothing like surfing a wave made by wind and weather. It is unpredictable and raw. The power of storm driven waves is something you have to experience to believe." Laird got a faraway look in his face, like he was remembering some amazing adventure when he had ridden gigantic, powerful, natural waves.

"I wish I could travel to your world the way you travel to mine. Why is it only a one-way trip?"

Laird shrugged. "I guess only Notch knows. Maybe should ask him next time you see him?"

"Yeah, well, I suppose I could. I'm sure he won't tell me a thing."

At that moment, Emma approached us. The sun was low on the horizon and there was probably only about a half-hour of daylight left.

"I think it's ready to test," she said. "You want the honors?"

I shook my head. "You're the one who knew how to build it. You should be the first person to ride it."

Emma smiled. "Really? You'll let me go first?"

I rolled my eyes. "Of course I'll let you go first. Why would you think otherwise?"

"I'll go first," said Laird, hopefully.

The Ender King walked over. "Why don't all three of you go first? There are three different waves, after all."

As usual, he was right. Well maybe I shouldn't say "as usual," since he wanted to fight a war rather than have a surf contest. But, he was usually right about things.

"Actually, there are four waves," I said. "There's the mushburger wave, the A-frame which really is two waves since you can go right or left, and then the point break. So we could all go at same time."

"It's a deal," said the Ender King.

I volunteered to paddle out at the mushy wave. Laird paddled out to the point break while Emma paddled out to the left side of the A-frame. The Ender King grabbed a surfboard and teleported himself out into the ocean so he could ride the right of the A-frame.

I wish I could teleport.

I looked back to shore at the ender soldier who was near the control box for the wave pool. "Okay, Thomas, press the button."

I could see the enderman's long slender arm raise up in the air and then move down, pressing the button. The Redstone circuit fired to life and began to move some pistons and push the wave making contraption. I saw the bump in the water as the ocean swelled. The swell came closer and closer until it hit the structures on the bottom of the ocean designed to break the wave in a certain way. It was working perfectly.

We all caught our waves and ripped them to shreds. The Ender King was a surprisingly good surfer.

I paddled over to the Ender King before the next wave came and asked, "How did you learn how to surf? I didn't think you had ever surfed before."

The King looked at me with his flat purple eyes and said, "I never have. I'm just naturally good at everything." He didn't say it like he was an arrogant poser. It was simply true.

"Well, that's ... hurrr ... pretty awesome. You'll have to ... hurrr ... practice some tricks so you can get really high scores."

"Perhaps, I shall. Perhaps, I shall not. I will study this peculiar sport some more prior to the contest and design a routine to impress the judges."

That was a bit weird.

"Cool. Um, hey, King, you mind if I take this right and you ride the mushburger?"

"I mind not at all."

After we rode a few more waves it was getting quite dark. We turned off the wave machine and teleported back to the Ender King's dwelling.

The Ender King invited us to dinner, but we had to decline because we needed to get home.

"Tomorrow, you will stay for dinner," the King insisted. "Your parents are invited as well. We can teleport you home after dinner, if you are worried about zombies and other nighttime vermin."

The Ender King's servants teleported us to each of our houses, and Laird to a hotel near the center of Zombie Bane. We agreed to meet the next morning at the Ender King's house in order to spend the entire day practicing.

Day 33

Today surf practice was very promising. Laird, of course, was ripping. In particular, he was able to ride deeper in the barrel than anyone else.

Emma was improving quickly. She was really good at doing turns and floaters on the mushburger wave and on the point break wave. She wasn't very good at riding the barrel yet, but she was practicing hard.

The Ender King was ... hurrr ... an unorthodox surfer. While he could do the normal things fairly well – turns, slashing maneuvers, and barrel riding – he preferred to do unexpected maneuvers.

For instance, he would drop into a wave and then just before he got in the barrel he would shrink down to baby zombie size to make the wave look a lot bigger. Then when he came out of the barrel he would grow to twice his normal size to make the wave look really small. Other times he would teleport off his surfboard and then teleport back on.

Steezy.

It was very strange. It was interesting, but strange. It was hard to know how the judges might score the King's waves.

We practiced from the morning until noon and then took a break for lunch, which was prepared by the Ender King's servants. After eating lunch and relaxing for an hour under oak trees, we practiced again for another four hours until the sun was beginning to set.

As we put our surfboards away, Laird said, "I think we are doing really well, but I heard Clayton was going to try to recruit some professional surfers from the human world who also play Minecraft. Depending on who it gets, he could have a formidable team."

I slapped my fist against my open hand. "That's not fair. What if he got three professional surfers? He'd easily win."

"Maybe," said Laird. "But strange things have been known to happen in surf contests. And, in any event, this is not a traditional surf contest. Who knows what additional rules Notch may impose upon the contest?"

"I agree," said the King. "This is the world of Minecraft, not the world of the humans. Things work differently here."

"Well, I don't know anything about the world of the humans," said Emma. "But, I do know that if we really want to win this contest and we practice really hard, we'll have a good chance."

"I'm getting hungry, King," I said as my stomach rumbled embarrassingly loudly. "Let's get back to your place and eat."

The King, who was still getting used to my familiarity as opposed to me being super polite and calling him 'your Highness' all the time, sighed but then wordlessly wrapped his arms around the three of us and teleported back to his Zombie Bane palace.

When we got to the palace, the Ender King told us to wash our hands and then go into the dining room. He instructed his servants to go to my house and Emma's house and pick up our parents. The King then left to prepare for the evening.

After we had washed our hands, we went to the dining room just in time to see two endermen teleport back with our parents.

My mother stumbled slightly when she realized she was no longer at her house. The first time teleporting is very disorienting because it lasts less than a second and you are suddenly somewhere completely different. My dad looked dizzy. Emma's parents were in the same predicament.

My dad shook his head rapidly from side to side and then said, "Whoa! That was ... hurrr ... something else."

My mom reached a hand out and grabbed my dad's shoulder to steady herself. "Oh my Notch," she said as she checked that her hair hadn't been messed up by the teleport.

Emma's parents, having already regained their balance, walked over to Emma and gave her a hug. My parents did the same to me.

It was then that I finally looked around the dining room and appreciated the grandeur of the situation. There was large table with seating for 10 people: Emma, me, our four parents, Laird, the King, the Queen, and Princess Tina.

A servant came in and announced that the Ender King was about to arrive. We stood quietly as the Ender King entered, leading his wife and daughter.

They were all dressed in fine clothing, mainly black of course, and they looked extremely impressive. The Ender King helped his wife sit down and then told everyone, "Please be seated."

My parents and Emma's parents sat close to the king and queen. Laird sat next to my father while the Ender princess set in between Emma and me.

"Isn't this fun?" said Tina, extremely excited.

"Yeah, I guess. Is the food good?" I asked.

The Ender Princess nodded her head rapidly. "Oh, of course. My dad's chef is the best chef in the entire End. I would guess he might be as good as anyone in the Overworld too."

Emma rubbed her hands together greedily. "Good. I'm starving. Surfing for eight hours a day will really make you hungry."

The Ender Princess suddenly looked sad. "I wish I could go surfing. My dad won't let me."

I rolled my eyes. "That's lame. You should come with us tomorrow. It's easy to learn how to surf, though getting good at it takes some practice."

Emma agreed. "Yes, you should come with us."

The Ender Princess put a tiny black hand on each of ours and said, "I don't know if my dad will let me. But I'll ask. But first, let's eat."

It was then that the servants brought out the first course. The meal was an extravagant one, similar to the meals I had enjoyed at the Dretsky household. It was as if there was a gigantic food factory inside the other room where the servants would go and retrieve dish after dish.

I was rather surprised at how much the enders ate. Tina ate about five times as much as I did. Her mother and father each ate ten or twenty times as much as I did. It was astonishing, especially when you consider how skinny they all were.

Maybe they needed all that energy in order to teleport?

It was a great meal, but I was so tired from surfing, the more I ate, the sleepier I became. In fact, I must've nodded off because the next thing I knew I was on top of my bed at home!

I sat up and rubbed my head. Then, I put a hand on my stomach. I felt so full.

I got up and changed into my pajamas and brushed my teeth. I fell back into bed, and there was a knock on my door. It was my mom.

"I was wondering when you would wake up. You fell asleep right before they brought out the plate of chocolate chip cookies."

"I hope I didn't snore or anything," I said, feeling anxious about the answer.

My mom laughed. "Oh, you didn't snore. But, when you fell asleep, your face landed in the apple pie."

I reached up and touched my face and felt a little crusty thing by my ear. I picked it off. I inspected it and realized it was hardened apple pie filling.

I suddenly turned bright red. "How embarrassing."

My mom laughed again and said, "Maybe a little, but it's a great story. Emma was calling you Jimmy Appleseed."

Oh great, I thought, *a stupid nickname. I bet Emma will keep using that forever.*

"Did the Ender Princess say anything?"

My mom smiled. "Yes, she said she hadn't seen anyone fall asleep at the dinner table since her one-month-old cousin did it. She was calling you Baby Jimmy."

I turned a deeper red from the additional embarrassment. I slapped my head. *Another stupid nickname*, I thought.

I tried to smile at my mom but it came out looking like I had indigestion and needed to vomit. "Great. Really funny."

"Well, get some sleep Jimmy. You have a big day tomorrow filled with surfing practice. And, Biff told me earlier today that his cousin Claire is stopping by tomorrow." And having dropped that news bomb on me, my mom walked out of my room and shut the door.

Claire! What was she doing? Why was she coming? Was she going to spy on us? Was she going to try to sabotage our practice? Or, was she actually just coming to talk?

Day 34

It took me a while to get out of bed this morning. I was so tired from surfing so much and from eating so much that I really just wanted to stay in bed all day. But I knew I couldn't. I had to practice.

And, I had to find out what Claire wanted.

After breakfast I stopped by Emma's house and the two of us walked to the Ender King's palace. Laird was already there.

"I'm so tired guys. Do we have to practice today?" I asked.

Laird shrugged. "I don't care. I'll probably go surfing anyway, but just cruisy, not like when I'm practicing for a contest."

"I'm kind of tired too," admitted Emma.

The Ender King looked at us. "Maybe we overdid it yesterday. When you fell asleep and smacked your face on the apple pie, I could tell you worked really hard yesterday."

I'd forgotten that the Ender King had seen it all too. "Yeah, I'm sorry about that," I said, turning red.

"It was pretty funny, dude," said Laird.

Emma laughed. "Yeah, Jimmy Appleseed, it was funny."

At that moment Tina walked in and said, "Hey everyone! Hi, Baby Jimmy."

I let my head fall forward until my chin was resting against the front of my robe. I slapped my forehead with my right hand. After everyone stopped laughing, I looked up and said angrily, "I get it. I get it. Hurrr. I fell asleep and my head landed on an apple pie. Can we just stop talking about it?"

"Not a chance," said Emma.

"No way," said the Ender Princess.

"No way, José," said Laird.

"I declare as his Royal Majesty that the answer is no," announced the King.

I sighed. "Whatever. Have your fun. My mom told me Claire's coming to town. Visiting Biff. I'm going over there to see what's happening. I'll practice with you guys this afternoon."

I could tell this information came as a shock to them all. Emma looked angry that I was going to talk to Claire. Laird looked confused, and the Ender King was disturbed.

"She's a Dretsky," said the King. "She's not one of us. You should stay away from her."

"I agree," said Emma crossing her arms across her chest. "She didn't do anything to try to stop the war. She was right there with Clayton and her father."

"Guys, she's just a kid. Just like you, Emma; just like me. Maybe she didn't have a choice." I said.

I could tell I got to them. She *was* just a kid. And kids don't always have control over what their parents do. "Okay, maybe you should give her a chance," said Emma, realizing she had rushed to judgment.

Laird continued to look confused. I don't think he'd ever met Claire or heard about her.

Tina looked at her father and said, "Yes, Daddy, would you have people hate me just because they hate you?"

The Ender King's head snapped in his daughter's direction. "Who hates me?"

She shrugged. "I don't know. I'm sure there are some people who hate you. You're the King and you tell people what to do. People don't always like being told what to do."

The King realized that she had just been speaking in generalities as opposed to some specific example of royal hatred. He was always too quick to jump to the conclusion that someone was trying to mess with him. I'd noticed that about him. He was on edge and anxious all the time. He really needed to chill if he wanted to be a good surfer.

"So, um, hurrr, I guess I'm going to head over to Biff's house now. If anyone wants come with me, let's go," I said.

"I'm going surfing," said Laird.

"I'm staying here and doing kingly things," said the King.

"I'll come with you," said Emma.

"Me too," said the Ender princess.

"You'll do no such thing young lady," ordered the King.

"Oh come on, Daddy, when am I going to be in the Overworld again? Emma and Jimmy are nice. Let me hang out," she said with a slightly whiny voice.

The Ender King softened a bit. You could tell he realized he was being an overprotective dad. "Well, okay, but I'm sending Gretchen with you."

Tina rolled her eyes. "Why Gretchen? Why not Ariana, Taylor, or Rihanna?"

"Because they're young and inexperienced like you, and Gretchen is older and wiser and smarter."

"She's older all right," said Tina sarcastically.

At that moment an elderly ender woman entered the room. She was hunched over and wore ill fitting clothes. Her hair was crooked and her teeth were missing. The purple of her eyes was turning into a light pink, so advanced was her age.

In a crackling squeaky old lady voice, she said, "Now, now, Tina. Someday you will be as old and ancient and decrepit as I am. And then you'll know why it is your father sent me with you."

Honestly, that didn't make any sense at all. I was a little concerned that Gretchen might be losing it. Her mind, that is.

Tina sighed. "I'm sorry I called you old, Gretchen. You know I like you."

"That's okay sweetie," said Gretchen moving in and pinching the Ender Princess's cheek. "I am old. But I also love you and will protect you with my life. Don't forget that."

"Yes ma'am," said Tina.

Gretchen smiled and said, "Well, I would teleport all of you to our destination, but I'm so old I don't know if I can get there with all of you. I'm not even sure I could manage it in a single leap all by myself!"

"That's okay," I said. "We can walk. It's good to walk sometimes. It's only about ten minutes."

"Besides," said Tina, "I want to take Isabel with me. She needs a walk."

"Isabel? Who is that?" I asked.

"She is my pet llama," said Tina.

We followed Tina out of the palace to the stables. In one of the stalls was the same llama we had seen hitched to a tree a couple days earlier.

As Tina approached, Isabel pricked up her ears and trotted happily in the stall. "Oh, Isabel, you are so cute," cooed Tina.

I looked over my shoulder and saw that Gretchen had waited outside the stables. I looked at Emma knowingly and then asked Tina in a soft voice, "Did you come here a day before your father?"

Tina stiffened. "Why would you say that?"

"Well, hurrr, I stepped in some llama poop and Biff said he saw a llama earlier that looked a lot like this one."

Tina swiveled her head around to make sure it was just the three of us. "Yes, I was here. Don't tell my parents. I just wanted to see the surf park. I wasn't sure he would let me out of the palace, so I snuck here a day early."

"It's cool," I said. "At least I know who to blame for my stinky foot."

"Sorry," said Tina. "Llama's just go when they go."

Emma laughed.

"What's taking you kids so long in there?" squeaked Gretchen.

"Nothing. I'm just putting a leash on Isabel," said Tina.

With Gretchen along, the walk took about twenty minutes instead of ten. Tina had offered to let her ride Isabel, but Gretchen refused. She was a very slow walker. Plus, she had to stop and point things out and talk about them. Every single souvenir shop, restaurant, storefront, and house. Everything was amazing to her. Apparently, she had never been outside of the End in her entire life, which apparently was several hundred years.

I didn't realize enders lived so long!

So, it was easy to excuse her excitement. She was basically like a little kid on her first trip away from home.

Her favorite building was the library. "So many books," she had said when she looked in the window. Apparently Gretchen loved to read. She told us that … only about twenty-five times during the walk.

When we, at long last, arrived at Biff's house, Gretchen said, "I'm going to sit under this tree. You kids have fun. When you're ready to go, wake me up."

"How do you know you will be asleep?" I asked.

"Because I'm old. That's what old ender women do. We sleep."

"Oh, yeah, that makes perfect sense," I said, not meaning a single word that came out of my mouth.

Tina hitched Isabel to the tree near Gretchen. Then, Emma, Tina, and I walked up to the front door of Biff's house and knocked. A few moments later, Biff's dad, Phill, opened the door.

"Are you here to see Biff?" he asked, eying the Ender Princess suspiciously.

"Yes, sir," I said.

"Hold on. I'll go find him."

We waited on the front porch for about thirty seconds before Biff arrived. "Hi, guys," he said happily.

"Biff, this is Tina, the Ender Princess," said Emma.

Biff reached out his hand and shook Tina's tiny hand. "Wow, I've never met a princess before."

I think Tina might've blushed, but it was hard to tell with her obsidian-colored skin. "Well, I've never met a Biff before," Tina said with a smile. The joke was lost on Biff.

Biff was about to invite us into the house when he saw Gretchen sleeping under the tree. "Oh my Notch, why is a husk sleeping under my tree!?!"

I slapped my head. "That's Gretchen. That's Tina's guardian."

"Guardian? It looks like she's the one who needs the Guardian."

I nodded. "Yeah, she is some crazy old lady who the King sent to guard Tina. We told him it wasn't necessary, but he insisted."

Biff shrugged and then noticed the llama. "That's the llama I saw the other day!"

I nodded. "Yeah, it's Tina's pet."

Biff was too dense to ask any questions about how the llama was here before the King had arrived. Tina was relieved. Biff invited us in. We went inside and saw that Claire was sitting at the kitchen table talking to Biff's parents.

"Yes, Uncle Phill," she was saying, "it was a fine trip. I was glad that Herobrine and Notch came up with this surf contest idea, otherwise we would be at war right now. I might've already respawned!"

When she heard us come inside, Claire looked over. I smiled and waved. Emma glared, and Tina stood there, not really knowing what to do.

Biff made the introductions. "Claire, you know Emma and Jimmy ... hurrr ... from before, and this is Tina, the Ender Princess.

Claire stood up and did a slight curtsy to the Princess and then walked over and shook her hand. "It's nice to meet you. I want to apologize for my brother's behavior. Believe me, we're not all like him."

Did she mean it? Or was this an act?

"Thank you. I know that children are not always like their parents or their siblings, but they can be," said Tina cautiously.

Claire nodded. "Sure they can. But I'm nothing like my brother or my father, believe me."

Emma let out a snort. "Words don't mean much, Claire. Actions do."

Claire swallowed hard. "I deserve that. I stood by while Clayton and my father were ready to go to war the Ender King and I did nothing. I apologize, but I was scared. He wanted me up there so that we would look like we are presenting a united front, but I didn't want to be there, believe me."

"Why do you keep saying 'believe me'?" I asked.

"Because I want you to believe me, because I'm telling the truth."

I suddenly felt my vibe-sensing ability kick in. I was getting good vibes from Claire. Not one hundred percent perfect, but good. I did believe her, at least at that moment.

"Are you going to come to the surf contest in a few days?" asked Tina.

Claire nodded. "I should. Actually ... hurrr ... I'm on the team," Claire said sheepishly.

My mouth fell open in shock.

Emma shook her head and said angrily, "You want us to believe that you're not on Clayton's side yet you are on his surf team?!? The whole point of the surf contest was to see who – the Ender King or Clayton – wins the right to humiliate the other for the rest of eternity. Why should we believe you that you are not like Clayton?"

I had to say, Emma had a good point. I was still getting good vibes from Claire though, so I wasn't sure what was going on. I was confused.

"Just because I'm on the team doesn't mean I support Clayton's evil ways. I was never in favor of his enslavement of villagers or of his... hurrr ... exploitation of the ... hurrr .... resources of the End."

Now, Tina was upset. "Exploitation of resources?!? Don't you mean the murder of my people!"

Claire sighed. "Yes, but I didn't want to say that in front of you. I didn't want to hurt your feelings."

"I am a royal princess. My feelings can't get hurt. That's what happens when you are leadership quality," said Tina resolutely, crossing her skinny black arms in front of her chest. Her purple eyes glowed with rage and, despite what she had said, beginning to shine with the mist of sorrowful tears.

Biff could sense the situation getting out of control. He stepped in between Claire and the rest of us. "Hey, guys, can we just try to chillax for a bit? I know everyone's upset, but I don't want any fighting inside my house, okay?"

"Yeah, sorry man," I said. Emma and Tina remained silent, but they backed off a bit. Claire nodded her head and sat down on a chair.

Claire looked up at us and into each of our eyes and tried to convey her thoughts without words. Her good vibes increased. *She must be telling the truth,* I thought.

"Look, everyone, you don't have to believe me. I want you to, but I understand why you might not. But, I'll prove it to you ... hurrr ... one of these days. Just you watch."

"I hope so, Claire, I hope so," said Emma as she turned and walked out of Biff's house.

Tina followed and said, "Come on, Baby Jimmy, let's go."

Why did she have to say that?

Biff looked at me and laughed. Even Claire had a slight smile on her face.

"Baby Jimmy? What's that about?" asked to Biff.

I sighed. "It's a long story. I'll explain it later." Then, I looked at Claire and nodded sympathetically to her but said nothing before I walked out of the house.

I walked over to Emma and Tina who were attempting to rouse Gretchen from her sleep. For a moment, I thought she might be dead until I realized that if she were dead she would have already evaporated into a puff of smoke. I shuddered at the thought of what sort of dessicated drops she might leave behind.

Yuk!

After a couple minutes of forceful shaking, Gretchen finally woke up and we helped her to stand up. She's stretched her back and cracked it a few times turning from side to side. She then announced, "Ready to go."

We unhitched Isabel and walked to the Surf 'n Snack, which was already doing lots of business. A couple hundred villagers were out in the water, mostly kids.

"I've never seen so many kids in the water," said Emma.

"Yeah, this is crazy," I said. "I don't even recognize half of these kids. Where did they come from?"

At this moment, one of our employees walked up to us and, having overheard our conversation, said,

"They're coming from Creeper Junction and Capitol City, sir."

"Knock off the 'sir' stuff, Geronimo," I said, feeling uncomfortable that another twelve-year-old villager would address me as "sir." I continued, "What do you mean they're coming from Creeper Junction and Capitol City?"

"They're all using the DOTS. Apparently, Clayton has been shutting his wave pool so his team can practice, and the kids who would normally go there have been coming here. Plus, they all want to surf where one of the contests is going to happen. We've made more money in the last couple of days, than we made in the last week."

I felt the greed swelling within me.

This rate of earnings was amazing. I had a vision of a pyramid stacked high with emeralds. Of emerald rings, of emerald crowns, of emerald necklaces, even of an emerald house. Then I realized I was falling into the trap that keeps most villagers from being anything other than greedy workaholics. I shook my head, clearing it of the horrible thoughts of greed.

"Wow, that DOTS sure is amazing," I said.

Emma had a concerned look on her face and said, "I'm a little wary of all these people from Creeper Junction, Jimmy. What if they are part of the rainbow creeper religion?"

Tina looked at us confused. "What is the rainbow creeper religion?"

I explained it to her quickly. The part about breaking away from Notch and being exiled. The part about the exploding creepers leading the exiles to what is now Creeper Junction. The rumors that the ancient religion lives on and that it's all about absolute power and absolute, insatiable greed.

Tina was horrified. She put her tiny little black hand in front of her mouth in shock. "That sounds horrid! Why would anyone want to follow such a religion?"

I shrugged. "I have no idea."

At that moment we were surprised by Mr. Blaze. "Hi, kids. And who are these fine ender people with you?"

We introduced Tina and Gretchen.

Mr. Blaze bowed slightly and said, "Nice to meet you Gretchen." Then he turned and, bowing deeply, said, "It is a pleasure to be in your presence, your Royal Highness."

Tina laughed and said, "I'm just a princess. When I'm queen you can do all that formal stuff. For now, you can just call me Princess Tina."

Mr. Blaze smiled. "Well, Princess Tina, I overheard your question about the rainbow creepers. I can tell you why people would follow that religion, if you would like to hear."

This was getting interesting.

"Ok," said Tina.

Mr. Blaze continued. "The rainbow creeper religion is actually somewhat misunderstood. While there is a strong strain of authoritarianism and end-of-the-world thinking in the religion, there's also strain of it, followed by a small handful of adherents, who believe in world peace and fairness. Unfortunately, they've never held leadership positions, so no one in the Overworld has really heard of them."

"How come you know about all that stuff?" asked Tina, curious and suspicious at the same time.

"I read a lot of books."

Tina nodded her head in understanding. "Yes, books. Books are good."

Mr. Blaze smiled. "Anyway, kids, don't generalize about people who believe in a religion. Some are good and some are bad. They'd probably be that way whether or not they believed in the religion. Anyway, I'm off. I just thought I'd say, 'Hi.'"

"Are you going surfing, Mr. Blaze?" I asked. "Is that why you are at the Surf 'n Snack?"

Mr. Blaze seemed a little nervous for some reason. I got a strange vibe from him just briefly. His eyes darted back and forth and he said, "I'm not. I was just taking a long walk from my house to my bookstore instead of the short walk that I normally take. I just wanted to see what was happening out here."

"Okay, see you later," I said, eyeing him suspiciously.

When Mr. Blaze was gone I looked around and asked, "Did that seem a little weird that he was here just at the right time to tell us something about the rainbow creepers?"

Emma shrugged. "Maybe. Or, maybe he was just taking a long walk. People *do* take long walks."

71

Gretchen cracked her back and in her squeaky old lady voice said, "Yes, they do. Walking is great exercise. You kids should make sure you walk a lot. Five or ten thousand steps a day is what they recommended for endermen and women."

What a crazy lady!

"Tina, do you want to learn how to surf?" I asked.

Tina smiled. "I do, but I think I should wait until we are at the more private surf location. I'd be kind of embarrassed trying to surf out here. I really don't know what I'm doing."

"Suit yourself. I'm going to paddle out and grab a couple waves. Then, we can get some lunch, okay?" I asked.

Tina smiled and petted Isabel's neck. "Okay."

I looked at Emma. "You want to come with me?"

"No, that's okay. I'll stay here and talk to Tina and Gretchen."

"Okay, see you guys later."

* * *

After I finished surfing, we all got some food at the Surf 'n Snack restaurant and then walked another ten minutes to our secret surf location.

Unfortunately, it wasn't so secret anymore. There were about 200 villagers being kept away by the Ender King's soldiers. They weren't all from Zombie Bane either. There were definitely some from Creeper Junction and Capitol City. When we arrived, it was starting to get out of hand.

I saw an ender soldier teleport away and then teleport back with five Zombie Bane policemen. The policemen stood in front of the ender soldiers and barked orders at the villagers to disperse or they would be arrested. They were trespassing on private property and they had to get off.

It actually wasn't private property. It was just some part of the ocean that we had taken over for a practice surfing location, but that's what the police said. It worked. Everyone left, but they were grumbling.

We walked past the ender soldiers and said hello to Laird and the King who had arrived some time earlier.

"I feel like such a celebrity," I said. "Everyone wants to see what I'm doing and see our surf park."

"Welcome to my world, Baby Jimmy, welcome to my world," said the King sadly.

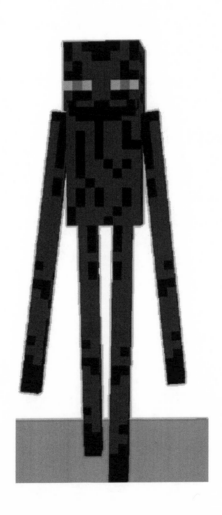

After everyone finished laughing at my stupid nickname, we grabbed our surfboards and practiced. Tina even managed to stand up a few times on the mushburger wave.

We practiced for about three hours until the sun began to set. The King and Tina, along with Gretchen and Isabel, teleported back to the palace, while the King's soldiers took Laird, Emma, and me to our respective dwellings.

Another day in the books.

Day 35

Another morning, and as usual, Emma and I were walking to the Ender King's palace so that we could teleport to the practice facility. It is kind of amazing that I was already getting bored. The surf contest existed to stop a war, but I was getting bored of preparing for it already. What was wrong with me?!?

We were just a few buildings away from the Ender King's palace when Mr. Blaze waved to us from across the street and then came over.

"I have something disturbing to share with you," he said, his face displaying concern and worry.

I suddenly felt sick to my stomach. It wasn't a good or bad vibe situation, but I actually felt physically ill for some reason.

"What is it?" asked Emma.

Mr. Blaze took in a deep breath and then let it slowly out before speaking. "You knew that the librarian had been arrested, right? As a conspirator with Clayton to enslave villagers?"

We both nodded our heads. We heard that after Notch freed all the slaves, those returning to Zombie Bane immediately went to the police department and complained about the librarian. The librarian had led the police on a brief chase through the stacks of books, but she was too old and slow to escape capture. Her zombie pigman guards had already abandoned her and returned to the Nether.

Mr. Blaze continued. "The police asked me to speak with her. Because I have a fairly substantial knowledge of the occult and because of my special ... hurrr ... powers, they thought I could get some information from her."

I was at the edge of my seat, even though I was standing up and there wasn't a chair in sight. "What did she say? What did she say?"

"Nothing at first. She swore her allegiance to Clayton and refused to believe that Notch had actually appeared and done anything. But as the people whom she had enslaved were paraded in front of her one by one, she realized they had gotten out somehow. Finally, she was convinced that I was telling the truth about Notch's intervention. Still, she said nothing for a few days, until last night."

Mr. Blaze paused for a moment. A shiver ran up and down his body. I could tell something heavy was coming.

"When she finally was willing to talk, she told me that after she had joined Clayton, on the promise that Clayton would give her 5% of all his earnings generated by any villagers she helped enslave, she revealed something horrific."

"Isn't it horrific enough that she would sell her fellow villagers for only 5%?" said Emma.

I shrugged. "That's a pretty good percentage, when you consider you don't have to feed or clothe them or do anything, all you have to do is capture them and send them off to Clayton."

I suddenly put my hand to my mouth. I couldn't believe those words had just come from my mouth. I sounded just like Clayton. *What was happening to me?*

Mr. Blaze looked at me curiously. It was as if he was reconsidering revealing what he was about to say. Maybe he thought I was not on the right side or not of sound mind. But he continued nevertheless.

"She told me that after she joined forces with Clayton, Clayton had to be sure her loyalty was complete. Therefore, two zombie pigmen took her to the Nether. She was blindfolded and led through passageways for at least an hour until they entered a very large chamber. Her blindfold was removed and she saw some sort of altar with a priest standing in front of it. The priest was wearing a rainbow colored robe."

I fainted. Fell down right there in the street.

When I regained consciousness, Emma was slapping me in the face and Mr. Blaze was repeating, "Are you all right, Jimmy?"

I sat up and shook the cobwebs from my head. "Sorry, I passed out. It's just when you said rainbow colored robe, it reminded me of a gift Claire Dretsky had given me."

Emma helped me to my feet held me up until I could lean against the wall of the building nearby. "Are you sure you're okay, Jimmy?" asked Emma.

I nodded my head. "I want to hear the rest of Mr. Blaze's story."

Mr. Blaze looked at me and, assuring himself that I was able to bear the weight of what he was about to tell me, said, "The priest approached her and performed some sort of ritual she didn't understand.

He spoke a peculiar language. She understood a few words, but they made no sense. After that was done, the priest backed away and the door behind the altar opened. The librarian couldn't see anything other than bright multicolored lights coming from the room which cast a shadow on the wall behind her. Only, the shadow wasn't black, it was all the colors of the rainbow."

I fainted again.

When I came to Mr. Blaze was slapping me in the face and Emma was repeating, "Jimmy, are you okay?"

I sat up and leaned against the building. "I feel fine except for my face. It's all hot and red from being slapped so much."

"I'm sorry," said Mr. Blaze. "But you were passed out a lot longer this time."

"Well, why shouldn't I be?" I said angrily. "It sounds like the librarian may have actually met the Rainbow Creeper itself!"

"Now, now, Jimmy, I wouldn't go that far," said Mr. Blaze. "It's probably just some series of torches with different colored glass around them. You think the Rainbow Creeper really exists?"

"Why wouldn't he or she or whatever it is? Notch is real, right? We saw him with our own eyes."

"Yes, but Notch is the true creator of the Overworld," said Emma. "Why would the Rainbow Creeper even be real? It's probably just some fake god invented years ago to try to distract people from the true worship of Notch."

I shook my head. "I really don't know if that's true or not but I've learned a lot of weird things in the past few weeks about evoking and Herobrine and the Ender King, and all sorts of stuff. Things that I thought were true are false and things I thought were false are true and I'm just really confused right now."

"You are right, Jimmy. This has been a strange few days," said Emma.

"And," I said, standing up, "what about the strange language the librarian heard? What if it is some ancient language of the gods? What if ... hurrr ... what if it is ... hurrr ... hexadecimal hieroglyphics!?!"

Mr. Blaze looked shocked and his eyes darted from side to side. "Don't say that. Herobrine's own language? Like in the diary we saw at his fortress?"

"We are assuming it is Herobrine's language," said Emma. "What if there were others who spoke it at the dawn of time? Think of the knowledge it contains! Or, maybe it is an entirely different ancient language? The language of the gods!"

Mr. Blaze shook his head rapidly. "No. No. No. You children cannot concern yourselves with this. I only told you about the librarian because I wanted to warn you to be on the lookout for strange forces and strange doings. Report anything you see to me at once!"

"Yeah, okay, I guess," I said, not entirely convinced. Emma looked at me out of the corner of her eyes. She wasn't entirely convinced either.

Why should we report to Mr. Blaze? Why not the Ender King? Of course, Blaze and the King we homies, so maybe telling one was like telling the other.

"Good," said Mr. Blaze. "All this talk of linguistics, philology, and paleo-linguistic analysis aside, I can tell you that my conclusion is there is definitely a group of people, apparently including Clayton Dretsky, who are involved in the worship of the Rainbow Creeper, and are using it not simply to express their faith but to violate the law and destroy the lives of others. Who knows how far they'll go?"

"I have no idea, Mr. Blaze," I said. "All I know is that I have a surf contest to win. If I can solve the mystery of the Rainbow Creeper along the way, so be it."

I brushed the dirt accumulated from fainting twice from my robe. I thanked Mr. Blaze for telling us about the librarian and then waved goodbye to him as Emma and I began to walk away. But, then I stopped, turned around, and asked, "So what's going to happen to the librarian?"

Mr. Blaze stiffened and said, "She perished last night, alone in her cell. The only thing remaining were her drops: one book and a single pile of gunpowder."

Emma and I both gasped. "A villager dropped gunpowder?!?" said Emma. "I thought only witches or creepers dropped ---." She couldn't finish her thought; it was too horrific.

Had the librarian's sole been merged with a creeper? Was the librarian a witch? Or, was the gunpowder a way for the evil priest to somehow control her?

I was totally shook. In fact, I'd go so far as to say I was shook-eth.

Mr. Blaze could tell what we were thinking, I was sure. He said nothing, but simply walked slowly away.

Emma and I, still in a daze, approached the ender soldier guarding the King's temporary palace and asked to be let inside.

As we walked down the hallway to the Ender King's chamber, I asked Emma, "Should we tell the King about what Mr. Blaze just said?"

Emma pondered this for a moment and said, "No. Let's keep this to ourselves, for now. I think Notch must have this all under control."

"Maybe."

* * *

The rest of the day was basically just like the other days, so there's probably no reason for me to write anything down about it. The Ender King teleported us and Princess Tina to the practice facility. Princess Tina was getting pretty good at surfing. She was nowhere near as good as Emma or me or Laird, but she was getting the hang of it. A few more weeks and she'd probably be one of the best surfers in the Overworld.

The Ender King continued with his bizarre surf style. He was doing handstands on the surfboard. He was curling up in a little ball. He would lie down on the surfboard like a stiff corpse. He would teleport here and there and everywhere while the surfboard rode the waves without him. I just didn't know if his approach was the right one to win this contest.

But he was the King and I was on *his* team he was not on *mine*. He could do whatever he wanted.

* * *

At the end of our day of practice, the King said, "Tomorrow, we should get a morning practice in and then travel to the Capitol City. That way, we can get situated and prepare for the contest the day after tomorrow."

"That sounds like a good idea, King," I said.

"Excellent. I will arrange for my people to teleport you to Capitol City."

"Well, hurrr, actually, I was kinda hoping to try out the DOTS," I said.

The Ender King swelled to five times as normal size and pointed his long black finger at me and said, "Are you going to betray me? Why would you use the DOTS? That was created by my arch enemy!"

"Chill, King. I just want to see how it works. I was thinking of maybe trying to build my own DOTS, except I'd call it the SOTS because it would be the Slade Overworld Transportation System."

The King returned to his normal size and had a belly laugh. Although, as an enderman, he really has no belly because he's super skinny, so maybe there's a different term I should use here, but that was the best description I can come up with.

"SOTS? That is the stupidest name I've ever heard in my life. You need to think of something better or else no one's going to want to use it."

"How about the LOTS?" said Laird.

"Or the WOTS?" said Emma.

"Those names are even worse," I said, sticking out my tongue.

"So you admit your name is terrible," said the Ender King.

I couldn't believe I had been entrapped into admitting my own name was bad. I didn't like people who played that sort of passive-aggressive insult game.

"Whatever," I said, crossing my arms. "I'll come up to something."

I turned around and looked out at the ocean as it reflected the final rays of sunshine. Staring at the water helped me calm down before I went any further and said something I'd regret.

After a few minutes, the Ender King said, "Okay, let's teleport back. You want to stay at my palace for dinner?"

We all said we would as long as his people could teleport us home after dark. Of course, the King agreed.

The King wrapped his spaghetti arms around us next thing we knew we were in the dining hall.

Day 36

When I got up in the morning I packed my clothes for the trip to Capitol City.

My mom made me a delicious breakfast, and both my parents ate breakfast with me. It was nice.

"When are you leaving?" asked my dad.

"This afternoon. We are going to practice this morning for a couple hours and then the Ender King is going to take us to Capitol City. Well, I'm going to try out the DOTS, but I think everyone else is just going to teleport there."

My mom clutched her robe tightly against her neck. "Doesn't the DOTS go through the Nether? Do you think you should go back there?"

"It won't be a problem, Mom," I said with my mouth full of watermelon. "Now that Notch has freed all the slaves and forbidden slavery, I don't think there's any danger."

"But what about the zombie pigmen? Maybe they'll be really upset that you cost them their livelihood?" said my mom.

I had to admit, I hadn't thought about how the zombie pigmen might feel about all this. First, Notch creates them as a race that dwells in the dank, dark Nether, and then he takes away their main source of income. That might make you upset.

"It's not like I'm going to go on a walking tour of the Nether. I'm just going to transit through the DOTS to see how it works. I was thinking maybe of building a transportation system myself."

My dad looked at me and smiled. "That's the spirit, son. Your entrepreneurial muscles are sure working well. First a surf park and now a transportation system. I'm proud that you're in the Slade family."

I could feel the desire for emeralds radiating from my father. His greed was strong.

"Thanks, hurrr, Dad. Besides, I don't want to keep using something Clayton invented the rest of my life, and I'm sure other people don't want to either."

"Well, I guess a quick trip through the DOTS should be safe. That's how your father and I are going to get there to watch the contest anyway. I was just worried that maybe you'd have some anxious reaction to being back in the Nether," said my mom.

"I'll be all right," I said before stuffing the rest of my food into my mouth. I chewed quickly and swallowed, somehow avoiding choking on the giant unchewed hunks of food.

But, would I be all right? What if the same forces that indoctrinated the librarian captured me while I was in the Nether? What would they do?

I shuddered before pushing away from the table and standing up. "Okay, I'm off to see the Ender King. I guess I'll see you guys tomorrow in Capitol City."

My parents stood up. My mom hugged me and kissed me on the cheek. My dad shook my hand and put his other hand on my shoulder and gripped tightly. "Go get them, son," he said.

I smiled and picked up my bag with my clothes and snacks. "I'll try," I said as I walked to the front door and out into the street.

*   *   *

Our morning practice was successful. Everyone was ripping still. After that we teleported back to the Ender King's palace and had a delicious lunch. When we were done, I gave my bag to the Ender King's men who were going to transport it along with my surfboard to our hotel in Capitol City. The Ender King had managed to locate a hotel that was not owned by the Dretsky family. He'd rented out the entire hotel so that we wouldn't be bothered by anyone else.

"Are you sure you want to take the DOTS?" asked the Ender King.

"Yeah, I want to see how it works. Like I said yesterday."

"I want to try the DOTS too," whined Tina.

The King looked over at her angrily. "I refuse to permit you to use the DOTS now or ever. Besides, you can teleport. You don't need to use some stupid contraption."

Tina slumped her shoulders and stomped her foot on the ground like an angry toddler. "You never let me do anything."

"What about all the surfing you been doing the last few days?" said the Ender King.

"Well, you never let me do anything by myself. You always have to be there to watch me or you send Gretchen along with me."

The Ender Queen intervened. "Now, now, stop arguing. We have a surf contest to win!"

The Ender King reached his hand over and held his wife's hand tenderly. "Meredith, you always know the right thing to say. We should focus on the contest."

Princess Tina lowered her eyelids, slightly ashamed of herself. "Yes, mother. I will focus on the surf contest, too. Maybe I can come up some sort of cheers or rallying cries we can shout when daddy is surfing."

Queen Meredith looked proudly at her daughter. "Yes, that would be nice."

All this strange ender royalty discussion was making me a little woozy. Cheers? Rallying cries? This wasn't a game of Quidditch; this was surfing. It was all about style and slashing moves and throwing lots of spray, not "2-4-6-8 who do we appreciate"-type stuff. Sheesh!

Anyway...

"Okay, hurrr, well, now that that's settled, I'm going to head over to the DOTS and I'll meet you at the hotel," I said as I waved goodbye.

When I was halfway to the DOTS hub at the library, I heard a voice behind me, "Jimmy Appleseed, wait up."

I turned around and saw Emma running along the street.

"You don't have to come in the DOTS with me," I said.

"I wanted to. I want to see how this thing works too. Besides, teleporting places is cool and all but it's kind of boring. You don't get to see anything. You are just in one place one moment and then another place the next. There's no journey in between. The journey is usually the best part," said Emma, sage like.

I shrugged. "I guess so. Come on then, let's go to the DOTS."

The trip on the DOTS was actually kind of boring. We walked into the library, bought our tickets for three emeralds each, and then walked into the appropriate nether portal. We then materialized in the Nether, where there were another ten portals waiting for us. Each portal was labeled with a number that corresponded to the destination.

According to our map we needed to enter portal 7 which would take us to a location near the Capitol City museum district, which was about 4 blocks from our hotel. We walked into the appropriate nether portal and sure enough, within a few moments we were inside the museum district transportation hub. We showed our ticket to the villager guarding the exit and once he had assured himself that it was a valid ticket, he let us leave.

We then walked out on to the wide boulevards of the Capitol City museum district.

Emma ooo'd and ahhh'd at the sights. Five, ten, and even fifteen-story tall stone buildings graced the wide boulevard. Stylishly dressed villagers walked up and down the street, peering in the shop windows and discussing art and politics and especially money.

"Isn't this exciting, Jimmy?"

"It's a bit frantic for my taste."

"Oh, relax. Just soak it all in while we walk to the hotel. Maybe we'll see something interesting."

I doubted that. However, I was fairly certain I'd would see things that were expensive and extravagant and stupid, but probably not interesting.

I could describe the various shops to you and the fancy doodads you could buy in them, but this is not a shopping guide to Capitol City, this is my diary, and I don't really care about those sorts of things. Suffice it to say, we walked by all sorts of shops in which people were spending tons of emeralds on things that looked a lot like trash to me.

The only thing that intrigued me was the Museum of Redstone circuitry. I thought that might be worth checking out after the surf contest. For now, I wanted to concentrate on winning absolute victory.

When we finally got to the hotel, we walked up to the front desk and were about to tell the desk clerk who we were, when she said, "Hurrr, you must be Jimmy and Emma. The Ender King told me to expect you. My name is Rachael."

"Correct," I said.

Rachael reached behind her and stuck her hand into two cubby holes and pulled out two keys. "You are in room 204," she said to Emma, "and you are in room 205," she said to me.

"Thanks," said Emma. "Have our bags been put in our rooms?"

Rachael nodded. "Of course. If you need anything, pull the string near your bed. It will ring a bell over here," she said, pointing to a panel of bells with numbers above them, "and I will send a servant up immediately to attend to your request."

"This place is pretty fancy, no?" I asked.

Rachael rolled her eyes. "Of course it is. We've been in business for over 300 years. Only the best for the best clientele, meaning the Ender King of course, not you."

Ouch!

"Okay, thanks for that enlightening explanation," I said. "See ya later."

Emma and I walked over to the stairs and went up to the second floor. We each went in to our rooms. My room was pretty nice. I'm sure this room would cost 50 emeralds a night or something completely ridiculous like that.

I went over to the sink and washed my hands and face. I checked my hair in the mirror and then realized I hadn't asked what room the Ender King was in. I rang the bell and there was soon a knock on the door.

When I opened the door, there stood a smartly dressed villager wearing a dark red robe who said, "How may help you?"

"Oh, I was just wondering which room the Ender King is in. I forgot to ask at the front desk."

"He is in the penthouse suite, of course."

"Of course," I said. "How do I get there?"

"Take the stairs all the way to the top. There will be a door. It's behind the door. Of course, you have to get through the Ender King's guards."

"No problem with that, they know me," I said. "Okay thanks." I began to close the door but the servant put his foot in the door and kept me from closing it. He reached out his hand and flicked the ends of his fingers towards himself, indicating that I needed to give him something.

A tip? For that?!?

"Oh, yeah, sorry about that. I don't travel much." I reached into my pocket and pulled out two emeralds and put them in his hand. His hand remained open and he flicked his fingers toward himself some more.

"Two emeralds isn't enough? What's a normal tip around here?"

"Five emeralds," he said without a hint of sarcasm or levity.

"Five emeralds, just for giving me a little piece of information?"

The servant nodded his head and flicked his fingers towards himself again.

"Fine," I said rolling my eyes. I reached into my pocket and dug out three more emeralds and dropped them in his hand. His greedy villager fingers closed on the emeralds and a smile came across his face. He tucked the emeralds into his inventory and said, "It was a pleasure to serve you, sir." Then he walked away and I slammed the door shut.

After a few minutes I went over to Emma's room and knocked on the door. After she opened it, I told her where the Ender King was and we both walked up the stairs to the penthouse. We said "hi" to the ender soldier guarding the door and were let inside.

The Ender King's penthouse suite was almost as fancy as his palace in Zombie Bane. The Ender King sat talking to Queen Meredith and Princess Tina. The King watched us walk in and then said, "Welcome. Laird is taking a nap in his room, but I'll send someone for him. We should go over to the Capitol City surf pool and practice."

"Should we? Won't it be crowded?" I asked.

Then the King shook his head. "Actually, Clayton Dretsky sent over one of his henchmen – err, servants – and told me that he would shut the park down at three o'clock today to let us practice in it. Even though he's an evil person, at least he seems to be playing fair by letting us practice."

I did not for one second think that Clayton was really playing fair, but I said, "Okay ... hurrr ... so what should be do until then?"

"Let's wait for Laird to get here, then we can discuss contest strategy," said the Ender King. "Or, you can go back to your room and take a nap. I really don't care."

"Aren't you being a bit nonchalant about all this, King?" asked Emma.

"What is there to worry about?" said the King. "Worry just steals happiness from the present moment."

Mind blown.

"But, what if I'm not happy and I'm not worrying?" I asked, trying to back the King in to an intellectual corner. What could possibly explain the absence of happiness without worry? The King was finished.

The King rolled his eyes. "In that case, Jimmy, you would be sad."

"Aaargh!" I yelled at the pain of my defeat.

"Don't try to play a player," said the King as he winked.

"My brain hurts," I said.

At that moment Laird materialized in the arms of an enderman. "What's up, King?" asked Laird.

"It is time to practice," said the King. "Everyone, return to your rooms and put on your surfing clothes and grab your surfboards. Be back here in ten minutes."

When everyone had returned, the Ender King teleported us directly into the water of the Capitol City surf pool.

After splashing down, I looked over and saw Clayton standing on his private pier where he had taken Biff and me surfing that one time. Clayton waved at us. Laird waved back, but the rest of us didn't.

"You have the place to yourself for two hours," yelled Clayton. "At five o'clock, my team wants to practice. You can stay and watch us if you want."

"Thanks, but no thanks," I yelled back.

"Suit yourself," Clayton yelled before retreating along the wooden pier into his private room.

Someone turned the waves on and we started practice.

I was surfing the same way that I had been surfing at our practice pool, same goes for Emma and

Laird. The Ender King, however, was surfing in a very lethargic style. He would simply catch a wave and stand straight up and stiff on the deck of his surfboard. He performed no maneuvers. In fact, he looked like ... well ... a kook. He looked like one of the worst surfers there ever was. He was boring and pathetic.

After about an hour of this, I paddled over to the King and said, "King, what's up? You were ripping back at our practice facility. Why are you acting like a kook?"

The Ender King snapped his head around and looked at me. I could tell he was upset, but he did not increase his size. Instead he simply said, "It's a surprise."

I wasn't sure what he meant by that. Would I see a surprise at the end of the practice or was he holding back so Clayton would not know what he was capable of? I discovered the answer shortly, because, by the end of the practice, the Ender King had done nothing other than be a kook the entire time.

At exactly five o'clock, Clayton came out onto his pier and yelled, "Okay, time's up. Please leave the pool."

I was going to paddle in and dry off, but the Ender King said, "Everyone paddle to me, and we will teleport away."

"Don't you want watch Clayton's team and see what they're like?" asked Laird.

"Absolutely not," said the Ender King.

Well, he was the coach of the team, so what could we say? We all paddled close to the King and he wrapped his scrawny arms around us and teleported us to the penthouse.

When we appeared in the Ender King's suite, one of his servants tossed each of us a towel so we could dry off. Once we were dry, then King told us to go back to our rooms and rest for an hour. He would have dinner brought to our rooms. He wanted us to eat and then go to sleep. We had to get up early because the surf contest was supposed to start at eight o'clock the next morning.

"I will send an ender soldier to wake you up at 6:00 in the morning. The soldier will bring you breakfast as well. Once you've eaten, put on your bathing suit, grab your surfboard, and come up here. We will teleport to the surf pool at precisely 7:30 a.m..

Then we'll see what Notch's surf contest is really all about."

* * *

The dinner the ender soldier brought to my room was delicious and filling. I thanked him as he gathered the dirty dishes and teleported away.

I thought about knocking on Emma's door and hanging out with her for a while, but realized I was very tired. So, I put on my pyjamas and crawled into bed. I was asleep before I knew it.

The dream began immediately.

A hooded, cloaked figure appeared and tied my wrists with rope. He led me down one of the hotel's hallways to a door. When the door opened, I saw a nether portal inside. The figure pushed me through, but he remained in the hotel.

When I emerged in the Nether, another hooded figure led me through a series of passageways. It was hot and humid. Zombie pigmen lurked in the shadows hissing their hatred at me.

After several minutes, we came to another room. Inside it was an altar. I was screaming to myself in my dream.

Was this the same altar the librarian had seen before ... hurrr ... before she was corrupted by the Rainbow Creeper?

I turned away from the altar, not wanting to look. It was at that moment I caught a glance of the hooded figure's face: It was Clayton! I reached up to pull off his cloak, but my bound hands did not permit me to reach that far.

Clayton pushed me away, knocking me to the ground. He grabbed my head and forced me to look at the door behind the altar. The door was opening. Colored lights were streaming forth. I heard a mysterious language being spoken.

I screamed and passed out.

The next thing I knew, I was back at the nether portal and was being shoved from behind. I entered the portal and emerged inside the hotel. The first cloaked figure was awaiting me. I looked at his face and saw: Clayton!

Again? Had he been in both locations at once? It was a dream after all, wasn't it? Or were there two Claytons?

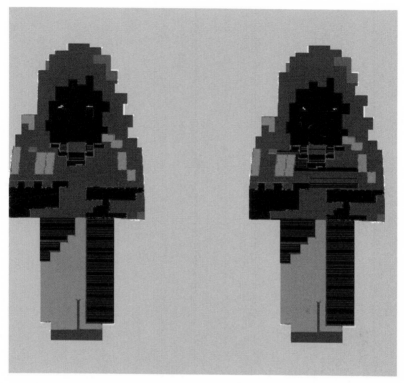

I screamed again. This time, I woke up in my bed. My wrists ached, as if they had really been tied.

I cast furtive glances around my room, not convinced I was really awake. I expected to see another cloaked figure or Entity 303 or an evoker.

But, I saw nothing.

Nothing except the rope marks embedded in my wrists!

It was too much to take, and I passed out.

Day 37 – The First Surf Contest

True to his word, a soldier arrived at my door at 6:00 in the morning.

I woke immediately at the sound of his tiny black knuckles smacking on the door with a staccato sound. He continued to hit the door every second.

I checked my wrists and ... nothing! No evidence they had ever been tied with rope or anything else.

What was going on? The dream had seemed so real last night. I had seen the marks on my wrists plain as day!

I rubbed my eyes, trying to wake up enough to be able to get out of bed. The noise of the soldier's little bony fingers against the hard wood of the door was nothing short of horrific so early in the morning. Finally, after about one minute of enduring this horrible sound, I jumped out of bed, threw on my robe, and rushed over to the door, pulling it open angrily.

"Will you give me a minute!" I yelled.

Before me stood an exceptionally skinny ender soldier holding a tray covered with food. He looked at me with a confused expression. "A minute for what?"

I realized my request made no sense to someone used to following orders. Leaps of logical reasoning were impossible if you never thought for yourself.

When I had yelled at the soldier, I had wanted a minute to wake up. But now I was awake and I was standing. "Nevermind. You can put the food on the table."

The soldier entered my room and walked to the small table and two chairs located under the solitary window in the room. He gently placed the tray of food on the table.

"The King requests your presence at seven o'clock in his penthouse. Do not be late." And with that, the ender soldier teleported away.

I walked over to the door to my room and shut it, upset that this ender soldier had rudely awakened me before I wanted to be awake and then left without closing my door. I mumbled out loud, "The king requests your presence. The king request your presence. Bah!"

I sat down and ate my food absentmindedly. I ate a big pile o' food, but I didn't really taste it. I was thinking about the contest already.

Who would Clayton have on his team? Would they be any good? Had he managed to get some professional surfers on his team? Did we even stand a chance?

After I finished my meal, it was still just 6:30. I lay down in bed again. I could feel myself drifting back to sleep but shook myself awake because I didn't want to miss the surf contest and incur the wrath of the Ender King.

I got back up and paced around my room. Eventually, I put my surf trunks and robe back on and then checked the time. It was 6:55: Go Time!

I opened my door and walked over to Emma's room and knocked. Through the wooden door, I heard Emma say, "Come in."

I open the door and walked in. Emma was sitting in a chair staring out the window at the crush of people in the streets below.

"I can't believe how many people live in Capitol City," she said. "I bet if I counted the people I can see right now, it would be at least half the population of Zombie Bane!"

"Yeah, this place is something else," I said, glancing out the window at the thick crowd of people rushing around like frantic cave spiders. "But, I prefer the simple life of the country."

"You're probably right, but I'd love to come here for college to learn about science from the top scientists of the villager world."

I nodded my head in agreement. "I suppose if I were any good at science, I'd want to come here to."

Emma stood up and closed the blinds across the window. She flattened her robe and said, "I guess we should go."

"Yes, but...," I said, letting my thought trail away. I realized I should not burden Emma with my dream. Not until after the contest was over, anyway.

Emma looked at me with concern. "What is it, Jimmy? You don't look so good."

I shrugged. "Just nervous, I guess."

Emma smiled. "Well, hurrr, don't be. We can win this."

I smiled back. *Worry is just stealing happiness from the present moment.* "Yeah," I said. "I suppose we can."

* * *

When we arrived at the Ender King's penthouse, he was relaxing in a chair, his long, skinny legs stretched out in front of him.

Laird was already there, sitting in another chair twiddling his thumbs. Literally. It looked like he was having a thumb war with himself.

Queen Meredith and Princess Tina were nowhere to be seen. Probably still sleeping. Or, maybe getting dressed up in some fancy ender couture so they could look stylish while watching the surf contest.

The four of us spent the next thirty minutes discussing contest strategy. Basically, the strategy was to go out there and rip as hard as possible. However, we needed to pay attention to the scores the judges were giving and adjust our surfing accordingly.

If they were scoring the barrel, then we should try to get deeper in the barrel. If they were scoring turns, then we should gouge our turns as deeply as possible and shoot as much spray in to the air as possible. If they were giving good scores to airs, then it would be up to Laird to get the points, since the rest of us couldn't do airs. Well, maybe the Ender King could, but I'd never seen him do an air.

After the discussion was over and the clock showed 7:30, the King wrapped his arms around us and teleported us to the artificial beach inside the Capitol City wave pool.

* * *

When we materialized on the beach, there were fifty ender soldiers waiting for us, ready to protect the King. General John was in charge. Even though Notch himself had created this contest, the King was still worried Clayton might try something. After all, the King had threatened to kill Clayton and destroy Capitol City in the process.

After my dream, I was worried Clayton might try something too.

When we appeared, the crowd went wild. I looked up and saw there were several thousand villagers in the bleachers, which had been constructed just for this event. About a quarter of the villagers were from Zombie Bane. I assumed the rest were from Capitol

City, with a handful of villagers from other locations. I suddenly felt very anxious and nervous.

I scanned the crowd and saw my parents and Emma's parents near the front of the bleachers. I elbowed Emma gently in the ribs and pointed to where our parents sat. They waved and smiled at us and we waved and smiled back.

"I didn't realize that so many people would be watching this!" I said.

"It's a surf contest," said Laird. "People watch these things. They're exciting."

"Yeah, Jimmy Appleseed," said Emma. "Plus, this is for an eternity of bragging rights. Pretty high stakes."

The King said nothing.

It was then that I noticed a small section of the bleachers had been reserved for mobs. The majority were zombie pigman, obviously they would cheer for Clayton. But there were also some endermen, a few skeletons, and two husks.

"Who do you think the skeletons and husks are cheering for?" I asked Emma.

She shrugged. "Maybe they just want to see the contest and don't care who wins?"

Normally, if I saw a skeleton or a husk, I would run away or kill it. Now, they were going to watch me surf? I was simultaneously creeped out and in awe.

Was it possible surfing would bring everyone together and end the generations of killing in the Overworld? Was surfing the bridge to peace between mobs, NPCs, and players? Was that the real reason Notch had ordered the surf contest? But, then I remembered this was Herobrine's idea originally. He couldn't want peace, could he?

The King motioned for us to come near him. When we were close enough, he whispered, "I can sense you are all nervous. Stay calm. Just pretend you're surfing at the practice facility. Don't worry about it."

"Easy for you to say, King," I said. "The crowd. The stakes. This is nerve wracking!"

"Dude, chill. Are you a surfer, or an uptight villager kook?" said Laird. "Let the stress go, man."

I could feel the chill vibes coming from Laird. I embraced the chill and let it come to me. I could feel myself relaxing already. I was no kook!

At that moment, Clayton and his team walked on to the sand and the crowd erupted with a great roar. I strained to see who was on Clayton's team. To my surprise, it looked like there was a zombie pigman on his team. The pigman looked familiar somehow....

"I didn't know zombie pigmen could surf," I said nudging Emma in the ribs.

"Well, I didn't know endermen could surf either, but they can," she said.

As Clayton's team approached us, I saw that the other participants were a male player I didn't recognize and Claire. I would have been surprised if she hadn't told us already that she was going to be on the team.

"Claire!" I shouted. "Who's the player?"

The tall thin player with curly blonde hair said, "My name's John John. You must be Jimmy Slade."

"Yeah, I am. Why do you have two first names?"

Before John John could answer, Laird said, "Hey, John! I didn't know you played Minecraft."

John smiled and walked over to Laird and gave him a bro hug. "Yeah, I've been playing Minecraft for years. It helps me relax before surf contests."

"Cool man."

I was dumbfounded. "What you mean it helps you relax before surf contests?"

Rather than letting John respond, Clayton interrupted. "Yeah, this John. He's a professional surfer in the human world. He's won a couple of world titles. He rips."

I looked over at John and squinted my eyes at him. "Is all that stuff true?"

John looked uncomfortable with all the attention, but said, "Yeah, I guess it is."

I looked over at Clayton and said, "That's cheating! You brought in a ringer!"

Clayton laughed. "It's not cheating. Besides, Laird's on your team. He used to be a pro surfer, back when he was young."

"That's different. He's not a professional surfer now."

"It's not different at all. You have your own ringer and I have mine."

"Why you –"

Before I could finish the brilliant insult I was about to deliver to Clayton, there was a flash of light and Notch appeared above the water and then slowly floated down to the sand at the water's edge. Everyone was silent for a moment and then applauded wildly. I had forgotten what an amazing entrance he could make.

He walked up the beach until he was standing between the two teams. "This is to be decided in the water, not on the beach. I want the King's team to go over to the right and I want Clayton's team to go over to left. I don't want the two teams talking during the contest."

Notch stood there as we made our way to our respective locations.

Once we were situated, Notch floated up into the air and announced, "Ladies and gentlemen. Mobs and villagers. The contest will begin shortly, but first I want to go over the rules and introduce your judges."

Finally, I get to hear how this contest will be judged.

"The rules are simple. Each member of the team will ride each of the three kinds of waves available in the wave pool twice. Where a wave offers the choice of going in either direction, the contestant must ride it in each direction at least once. Therefore, each team member will perform four rides. The winning team will be the team with the highest total score of the top two waves of each team member.

"The judging criteria is also very simple. We want to see exciting radical maneuvers, barrel riding, and creativity. This may sound somewhat nebulous, but you will understand why we give certain scores the moment we start.

"Each team will take turns riding a wave so the judges can focus on a single wave at a time. Once each wave is completed, the judges will confer and announce the final score. Then it will be the next person's turn on the opposite team."

Notch looked at the Ender King and Clayton and then asked, "Are there any questions?"

The King shook his head. Clayton also had no questions.

"Excellent," Notch continued. "Now I will introduce your judges for the day. The first judge comes all the way from the Nether. Ladies and gentlemen, put your hands together for the Ghast King." Notch snapped his fingers and suddenly there was a large ghast floating above the sand next to Notch! The crowd gasped in awe and horror. They recoiled at the thought of the Ghast King shooting a fireball at them.

The Ghast King then spoke with a deep hollow voice. "Thank you for having me, Notch. Do not worry villagers, I will not try to kill any of you today."

The crowd went wild, cheering the Ghast King.

"And your next judge is the Witch Queen," said Notch, snapping his fingers. The Witch Queen instantly appeared next to Notch, floating in the air.

The Witch Queen addressed the crowd. "Hello, everyone! I can't wait to judge the contest. Also, after the contest is over I'll be selling potions for 50% off the normal price. So come check out what I got."

Notch laughed. "And your third judge ... will be ... me! In fact, I will be a judge at all three of the scheduled contests to ensure they are conducted properly. However, the other judges will change for each contest."

Oooo, mystery judges!

There was a momentary pause while Notch and the Witch Queen floated down to the sand and walked over to a judging platform. The Ghast King floated next to the platform.

Once the judges were situated, Notch announced, "Let the contest begin! We will start on the mushy wave. The first contestant will be Jimmy Slade."

Of course, Notch had to make me go first. The chill vibes I had gotten from Laird vanished. I was a nervous wreck. Plus, the mushy wave was pretty boring to ride. You couldn't do much except for some really basic turns and some floaters. If I knew how to do an air, I might be able to fit one of those in, but I didn't.

I looked over at my teammates and said, "Here goes nothing."

I paddled out and waited in the takeoff zone. The villagers from Zombie Bane were chanting, "Go

Jimmy! Go Jimmy." I made the mistake of looking at the crowd and saw my parents holding their breath looking as nervous as I felt.

The wave pool turned on and waves came towards me. I let two waves pass underneath me before catching one. I paddled into the wave, did a bottom turn to a nice cutback, another bottom turn, a slashing top turn, another bottom turn, and then a floater at the end. The crowd went crazy. I wasn't sure if they liked my ride or if they were just excited to actually see surfing in person.

I walked up the beach to my team and waited anxiously for the score to be read. The judges decided on the score quickly and Notch announced, "6.5 points out of 10."

I felt ashamed. That was a very low score. Or was it? I had no idea. Being the first surfer of the day is always the hardest because you have no idea what the judges are thinking.

"The next surfer is Mateo, the zombie pigman."

Mateo?

"Hey!" I shouted. "Weren't you the pigman who tried to keep me and Emma from escaping the Nether?!?"

Mateo looked over with a smirk. "Yeah, so?"

I was filled with anger and rage, but Notch had said we needed to settle this in the water. "I hope you wipe out!" I yelled.

"Whatevs, brah," said Mateo as he paddled out.

When the pigman caught his wave, he dropped in, did a bottom turn, a slashing turn to start, another bottom turn, then a really drawn out roundhouse cutback, and finished with a floater. He did all this quite quickly. When a score was announced, it was a 6.9 out of 10.

I walked over to Emma, Laird, and the King and asked, "What was different about my ride from his ride?"

"He opened the slashing turn and you did a more simple turn," said Laird. "Plus, that was a sick roundhouse. Otherwise, I think they were about same."

The Ender King agreed. "Yes, we need to try to be as exciting as possible as quickly as possible."

The next four contestants were Emma, then Claire; Laird, then John. They exchanged similar scores on the wave. I could describe their rides in detail, but you probably want me to get to the good stuff rather than describe each ride. If you wanted descriptions of all thirty-two rides in this contest, I apologize for disappointing you. But, remain calm, for I will describe a few of them....

The final pair of the first round was Clayton versus the Ender King. The Ender King surfed first. He paddled in and did a quick bottom turn, then a massive slashing move, his long back leg extending out so far and pushing his board so hard that it seemed like his board was going to fly into the crowd, but his front foot held onto the board and it returned under his feet just in time for him to do another bottom turn, then a huge cutback, followed with a floater where he teleported up into the air twenty feet above his board and then back on to the board so quickly that landing was not a problem.

The crowd went crazy.

"Dude," I said to Emma. "What the heck was that?!?"

Emma shrugged. "I guess the King had been holding back in practice. He rips."

After a few moments, the judges announced a score of 8.8 out of 10.

Only an 8.8?

The Ender King paddled in proudly, having earned by far the highest score so far.

Clayton looked angry as he paddled out. When Clayton caught his wave, he stood up on his board with the fins in front instead of the nose. He then jumped up, did a kick flip, and spun the board around in the correct direction before bottom turning and doing a slashing top turn followed by another bottom turn, roundhouse cutback, and a finishing floater.

I had to admit, his ride was pretty creative at the beginning, but then became similar to the rest of our rides.

Apparently the judges agreed because, even though the King's surfing was much more explosive than Clayton's, they gave Clayton the same score of an 8.8, as a nod to his creativity, I guess. The crowd was not impressed. There were rumblings from the villagers from Zombie Bane and the endermen in the crowd. Princess Tina, who had arrived after the start of the contest and was sitting in a VIP booth surrounded by ender soldiers, shook her head in disbelief.

I agreed that the King's ride was better, but not by much. The teams were evenly matched. If Clayton didn't try some underhanded, illegal, and immoral tactics, it was anyone's contest to win.

It was then that I felt a surge of bad vibes. Someone evil had just arrived. I looked in the crowd, but could not see anything suspicious. I looked at Clayton, but he seemed totally involved in the contest; he did not look like he was trying to communicate with anyone. Then, as suddenly as they had come, the bad vibes disappeared.

I could detail the entire surf contest for you, how we went blow for blow on the A-frame, some of us opting to get deep into the barrel and others opting for turns and aerials, but that would take up so much time that you might get a little bored. Suffice it to say, when we got to the final round, about an hour later, Clayton's team was ahead by only one point.

The final round would be contested on the long, point-break style wave.

Because the King's team was behind, Notch changed the order so that the Ender King would surf last, giving him the ability to know the score he needed and to win the contest on the final wave.

The rest of us surfed our waves, keeping the contest close. In fact, Emma pulled an air at the end of her wave and her score brought our team within 0.5 points with only Clayton and the King left to surf.

When Emma paddled in, I rushed over to her and gave her a high-five. "Sick air!" I said.

Emma smiled broadly. "Yeah, I was just trying to hit the lip, but my board got air. I didn't think I'd pull it off. Did it look okay? I felt like a kook."

"It looked sick," said Laird. "You'll have to practice those next week."

Even though Emma's air was awesome and we had pulled closer to a win, I was worried. Clayton's team had been in the lead since the end of the first round, and I wasn't sure we'd be able to catch up. I looked over at the King as he watched Clayton paddling out. The King was calm. I could tell he was planning something.

Clayton paddled out to the point-break style wave and proceeded to tear it to shreds. He opened with an air, then did a series of searing cutbacks, followed by another air, and ending with a dangerous floater where he was in freefall for eight feet before landing perfectly like an ocelot leaping from a tree. I had to admit, it was impressive.

In the end, the judges gave him a 9.4 out of 10. This meant that the only way our team to win would be for the Ender King to get a perfect 10 out of 10 score, which seemed impossible.

I looked over at the King who had already figured out that he needed a perfect score. "I'm sorry King," I said sadly. "We let you down. We should have ripped harder, scored higher."

The King looked over at me with rage in his eyes. "Never give up until it's over. I've been saving the best for last."

"What do you mean?" asked Emma.

The Ender King smiled – or, at least I think he smiled; it's kind of hard to tell with endermen – and said, "Just watch."

As the King paddled out, I heard Tina yell, "Go, Daddy! You rule!" The King turned around and then disappeared from his board. He reappeared next to Tina and gave her a hug, then teleported back to his board.

The crowd said, "Awwww," due to the cuteness of the King's gesture to his daughter, but then refocused its attention on the final salvo of the war in the water.

The Ender King paddled over to the start of the wave and waited for it to come. He paddled in and stood up. He then did a deep bottom turn, a slashing top turn, and another deep bottom turn followed by a mid-face hack that stopped his progress completely in its tracks but regaining top speed immediately.

So far his ride was at least as good as Clayton's, but he needed something extra to push his score to a 10.

At that moment the Ender King reached out with his right arm and stretched it to several times its normal length and then dug it into the face of the wave. Somehow this action converted the wave into a barrel and he disappeared for three [!] seconds before popping out the end of the tube with the spray. The crowd went nuts. This wasn't even a barrelling wave and he had gotten a three-second barrel. It was amazing.

And he wasn't even done yet.

He did a few more bottom turn, top turn combinations, throwing massive buckets of spray all over the place, and then he did a deep bottom turn, got up to the top of the wave and pumped his board a few times to increase his speed and then at the end section of the wave, he *launched* his board into the air. His feet somehow remained on the board and he spun it around multiple times like a top, but that wasn't the most amazing part. As he was spinning in the air, the Ender King disappeared.

But he hadn't really disappeared. Instead, he teleported onto the beach and did some jumping jacks while the crowd roared and then teleported back onto his board before it finished spinning in the air and then landed on the end of the wave.

The King raised his arms in triumph while the crowd exploded with cheers, even those people who are cheering for Clayton's team, erupted with cheers.

The judges had no choice. They had to give the King a 10 out of 10. We had won by 0.1 points!

Clayton ran over to the judges' tower and yelled at them, "That's not fair! He can't use teleportation to increase his score."

Notch looked down at Clayton and said, "Was that in the rules anywhere, Clayton? I don't think so. If there's no prohibition in the rules, then you can do it in the contest."

Clayton's face turned red with anger. But he didn't say anything. Instead, he got a strange look on his face and asked, "Anything goes?"

Notch looked down at him and said, "Anything within reason. No killing."

"Oh, I wasn't thinking about that," said Clayton as he walked away with a smug expression on his face. I got some bad vibes from him as he walked toward his team. I noticed that he glanced into the crowd and gave a little nod. I followed his line of sight and saw a figure covered with a dark cloak, just like the figure in my dream.

Was that Clayton's Evoker? Or something worse? Entity 303? Maybe it was Herobrine, who had been conspicuously absent in light of the fact that the surf contest was basically his idea. Herobrine always liked to be the center of attention, but he also liked to disrupt things. Maybe he was here to upstage Notch?

I squinted my eyes as I looked at the figure. The cloak obscured his face until, just for a moment, it moved its head and I could just make out his face and ... oh my Notch! ... it looked just like Clayton! Just like my dream: two Claytons! I was shook.

Emma could tell something was wrong as we walked toward Clayton's team. John, Mateo, and Claire all congratulated us even though we could tell they were disappointed. Clayton stood off to the side, still angry.

Then, he gathered himself together and came over to the Ender King. "I guess you beat us fair and square," said Clayton, reaching out a hand.

"Yes," said the Ender King, refusing to shake Clayton's hand. I couldn't blame him.

"See you next week at the Zombie Bane wave pool, right?" said Clayton.

"Right," said the Ender King.

Clayton bared his teeth and said, "Get ready to lose. Your teleportation won't help you next time."

"Is that a threat?" asked the King.

Clayton laughed. "Why? Are you scared?"

"No."

"Then, it's not a threat."

And with that, Clayton snapped his fingers and his team followed, all except for Claire, who hung back for a moment and walked over to me.

"You were ripping out there, Jimmy," she said. I noticed she was now wearing a robe with a little rainbow creeper logo on it. I didn't mention it, for now.

"You were surfing pretty good too. Especially for someone has only been surfing for a few days," I said.

Claire smiled. "Thanks. Hurrr ... there's something I want to tell you, but I can't do it here. Maybe I can stop by Zombie Bane next week and we can talk."

"Sure, that's fine," I said. I was picking up good vibes again from her. I wondered if she felt trapped or if something else was going on. "Say, Claire ... hurrr ... does Clayton have a twin brother?"

The blood drained from Claire's face. She turned as white as a bunny rabbit. I no longer felt any vibes — good or bad — coming from her. Her lips quivered as her brain worked to come up with a response.

But then, I felt the same bad vibes I had felt during the contest, and Claire's expressed went blank. Her eyes became placid and the color returned to her face. "No," she said in a monotone voice. "Why do you ask?"

Had I just watched Claire be possessed by an Evoker, or something else?

"No reason. I just saw someone who looked a lot like him."

Claire smiled. "Ok, then. Bye, Jimmy," she said as she walked away toward Clayton.

I watched her walk away and then caught Clayton's eyes. He was staring at me with pure hatred. I knew I had stumbled on to something he had been trying to hide. I needed to discuss this with Mr. Blaze once I returned to Zombie Bane.

The Ender King gathered us together and said, "Thank you, everyone. That was very close. We need to practice more for the next contest. We have to be faster and more precise in our turns. I was lucky to get that 10. I don't know if I can do it again."

We all agreed that speed and precision was the key to the judging criteria.

"What now, King?" I asked.

"Now, I will teleport you back to the hotel. You will get your things and my men will teleport you to Zombie Bane. Unless, of course, you want to use the DOTS. There is a station in here somewhere."

"No, teleportation's fine," I said. "I want to get home as soon as possible."

"Good. You all should take tomorrow off to rest and recover. I will return to the End with the Queen and Princess in order to see to the affairs of my kingdom. I will then return to Zombie Bane and we can practice some more."

"Sounds like a good plan to me," I said.

"Will Tina be coming back?" asked Emma. "I really like her."

The King smiled. "If that is her wish, she will come back."

At that moment, Tina materialized next to us. "Of course, it is my wish, dearest royal father," said Tina in an exaggeratedly formal voice.

Everyone, except me, laughed at Tina's joke as the King wrapped his arms around us and we teleported away. I couldn't laugh. I was still thinking about Clayton's doppelganger.

END OF BOOK 6

Book 7

AN UNOFFICIAL MINECRAFT BOOK

DIARY
OF A
Surfer Villager
BOOK 7

DR. BLOCK

Day 38 – Afternoon

I was very tired from the surf contest yesterday as well as my startling vision of the strange person who looked like Clayton's twin brother. To make it even more strange, I recalled seeing two "Claytons" in my dream the night before the surf contest, but now was wondering if I had dreamed about the "twin."

As a result of my fatigue, I had slept in quite late that morning.

After eating a late breakfast or an early lunch, whichever you prefer, I went over to Emma's house and we walked to the Surf 'n Snack. Along the way, we ran in to Biff and he suggested we all go out for a standup paddle session.

"That sounds like a good idea, Biff. I've been surfing so much the past few days, that I want to do something else," I said.

"Let's do it!" said Emma.

Biff smiled. "Okay, let's meet out in the ocean between your Surf 'n Snack and my SUP school. How about we meet in 30 minutes?"

"Agreed," I said.

Emma and I continued to the Surf 'n Snack and spoke with our employees there. They said everything was going along very well.

"Everyone is super excited about the surf contest being here in a few days. It is all anyone can talk about," said Michael, one of our employees.

"You guys, we are going to have to shut down the surf park the day before the surf contest and the day of the surf contest to allow for practice sessions," I said. "So, you can have those days off, if you want."

Geronimo, our other employee, smiled. "That'll be great. I haven't had a day off in a couple of weeks. Not that I'm complaining, you pay really well, but it does get a little tiring."

Emma looked at me sideways. "I told you we should hire more employees."

I nodded. "I guess so." I had hoped not to hire anyone else because the profit margins were pretty good with only two employees. With three or four the profits would go down, but I supposed the revenue is so good it wouldn't really matter.

"Let's try to find some new employees after the craziness from the upcoming surf contest dies down," suggested Emma.

"Sure, I'm cool with that," I said. "Anyway, let's grab our SUPs and meet Biff."

*   *   *

About ten minutes later, after exchanging our robes for swimsuits, we were paddling out to meet Biff.

As we were paddling past the spot where the evil squid had attacked the young villager and then had almost killed me when I rescued the young child, I felt a shiver of fear. I felt panic rising in my gut and a wave of nausea quickly pass over my body. I shook my head to shut out the memory.

"What's wrong, Jimmy? You looked terrible there for a moment," said Emma.

I wiped the sweat from my forehead and then continued to paddle. "I was just thinking about that evil, killer squid. I'm glad we installed that net to keep them out."

Emma nodded. "Do you think anyone would try to possess a squid again, hurrr, if we removed the net and let the squids swim freely in the surfing area?"

I shrugged and sighed. "Who knows? Maybe."

"I wonder if we should remove it once Notch implements his Update Aquatic? Maybe it would be cool to go surfing with those dolphin things he's creating?"

"Could be," I said.

Just then Biff came into view and paddled over. "Hi guys," he said.

We nodded a greeting to him. The three of us paddled around in silence for a bit, enjoying the warm air and the cool water. We could hear the sound of the waves breaking at the Surf 'n Snack and the shouts of joy as the young villagers rode the wave.

"Guys, I need to tell you something," I said.

By the concerned tone of my voice, Emma and Biff could tell I was about to bring up some serious stuff. They looked at me, giving me their full attention.

"I saw something really weird at the surf contest. When the crowd was filtering out, I saw someone wearing a strange cloak. I wasn't able to get a good look at the person, except for just a brief moment.

When I saw his face ... hurrr ... it looked like Clayton Dretsky's twin brother."

Emma and Biff were shocked.

"Clayton never had a brother," said Biff. "I've seen my cousins every year since I was three years old, and I never heard of someone other than Claire and Clayton."

"Yeah, it might just be someone who looks a lot like Clayton," said Emma. "Maybe he's Clayton's doppelganger. We villagers do tend to ... hurrr ... resemble each other."

I shook my head. "No, it wasn't a mere resemblance, it was identical. It was creepy. If Clayton hadn't been standing nearby, I would've thought it *was* Clayton."

Biff clucked his tongue in thought. "Jimmy, I don't know what to tell you. There never was a third Dretsky sibling."

"Maybe you could ask Claire when Clayton's surf team gets here for the contest," suggested Emma.

I nodded my head in agreement. "Yeah, well, I asked her at the surf contest, and she denied Clayton had a twin. But, maybe she was too scared to tell the truth. I could try again."

I felt better having told Emma and Biff about the mysterious twin.

"Come on," I said. "Last one to paddle to the far side of the ocean is a piece of rotten zombie flesh!"

Day 38 – Nighttime

After our race to the far shore, Biff, Emma, and I paddled around for about an hour before we went back into shore. I said goodbye to both of them and walked home. I ate dinner with my parents and then told them I was really tired and went up to bed a few hours earlier than usual.

In retrospect, I wished I had stayed awake all night because I had a strange dream. Or should I say, a nightmare.

My nightmare began about the same way my previous nightmare left off. I was tied up and dropped off in my hotel bed after being indoctrinated by the minions of the Rainbow Creeper.

Only this time, I was able to sit up in bed and remove my shackles. I began walking around the hotel room, sweating with fear, knowing something was about to happen but not what or when.

After a few minutes of dream time, I began to hear laughter. It was a maniacal, random laughter which seemed as though it could not come from the throat of a villager but rather must be coming from some sort of demon.

I backed into the corner of the hotel room and cowered there. Knowing that the laughing, raving thing would eventually reveal itself. After all, it was a nightmare. You always see what torments you, usually jump-scare style.

It was then that, emerging from the dark shadows on the other side of the room, came a cloaked and hooded figure. I knew instantly it was Clayton's twin brother. He pulled back his hood as he continued laughing. In my dream I screamed, "Get away from me, Clayton's evil twin!"

The evil freak laughed and laughed and ignored my fear and my screams. And then, just as quickly as the laughing had started and as quickly as the evil twin had appeared, he vanished into thin air.

I collapsed in the corner of the room and wrapped my arms around my knees, pulling them to my chest. I rocked back and forth like a scared little baby.

Again I saw movement in the shadows and emerging slowly from the pitch black depths came a creeper. Not just any keeper, the Rainbow Creeper himself!

I screamed, but no sound came out. The muscles in my throat straining against my vocal cords, hoping to squeeze some sort of noise out so that I could release the pressure of my terror. But, my fear was so complete, so paralyzing that I couldn't even accomplish that.

The Rainbow Creeper shuffled up to me and bent his rainbow colored body to look down upon me and said in a deep, ominous voice, "You are mine." And then, he too disappeared, vanishing into thin air.

I totally lost it inside my dream.

I had gone insane.

I was rolling around on the ground pulling out my blonde hair and scratching my face.

I screamed and laughed and cried, all the same time.

And then suddenly, I stopped moving.

I looked at my arms and legs and saw there were thin, nearly see-through strings attached to my limbs. The strings stretched up into the sky, but I could not see where – or if – they had an end.

What is this?

And then, I felt the string on my right arm being pulled upward, and my right arm raised. Then I felt the string on my left arm being pulled, and my left arm lifted. Then I felt all the strings pull up at once and I stood up.

I had no control of my movements. If a string moved, I moved; if it didn't, I didn't.

It was at that moment I had the realization that there was a string attached to my mouth. It moved up and down and my mouth opened and closed. I was like a marionette puppet.

I then felt a string pull on my head and it made my face look up to the sky where I saw that the strings were attached to a set of puppeteer's sticks which were being manipulated by ... Entity 303!

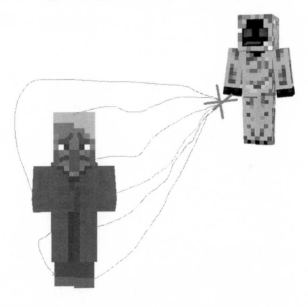

I woke from my nightmare screaming and covered with sweat. I sat bolt upright.

I was breathing hard and my heart was pounding as if I might have a heart attack and die. My health bar actually had decreased by three hearts *while I was sleeping*. Nothing like that ever happened to me before.

Suddenly my door burst open and my mother and father rushed in. "Jimmy what's wrong!?! Are you okay!?!"

I nodded. I licked my dry lips with my equally dry tongue, trying to get some moisture into my mouth so that I could respond to my parents. I swallowed a few times and then said, "It was just a nightmare. I'll be fine."

And then I flopped back down on my bed, onto sheets wet with sweat. It was kind of gross, but at least I did not have any strings attached to my body. I breathed a heavy sigh of relief.

"Do you think you can go back to sleep?" asked my dad.

I nodded. "Yes. Now that I know it wasn't real, I can."

But, was it fiction? This was the second dream in two days where the Rainbow Creeper appeared. And now, Entity 303 was involved?!?! To put it mildly, I was worried.

My mom smiled at me. "Good," she said as she stood up and walked to the door with my dad. "Just let us know if you need anything."

"Ok, Mom," I said, yawning. "I will."

Day 39 – Morning

After a breakfast, I went over to Emma's house and told her about my dream. I also told her about the dream involving Rainbow Creeper I'd had while we were in Capital City for the surf contest.

Emma was concerned. "I think we should go talk to Mr. Blaze about this. After all, he did tell us about the similar experience of the librarian."

I nodded my head. "I suppose we should. I doubt there's anyone else in Zombie Bane who would have any insight into … hurrr … comparative dream analysis."

Emma shivered a little bit even though it was a warm summer day. "And Entity 303 using you like a marionette. Super creepy."

It took us about ten minutes to walk to Mr. Blaze's bookstore. Although the bookstore was yet to open, we could see Mr. Blaze walking around through the window. I tapped my knuckles against the window to draw his attention. When he looked over at us, he smiled before coming to the door and opening it.

"What can I do for you two?"

"Mr. Blaze, I need your opinion about a couple of dreams I've had," I said.

Mr. Blaze's emotional intelligence quotient was apparently very high because he quickly became concerned and opened the door wider so we could enter.

Mr. Blaze closed the door behind us, locked it, and then said, "Have a seat over at that table."

Emma and I walked over to the wooden table and chairs and sat down. The chairs were very uncomfortable. I was squirming around trying to get into a position that was tolerable, but I was failing miserably at the task.

Mr. Blaze grimaced. "Sorry about the chairs. I had them made to be very uncomfortable so people wouldn't sit in here and read books like this is a library. I'm trying to get people to buy the books and then take them home and read them. People just think they can read for free these days. It's not right. Bookstore owners get nothing and the authors get nothing."

I looked at Mr. Blaze. "Hurrr, I guess I see your point."

Emma hit me on the shoulder softly. "Tell him, Jimmy. Tell him."

I kept shifting around in the chair trying to get comfortable and finally give up and stood up. "I can't take that chair anymore," I said.

Mr. Blaze smiled. "See, it works."

I slapped my forehead and then sighed. "Whatever. Let's talk about my dreams."

I recounted the details of both of my dreams. Mr. Blaze listened without saying a word, though his expression demonstrated that he was very concerned. When I finished narrating both dreams, I said, "Well, that's it. What you think?"

Mr. Blaze put his hand on his chin and rubbed it in thought. He rubbed it for quite a while, maybe fifteen or twenty seconds, without saying anything. I was starting to get upset at the delay, but I didn't want to interrupt him. He was clearly thinking it through, not simply ignoring me.

Finally, after about a minute, Mr. Blaze removed his hand from his chin and cleared his throat before saying, "I'm not sure those were dreams Jimmy. They may have been visions."

I was completely shocked.

"What do you mean, visions? Are you saying I'm seeing something in the future?"

"It could be that, or it could be that what you experienced as dreams were *actually happening to you* only without your body leaving your bed."

My eyes got wide. I felt the sweat forming on my forehead. I got nervous and nauseous at the same time. "I'm not quite sure I follow what you are saying, Mr. Blaze. Can you explain it a little better?"

Mr. Blaze took a deep breath and said, "Well, most people think of visions as a premonition of the future, and that's what these so-called dreams might be. However, there is another form of vision which some people call astral projection. It's where you observe your soul being manipulated in a certain way although your earthly body remains static. Normally, these sorts of projected visions happen when you meditate a lot and try to project your soul elsewhere, but it can also happen when someone takes your soul from your body and does things to it."

Emma sucked in a sharp breath, put her hand over her mouth, and whispered, "Oh, my Notch!"

I fainted before she finished the word "Notch."

When I regained consciousness, Mr. Blaze was slapping me in the face.

"Déjà vu," I said, in an attempt at a joke, thinking back to the last time I passed out and Mr. Blaze had to slap me back to reality.

"Jimmy, maybe you should ... hurrr ... see a doctor. You pass out a lot," said Mr. Blaze.

"Yeah, it's kind of scary," said Emma.

I stood up and shook my head to clear the cobwebs. "I don't need a doctor. I just need to figure out what's happening with these crazy dreams or visions or whatever the heck they are."

I leaned against a nearby bookshelf to steady myself and then asked, "So are you saying that the Rainbow Creeper or Entity 303 or Clayton and his evil twin are taking my soul out of my body and torturing me?"

Mr. Blaze put his hand to his chin again and rubbed it in thought for a few seconds and then said, "I'm not sure it sounds like torture. Are you ever in pain during these dream-like states?"

I shook my head. "No, never in pain, just scared and confused."

Mr. Blaze nodded. "I don't think these visions are to torture your soul, but instead ... hurrr ... to corrupt it."

I felt myself getting lightheaded again but willed myself to stay conscious. Emma looked over and saw that I was a little woozy and stood up and pushed her hand against my chest so I would be sandwiched between her hand and the bookcase.

Meanwhile Emma looked over at Mr. Blaze and said, "What do you mean corrupt his soul? What would be the purpose of that?"

"That's the 1 million emerald question, isn't it? If they viewed Jimmy as an enemy, it would be simpler just to kill him, we all know Clayton and Entity 303 are capable of that."

"What about the Rainbow Creeper's role in all of this?" I asked.

"I'm not sure if the Rainbow Creeper is there or is just being used to scare you or what is happening exactly," said Mr. Blaze sadly.

There was silence in the room while Emma and I pondered the horrible possibility Mr. Blaze had voiced. Mr. Blaze was quiet too. I could tell he was thinking again because his hand was on his chin.

After a few seconds, Mr. Blaze asked, "Do you expect the Ender King to be in town soon?"

I nodded my head. "I think he is supposed to be here sometime today."

Mr. Blaze pressed his lips together making his mouth at thin line of determination and said, "I think we should ask his opinion about all this. It might also be time for another visit to Herobrine, as much as I'd like to avoid being around him, he had a pretty good idea the last time we were there."

"Maybe we should ask Notch?" suggested Emma.

"If I knew how to contact Notch, I would," said Mr. Blaze. "However, I have no idea. At least, he will be here in a few days to judge the surf contest, so if you don't have an answer by then we can see if Notch will help us."

The thought of Notch helping us filled me with some comfort. However, the fact the surf contest was still five days away filled me with the fear and apprehension.

I really hoped the Ender King could help me figure this out.

Day 39 – Afternoon

After visiting with Mr. Blaze, I had returned home by myself to relax. Shortly after lunch time, there was a knock on the door and an ender soldier was there to inform me that the Ender King had arrived. He requested my presence as soon as possible.

"I'm ready to go now," I said to the soldier. "Is someone else going to pick up Emma?"

The ender soldier said, "Yes, someone else is fetching Emma. If you're ready to go now, shall we teleport?"

I nodded my head and stepped closer to the ender soldier. He wrapped his arms around me and the next thing I knew I was inside the Ender King's local palace.

The King, the Queen and Princess Tina were all there. Tina yelped with happiness when I appeared and ran over and hugged me. "Jimmy! How are you?"

"I'm okay," I said without any conviction. "How are you?"

"I'm fine. And so is Isabel. She's outside eating grass."

I smiled at the thought of Tina's ridiculous llama. "That's great. Maybe I should get a llama or a dog or something."

"Yeah, you should," said Tina. "Having a pet is cool."

At that moment, the Ender King walked over and said, "Hello, Jimmy. Welcome back to my palace."

"Thanks, King. But I have something else on my mind. Can we talk privately after Emma arrives?"

"Oooh, a mystery," said Tina in a conspiratorial tone. "I want to know."

"I'd rather keep this between me and your father. The only reason I'm involving Emma is that she already knows."

Tina stomped her foot on the ground like a petulant child. "No fair!" she said before stomping away to her room.

The Ender King's gaze followed Tina disapprovingly. "Ignore her. She's getting to that age."

"What age is that?" asked Emma, who had appeared just as those words came out of the Ender King's mouth.

"Never mind," said the King. "Welcome back to my palace, Emma. Jimmy tells me that he has a confound he wishes to discuss with me and with you."

"Yes, the dreams," she said.

The Ender King raised an eyebrow looked down at me and said, "Dreams?"

It took me a few minutes to explain what happened in my dreams or visions or whatever they were as well as Mr. Blaze's interpretation of them. When I finished, I asked, "So, what do you think, King? Are these dreams actually visions? Is my soul being manipulated? What? Inquiring minds want to know!"

"I suppose it could be any of those things. Without me being present inside your dream, I really have no idea how I can know the feeling of them. However, I am concerned. Either you are obsessed about the Rainbow Creeper and Clayton and Entity 303, and it is affecting your subconscious to the point that it interferes with your sleep, or you are being targeted for nefarious acts. Either way, it will affect your ability to surf well during the surf contest."

I couldn't believe this. The surf contest? Was that all he cared about? What about me? What about my soul?

"Yeah, I wouldn't want to ... hurrr ... affect the surf contest. I guess I will just let Entity 303 turn me into his puppet," I said angrily.

It was at that moment that the Ender King suddenly snapped to attention. "What did you say?"

"I said, I guess I'll just let Entity 303 turn me into his puppet."

The Ender King sat down in his throne and nodded his head sadly. "Maybe that's what it is. Didn't you say you had some visions of Entity 303 even before these dreams?"

"Yeah, but Clayton's Evoker basically told me that he had put those visions in my head just to scare me."

"And you believe the statements of an Evoker because...?" asked the Ender King.

"I guess I don't know why I believe him," I admitted.

"Exactly," said the Ender King slamming his tiny black fist against the armrest of his massive throne for emphasis. "Maybe this has been some sort of scheme all along to indoctrinate you or to program you to lash out at just the right moment. Maybe Entity 303 already can control you but just hasn't made you do anything yet."

I felt sick to my stomach. "You're not making me feel any better, King."

"I don't want to scare you, but I do want to explore the possibilities."

"Well then how do we figure out what's really happening?" asked Emma loudly. "Everyone's speculating about all kinds of crazy nonsense, but no one's trying to verify anything with objective data!"

A scientist to the end.

"Well, I think Mr. Blaze's idea was a good one. Herobrine has experience manipulating people and torturing their souls. If anyone's going to know what's happening, he would."

"So? Let's go now!" I demanded.

The Ender King shook his head. "No, it's already too late in the day and, besides, I want to surf. You could probably use a good surf also, to help you relax."

"But I won't be able to sleep again, not really, until we figure this out," I said.

"Look, Jimmy, we won't be able to go to Herobrine's lair until tomorrow. If it will make you feel any better, I can station an ender soldier at your door and even in your bedroom to try to prevent any nefarious activity."

"I guess that will have to do," I said, worrying about what might happen if the dreams returned. But then, I realized worrying wasn't going to help anything. "You know, maybe a surf will make me feel better. Let's go."

"That's the spirit, Jimmy," said Emma, trying too hard to be positive and encouraging, using the sort of voice you use when training a puppy to go to the bathroom outside instead of on the kitchen floor.

"Let me track down my daughter and we will go surfing," said the Ender King.

"Okay, but what about Laird?" I asked.

"Oh, I forgot to tell you, Laird says he has to go to a funeral for one of his best friends in the real human world. Therefore, he will not be able to play Minecraft on what he calls "Saturday" which is the date for the next surf contest. Therefore, we will have to find a substitute."

I slapped my head. This was disastrous. *Who the heck could we get to replace Laird, a professional surfer?*

"That's impossible! There's no one we can get on such short notice!" I said in a whiny voice, like a three-year-old toddler.

"Actually, there is," said Tina in a confident voice. I hadn't seen her come into the room. Maybe she had teleported.

"You?" I asked in disbelief.

She crossed her arms in front of her chest and said, "Of course, me. You yourself said that I was getting pretty good last week."

I slapped my head again. (It was starting to hurt.) I didn't care anymore. "Whatever. Let's go surfing."

Day 40 – Morning

When I woke up this morning, I said "hello" to the ender soldier who had stood guard in my room all night. His presence must have helped, because I didn't have any dreams last night.

As I stretched, I could feel my muscles were still tight from yesterday's surf session. It had been good. No one was ripping, but everyone was doing well. I wasn't sure we could win the contest with Tina, but it was best two of three, so even if we lost this round, we still had a chance to win the whole thing.

"Thanks for hanging out, Baxter," I said to the ender soldier. "You can leave now, if you want."

The ender soldier stood at attention and said, "Thank you, Jimmy. I shall return tonight." And then, he teleported away. I smiled at his formality before going downstairs to eat breakfast.

* * *

After breakfast, I met Emma as she was walking to the Ender King's palace. When we arrived, the Ender King was tending to some royal business and told us that he would be with us in about an hour. Instead of sitting around doing nothing, Emma and I, along with Tina, her llama, and their escort, the elderly Gretchen, decided to go for a walk.

As had happened the last time Gretchen tagged along, our walk was frustratingly slow. Gretchen was so old that she looked like a wrinkled black sock or a fossilized leaf that had somehow sprouted two skinny legs. It was as if a light breeze might blow her over.

We walked through the narrow streets of the village until we got to the main thoroughfare which passed through Zombie Bane. It was probably about thirty blocks wide. It was formally named the "Main Boulevard." Sometimes people called it the "main drag" or the "wide street." Villagers are creative like that.

We were walking along, or should I say *barely* walking along, looking into shop windows and listening to Gretchen's nostalgic comments about things she had seen when she was a child thousands of years ago, when I heard a strange noise coming from behind us. It sounded like a skittering noise. At first, I thought it might be horses, but I wasn't sure. As the noise came closer, I decided to turn around and see what was happening. When I turned around, I saw one of the most amazing and, at the same time, most horrific sights I had ever seen in my twelve years of life in the Overworld.

Coming down the main street of Zombie Bane was a herd of several hundred spiders. They were being herded by several zombies on zombie horses. The zombies were wearing helmets to protect them from the sun's rays.

I backed away from the street and said, "Oh my Notch! I've never seen anything like that. I didn't even know zombies herded creatures of any kind."

"It is very strange indeed," said Tina, holding Isabel's leash a little more tightly.

"I've never read about anything like this in any of my science books," said Emma.

Gretchen wheezed in and out a few breaths and then said, "We don't have zombies in the End, so I've never seen anything like it either."

The zombie horse and rider leading the herd of spiders was approaching us so I asked, "What's the meaning of this? Why are you herding spiders through my village? And, for that matter, why are you are herding spiders at all?"

The zombie horseman stopped his horse, and raised his rotten left arm, indicating that the herd and the other riders near the sides and back of the herd should also stop. The zombie looked down at me with his decaying eye sockets and said, "Jimmy Slade, correct?"

I was shook.

Why did the zombie know who I was? And, more particularly, why did a zombie riding a horse leading a herd of spiders know who I was?

"Yeah, I'm Jimmy Slade. Who wants to know?" I said, trying to act brave, but my cracking voice betrayed my fear.

The zombie chuckled slightly. I could smell the decaying flesh stink of his breath wafting over me. It was sickening. Then he said, "Jimmy Slade, progeny of Cornelius, bane of zombies, we have not forgotten the humiliation your family has brought upon zombie kind."

"That was generations ago," I said. "What does that have to do with you bringing a herd of spiders through town?"

"We are doing it as a favor to our patron."

"Who is that?"

"You've met him."

"Well, who is it then?"

"He did not want us to tell you. He simply wanted us to drive this herd of spiders through town and then leave. His only request was that we made sure that you saw it." With that, the zombie fell silent and smiled his rotten-gummed, loose-toothed smile at me.

I was shook again. I didn't know what to do. I could've kept asking questions, but it was clear he wasn't going to answer them. And that's when Gretchen intervened.

The elderly, tissue-paper thin ender woman, who looked like she would be knocked over by a light breeze, took two slow, laborious steps forward and said, "Hold on, you whippersnapper. You get off your high horse and come down here and tell Jimmy what he needs to know."

The zombie looked at the skeletal ender woman, smiled, and dismounted from his zombie horse. He walked over to her and said, "You don't want to get in the middle of this, old lady."

Gretchen bristled at this comment from the rude zombie. "You don't have the right to call me old, you undead thing."

Then, Gretchen extended a scrawny, arthritic ender finger at the zombie and pointed just inches from his face and said, "You tell Jimmy right now who sent you."

The zombie looked at Gretchen with disgust and then shoved her. Gretchen lost her balance and began to fall backwards. Tina screamed, "No," and tried to catch Gretchen before she fell. But it was too late.

Gretchen fell onto the hard cobblestone surface, hit her head, and vanished in a puff of smoke. The only remnants of her long life was a little doll she dropped and which, I learned later, she had been given as a child.

Tina screamed, "You horrible monster! I'm going to get you!"

Emma reached out and grabbed Tina's arm and restrained her. I reached into my inventory and found a knife and fork that I had for some reason left in there. I held the knife and fork out and said, "Come on, zombie! It's time for some dinner." Then I lunged at the zombie with the knife and fork ready to cut him into little tiny pieces.

But before I could begin to cut the zombie up like up plate of overcooked pasta, the Ender King materialized and restrained me.

"What has happened here?" demanded the Ender King.

"That zombie killed Gretchen, Daddy," said Tina through tears.

The Ender King reached his arm out and grabbed the zombie by the neck. "Is this true zombie?"

The zombie stared at the Ender King with hateful eyes and then said, "Of course it is. And I'd do it again."

After hearing the zombie's confession, the Ender King flicked his long, skinny arm and pulled the zombie's head off. The zombie flashed red and then vanished in a puff of smoke, leaving only two tiny rotten flesh drops as the disgusting remains of his corrupted, undead existence.

The Ender King kicked the rotten flesh into the gutter and then looked at the herd of spiders and the remaining zombie horsemen. "You leave town now or you will all die." For emphasis, twenty ender soldiers suddenly appeared around the herd, having teleported at that exact moment due to some unseen signal from the Ender King.

The zombie horsemen looked from left to right and then, realizing they were surrounded, said, "Get along little doggies." The herd of spiders began to move and within a few minutes they were beyond the borders of Zombie Bane.

As the herd left, I asked the Ender King if he had any idea what was the meaning of the herd and why the zombie had told me that his patron had directed they bring the herd through the village as some sort of message to me.

"I have no idea, Jimmy," said the King, rubbing his chin in thought and blinking his eyes as though he were startled. "I've heard of zombies controlling herds of spiders and other hostile mobs in the past, when the legions of the undead existed in much larger numbers than they do today, before the players came and started to exterminate them. But I haven't heard of something like this happening in generations."

I sighed. "Maybe Mr. Blaze will know something?"

The Ender King looked at us and said, "Sure, go ahead and ask him. I've arranged a meeting with Herobrine for this afternoon, so make it quick and then return to my palace so we can travel to Herobrine's fortress. But, if Mr. Blaze has any ideas, we might as well hear."

"Okay, we'll go talk to him right now," I said.

* * *

Emma and I arrived at Mr. Blaze's bookstore a few minutes later. We asked the young teenaged clerk working at the front desk if we could talk to Mr.

Blaze. The clerk told us that Mr. Blaze hadn't been in that day and he had no idea where Mr. Blaze might be.

"Okay, hurrr, if he comes in, can you tell him that Emma and Jimmy were looking for him?" I asked.

The clerk shrugged his shoulders. "I'll let him know. Is there any other message you want to leave for him?"

I shook my head. I did not want to tell the clerk the content of my conversation with the now dead zombie. It was weird enough that everyone saw the spider herd and saw the zombie talking to me. I did want to fan the flames of rumor.

"Okay then, see you later," said the clerk.

Emma and I began walking back to the Ender King's palace for our appointment with Herobrine. As we walked, I said, "The zombie horseman said he had a patron. The only people I could think of who could do something like this would be Clayton Dretsky, Herobrine, Entity 303, and maybe Clayton's father."

Emma nodded. "What motivation would any of these people have to do that? Even Clayton, if he wanted to scare you, why would he do it in such a strange, vague way?"

I sighed. "That's what's been bothering me. It doesn't make any sense. Why go to the trouble to find probably the only five zombies in the entire Overworld who can ride a horse, gather a couple hundred spiders and then ride through town? It doesn't make any sense at all."

Emma tapped her chin with her index finger. "What about that kooky dream you had. Were there any spiders in it? Or zombies?"

I shook my head. "No. Just shadowy figures, the Rainbow Creeper, and Entity 303."

"We forgot the Rainbow Creeper! Wouldn't it have enough power to do what we just saw?" said Emma.

"You're right!"

"Still, what would the Rainbow Creeper be trying to tell you?" asked Emma.

I shrugged. "I don't know. I have no interest in joining the Rainbow Creeper religion, so there doesn't seem to be any reason for this."

Emma sighed, shook her head, and said, "We aren't getting anywhere. It's just pure speculation. Let's see what Herobrine has to say."

Day 40 – Afternoon

We ate a quick lunch at the Ender King's palace and then teleported to the same wooded area where we had met Herobrine previously, about ten days ago.

The Ender King located the hidden entrance to the fortress and knocked. We waited for a minute without a response. The King knocked again. And, again, there was no response.

"I'm getting worried," said Emma.

"So am I," said the Ender King. "Stand back."

The King took two steps back from the door, lifted one of his long, skinny legs in to the air and then kicked the door as hard as he could.

The door swung open easily.

"Not even locked!" I said in shock.

But, the real shock was inside.

When we entered, we saw destruction everywhere. Furniture knocked over. Bookshelves destroyed. Herobrine's collections strewn across the floor.

"Who could do such a thing?!? And to Herobrine himself?!?" said Emma.

I looked at the Ender King. For the first time I saw fear etched on his face. I sensed a rising fear in place of his usual chill or authoritarian vibes. This was not good.

Just then, the chicken servant who had opened the door for us last time we were here staggered around the corner. I could see that one of his wings was broken, and he was covered with marks indicating quite a beating. We rushed over to him and he collapsed in our arms.

"Chicken," said the King. "Tell us who did this. Tell us where Herobrine is."

The chicken coughed and clucked and said, "So fast. Too much. Too many. It was ..." But, before he could finish, he flashed red and disappeared in a puff of smoke.

After a moment of silence for the valiant chicken, we searched the fortress for any clue as to what had happened, but found nothing. It was as if some invisible force had blown through the fortress like a hurricane, destroying everything and everyone in its path, yet leaving no other trace.

"Do you think Herobrine could be ... hurrr ... dead?" I asked, not believing the words were coming from my mouth.

The Ender King shook his head. "I would have ... well ... felt that. No, he is still alive, somewhere."

Emma, who had wandered in to the next room, suddenly screamed, "No!"

The King reached out and grabbed me and we teleported to Emma's side. She was safe, but she was staring at an empty shelf.

"This was where Herobrine's diaries were! The ones written in hexadecimal hieroglyphics! Do you think those were what the person who ransacked this place was searching for?" she said.

A bead of sweat formed on the Ender King's forehead. "I hope not. The power to destroy the world resides in those diaries!"

Day 40 – Late Afternoon

After we returned to Zombie Bane, none of us felt like surfing. Herobrine's disappearance, apparently at the hands of a very violent and very powerful force, had us too preoccupied to surf. The Ender King bid us farewell and told us to return tomorrow after he had pondered his next moves.

Emma and I walked back through town. We said nothing. We simply walked in each other's company.

About halfway home, I saw a stray dog walking through the streets of the village. I saw another villager throw some trash at it and tell it to "Get away, you filthy creature!"

"Don't say that to that dog!" I said. "He's just had some bad luck."

The villager looked at me and laughed while he rolled his eyes. "Whatever," he said before walking away.

I looked at the sad dog. It's head hung low, ashamed of what it had become. Once a noble wolf, it had been tamed and then degraded. But, I felt a good vibe coming from it. In fact, it was one of the most positive vibes I had ever felt from any living creature, villagers and players included.

"Dog," I said softly. "Dog. Come over here."

The dog stopped walking and looked at me. It's eyes seemed sad, but also intelligent. It sniffed the air and then cautiously approached me.

The dog stopped about three blocks from me and sat down.

I reached into my inventory and found an old piece of steak. I pulled it out and tossed it to the dog. "Here you go," I said. "It's all I have. I hope you like it."

The dog slowly approached the meat, sniffed it, and then gobbled it down quickly. It looked at me, hopeful for more.

"Sorry, that's it, boy," I said. "Do you have anything, Emma?"

"No, I don't. Sorry."

The dog seemed to understand our conversation and, upon hearing that Emma had nothing, turned around and walked away. But, before it got out of sight, it turned around and howled a long, soulful howl. Then, it walked around the corner of a building and was gone.

I sighed. "I wish I had a dog."

Day 41 – Morning

I had slept fitfully during the night.

Let's review. Herobrine was missing and his fortress ransacked. I was no closer to knowing who had sent the spider herd to town. And, we had not been able to practice much for the surf contest. I was stressed, confused, and worried.

I decided to eat some food in the hopes it would make me feel better.

Yes, I was eating to lessen my pain. Not emotionally healthy, but very tasty.

I was furiously eating my breakfast of toast and watermelon, feeling increasingly more at peace as I ingested larger and larger amounts of food, when there was a knock on the door.

"Jimmy, can you get that?" asked my mom.

I stood up and walked to the door. I opened it and my jaw almost hit the ground. I was so shocked that I was surprised I could talk. "Claire? What are you doing here?"

Claire looked from side to side, clearly worried about something, and then said, "Can I come in?"

I open the door wider and let her in. "I took the DOTS this morning," she said. "We need to talk."

"Okay, let's talk."

"Could we talk in your room. I don't want anyone to hear this."

I looked over at my mom who raised an eyebrow suspiciously but then shrugged her shoulders.

Claire and I went up the stairs to my room and she shut the door. She sat down on my floor crossing her legs. I sat on the end of my bed. After she let out a long sigh, she said, "My brother has…"

"Gone insane?" I said, trying to finish the thought for her.

She shook her head. "Returned."

"What you mean? I didn't know Clayton had gone anywhere."

"Not Clayton, Spike."

I knew instantly. *Spike must have been the one I'd seen under that cloak at the surf contest. Was he also the one I'd seen in my dream?*

"But you said at the surf contest you didn't have another brother?"

"He *made* me say that."

My eyes opened wide with disbelief. "What do you mean *he* made you say that?"

"Spike has the ability to control the minds of others. If he knows where you are, he can make you think things and do things against your will. That's why I came here to speak with you. He doesn't know I'm here so I can tell the truth without his influence."

My heart was racing. "Hold on a second!" I said, putting my hand up. "You need to give me some more background. Where does this guy come from and why is he not around anymore? How can a brother just ... hurrr ... disappear? Biff said he didn't know anything about him."

"When we were very little, Spike and Clayton must've only been about two years old and I was probably one, he did something terrible. Biff was just a little baby too, so he would not remember anything. Anyway, Spike had already discovered how to manipulate others using evoking powers and he..." Claire shuddered at the memory and then continued, "He made two of our servants kill each other in hand-to-hand combat."

"Oh my Notch!" I said, amazed and disgusted at the same time.

"My parents, knowing that he was troubled, had him committed to a mental institution, but when he was only 4 years old, he escaped. No one knew where. It turns out, he had gone into the Nether and began assembling a zombie pigman army to do his bidding."

I was so surprised I could feel myself getting lightheaded, as if I were about to pass out. But again, I willed myself to stay conscious. "So why is Clayton involved then? If your parents are against this sort of behavior?"

I could see tears forming in Claire's eyes. "We're all against the behavior!" Claire shouted through her tears. "Spike's just been controlling us. As Clayton's twin, he has an especially strong hold on Clayton. He might be able to make me say and do things against my will, but he's never been able to make me do *evil* things against my will, though he can prevent me from doing anything. I have spent many a day in my room sitting on my bed unable to move while Clayton is off committing horrible atrocities at the behest of Spike."

"So, are you telling me that Clayton actually isn't evil?"

She shrugged. "Who knows anymore? He wasn't evil when it started, but I'm not sure how much Spike has to do to control him anymore. It's almost like he's been trained to be evil for so long that now he doesn't know anything else."

"So, why are you telling me this now? It doesn't sound like there's anything I can do." I said, distraught.

"I'm telling you because Spike has no intention of honoring the deal about the surf contest. It was between Clayton and the Ender King, not Spike and the Ender King. He's letting Clayton go through the motions now before he returns to his plan to conquer the Overworld, the Nether and the End and become the ruler of all of Minecraft!"

I laughed. "What about Notch? We will just tell him when he shows up to judge the next surf contest."

The tears were streaming down Claire's face now. "Spike thinks he can take Notch."

I laughed. "How could he actually destroy Notch even if Spike is powerful and completely evil? Even Herobrine couldn't destroy Notch!"

"You're right, he couldn't do it all by himself, but he might be able to with the help of Entity 303."

My legs became weak and I slipped off the edge of my bed and plopped on the floor with a splat. I started to twitch. I thought for a moment I was going to completely lose it and have a fit but then I managed to regain control of my arms and legs and push myself into a sitting position. "But how? How could they? What's the plan?"

Claire was wiping the tears from her face. "I have no idea. He doesn't trust me enough to tell me these things. I just know he has something planned. I think it started yesterday. They went somewhere and captured what Clayton called 'a high value target.' He is imprisoned deep in the Nether."

Herobrine? Could they have captured Herobrine? If Claire thinks Spike could defeat Notch with the help of Entity 303 or the Rainbow Creeper, surely they could defeat Herobrine, right?!?

"I need to tell the Ender King about this. He'll know what to do!" I said.

Claire stood up. "Okay. I really should go before Spike realizes I'm missing."

I nodded but then stood in front of the door to my bedroom and said, "Claire, I have to know something. Are you a member of the Rainbow Creeper religion?"

Claire inhaled sharply and said, "Yes, but the Rainbow Creeper is not evil. He is whatever you want him to be. He is a good spirit, corrupted by those who quest for power."

"Like Spike?"

Claire nodded wordlessly.

"Will you tell me more about the Rainbow Creeper?" I asked.

Claire forced a smile and turned her frown upside down. "Yes, if Spike is ever defeated. I will show you the true meaning of the Rainbow Creeper."

"Thank you," I said, opening the door. I walked Claire down the stairs and to the front door. We exchanged a long, silent look.

"See you at the contest in a few days," I said.

"I hope so."

Day 41 – Fifteen Minutes Later

After Claire left, I sat down at the breakfast table and stared at my food. I wasn't hungry anymore.

Spike was a madman – or, I guess, a madteen, since he was only a couple years older than me. He had to be stopped. The only person I knew with the power to do that, other than Notch, was the Ender King ... maybe.

I stood up and yelled, "Bye, Mom! I'm off to surf practice!"

"Okay, be careful!"

"I will," I said, rushing out the door.

But, was it careful for me to tell the Ender King about all this? Was it careful of me to want to rush in to danger to stop Spike?

I ran through the streets of the village toward the Ender King's palace. I passed by one of the locations where my great-great-gramps, Cornelius, had killed one of the zombies during that fateful night so many years ago.

I felt a kindred spirit to my gramps for the first time. I was doing what I had to, just like he did. I finally realized what it meant to be an adult. You did things not because you wanted to, but because they were right.

I ran on until I reached the Ender King's palace. The soldiers knew me and let me in.

I rushed into the King's reception area where the Queen, Tina, and Emma were waiting.

"What is it, Jimmy?" asked Emma breathlessly. "You look frightened."

"I am frightened. I think Herobrine has been kidnapped by Spike and Entity 303!"

It took me a few minutes to explain everything, but when I was done, everyone in the room was as concerned as me. Silence filled the room. We were waiting for the Ender King to make a decision. This was his call.

The Ender King slowly arose from his throne. He swelled to about three times his normal size and yelled, "This deception will not stand!"

"Yeah, boy, of course it won't!" I shouted, doing a little dance.

Everyone looked at me like I was a complete idiot, and they were right. I tried to make myself as small as possible and sat down in a nearby chair.

The Ender King returned to his normal size and sat down in his throne. "We will go to the Nether tomorrow and locate Herobrine, or whoever has been kidnapped by Spike. Then, we will defeat Spike. There will be no surfing until this is resolved."

"Great," I said. "I'll just need to get a few things...."

The King interrupted me. "This is too dangerous for children. You and Emma and Tina will stay in Zombie Bane."

"No," Emma and I said in unison. "We want to come with you."

"Yeah, Daddy, no fair," said Tina, crossing her arms and sticking out her lower lip.

"Enough!" shouted the Ender King. "This conversation is over. Leave me."

Dang! He got all royal on us! Kicking us out like that!

Emma and I stood up and left. We waved goodbye to Tina and then walked toward our houses.

Day 41 – Afternoon

Emma and I stopped by Mr. Blaze's bookstore to see if he might have some ideas, but he still had not been seen by his clerk.

"It is strange for him to be gone for two days like this," said the clerk. "I'm a little worried."

After we left the bookstore, I said to Emma, "I can't believe I'm asking this, but ... hurrr ... do you think Mr. Blaze is involved in the kidnapping in some way or another?"

Emma thought for a moment and then said, "I can't imagine him doing something evil, but if Spike is as powerful as Claire says, maybe Spike wanted to use Mr. Blaze's power for his own gain. Maybe Mr. Blaze has been kidnapped too?"

I put my hands on the sides of my head, trying to keep my brain from oozing out of my ears. "I'm so confused. I can't tell who is good or evil anymore."

"The Ender King will figure this out," said Emma, though her voice lacked confidence.

"He could use all the help he can get. We need to get to the Nether and assist in the search for Herobrine."

"I don't know, Jimmy. It will be very dangerous."

"I know, but we've already escaped from Clayton or Spike, whoever it was, and the zombie pigman minions who enslaved us. We can do this."

Emma sighed. "I tell you what. Let's see if Mr. Blaze is around tomorrow. If he is, we can get his opinion about what we should do. Okay?"

I did not want to agree with Emma, but she was right. Going alone would be very dangerous. And, as much as I wanted to avoid it, I needed to ask my parents for permission.

I nodded. "Yeah, okay." I looked to the left and saw the street leading to my house. "Want to stop by my house for some watermelon?"

Emma smiled. "Sure, I love watermelon."

When we arrived at my house, I opened the door and shouted, "Mom? Dad? I'm home. Can Emma and I have some watermelon?"

There was no response.

I yelled again.

No response.

"That's weird. They always take the third day of the week off and let their employees run their shops. They should be here."

"Maybe they are outside?" suggested Emma.

I looked in the backyard and saw nothing.

I tried yelling again. "Mom? Dad?"

Nothing. But, then I heard it: a thumping noise against a window. I walked around the house and realized it was coming from a kitchen window.

I walked in to the kitchen and saw a stupid bat thumping against the window. I opened the window and poked at the bat with a stick. "Get away, fool."

The bat backed away and then hovered in front of the window, flapping its wings rhythmically. Suddenly, its eyes turned red and it opened its mouth. A voice somehow came from the bat, "Your parents are in my prison in the Nether. You will never see them again. Don't mess with me!"

And then, the bat charged at me. It was so fast, I did not have time to defend myself or even to react in any way, but someone did. At that moment, the stray dog I had seen earlier appeared as if from nowhere, leapt at the bat, and caught it in its jaws. The dog crushed the bat and it flashed red and disappeared with a puff of smoke.

My legs became weak and I sank to the ground, tears streaming down my face.

Spike! It had to have been Spike's voice coming from the bat.

"Spike has my parents," I said weakly, before looking at the dog with gratitude in my eyes. The dog approached and sat down next to me. I petted its filthy fur.

Emma got down next to me and hugged me. "I think you are right."

"He'll kill them," I said, still petting the dog. *Was he my dog now?*

Emma hugged me more tightly. "No, the Ender King will rescue them."

The Ender King! Now, there was no reason he could keep me from going with him.

I stood up, a renewed vigor in my body. "I'm going to pack my things and get back to the Ender King's palace," I said. "Spike messed with the wrong villager this time!"

The dog – *my* dog – howled in agreement.

End of Book 7

Book 8

Day 41 – Later that Afternoon

After the dog killed the possessed bat, I knew that I had to go to the Nether to find my parents. Nothing was going to stop me!

Emma agreed with me and went to her house to prepare for a trip to the Nether.

I'd seen what Spike, through Clayton, had done to me and Emma and the other villagers when we had been enslaved. I knew that the kidnappers of my parents were capable of *anything*.

I quickly packed what I needed in my inventory, and met Emma on the way back to the Ender King's palace.

"Do you think the Ender King will let you come, Emma?" I asked.

Emma shrugged and then asked, "Will he let *you* come along?"

I did not respond because I wasn't sure. But the King had better let me come along, because if he didn't, I was going anyway.

The dog trotted alongside us, covered with filth and grime, evidence of a streetwise existence, but somehow looking majestic and dominant at the same time.

I looked at the dog and then at Emma and said, "We need to give the dog a name. We can't just keep calling it 'dog' or 'hey, you'."

Emma nodded her head. "I think we should name it Sunbeam."

I slapped my head. "I'm not going to name a super dominant, bat-killing, grime and filth-covered dog, 'Sunbeam.' It needs a name that's more awesome and more frightening."

Emma shook her head. "What? You probably want to give it some sort of dude-bro name like Hunter or Rex or Killer, right?"

"No, just something that sounds a little more awesome when you call to it. How about 'Solar'? It's a compromise. It still has to do with sunlight but it's a little more cool, like a solar eclipse or solar radiation or solar flare."

Emma laughed. "Whatever. I think I'm going to call it Sunbeam."

"You're going to confuse it," I yelled, pulling at my hair.

Apparently the dog didn't like us fighting because it barked and growled. I said, "Sorry, Solar." The dog looked at me and nodded as if it understood and forgave me.

Then Emma said, "I'm sorry, Sunbeam." The dog looked at her and nodded as if he understood her. It was very strange.

Anyway, after we had agreed to disagree about the dog's name, we arrived at the Ender King's palace. The guard was reluctant to let us in, but we had been there so many times in the past that he assumed the King would likely want to speak with us.

When I walked into the King's reception hall, he looked at us in shock. "Didn't I tell you that you cannot come with me!" he said in a commanding voice which echoed against the walls.

"That ship has sailed," I said. "My parents have been kidnapped. A possessed bat told me they were in the Nether. I'm coming with you."

The Ender King was shook. The color of his face went from a deep obsidian black to an ashy gray, which is what happens when you are an enderman and all the blood runs out of your face.

"This is worse than I thought," said the Ender King. "It's one thing to kidnap someone with blood on his hands like Herobrine, but it's another thing entirely to kidnap the innocent. I thought Notch had put a stop to this when he started the surf contests, but apparently Spike isn't listening anymore."

At that moment the dog let out a loud howl and then growled several times.

Then the King looked at the dog as if it were the first time he had noticed it. "What is this filthy beast doing in my Reception Hall?"

I put my hand on the dog's head and gently stroked its disgustingly filthy fur and said, "This is Solar. He saved my life when the possessed bat was about to attack me. He's coming with us too."

The Ender King shrugged. "Fine, but keep him away from me. I can smell his filth from here."

Now that the King had mentioned it, the dog did smell rather disgusting. It was as if he rolled in some rotten zombie flesh every day for the past five months and no one had ever given him a bath. I was not sure how I hadn't noticed the stench before now.

I pulled my hand away from the dog's fur and saw that it had turned black. I barfed a little in my mouth but managed to swallow it back down, preventing myself from being embarrassed in front of the King. I wiped my hand on the tablecloth that was next to me, without anyone noticing.

That would never be clean again, I thought.

"I'm coming too," said Emma.

Then the King looked at her and shook his head. "Have your parents been kidnapped too?"

Emma shifted her feet a little and looked down at the floor before saying, "No, but I thought I could come with you."

The Ender King shook his head. "No, I will let you go only if you have your parents' permission, but I'm sure you do not have it, right?"

Emma sighed. "Right. I didn't even ask."

At that moment the Ender King clapped his hands together and Tina teleported into the room.

"Tina, you and Emma keep practicing for the surf contest. If Jimmy and I are back by the time of the contest, we will surf in it; otherwise, try to find at least one new person to be on the team, just in case."

"But Daddy, do you think they'll still have the surf contest after all these kidnappings? Isn't Spike honoring the deal Notch made with everyone?"

The Ender King shrugged his scrawny little pointy shoulders and said, "Who knows? It's up to Notch, and he acts in mysterious ways. We just have to be prepared."

"Okay, Tina and I can practice and try to find someone new for the team," said Emma. "I think there are some kids who have been ripping pretty hard lately from our village. I'm sure at least one of them would want to be on the team."

The Ender King nodded his head resolutely and said, "It's settled then." He turned toward the girls. "Tina. Emma. We will be leaving soon. I want you to keep ender soldiers with you at all times. Tina, be sure to listen when Ariana or Rihanna tell you what to do. Now that Gretchen is ... well ... no longer with us (***tear***), they are your best ladies in waiting for protection."

Tina nodded and said, "Sure thing, Daddy. I'll have Ariana and Rihanna come with us while we practice surfing."

The Ender King, his instructions to his daughter finished, wished them goodbye. Tina and Emma left the room, presumably to go to Tina's room.

Day 41 – Still Afternoon

After Emma and Tina left, the Ender King and I ate food. I wanted to go to the Nether immediately, but he insisted that we have a nutritious meal before what was likely to be long journey ahead.

The King's servants brought us a lunch of mushroom stew, steak and watermelon. Normally I liked all these foods, but right now, as I worried about my parents, my meal tasted like bitterness and rage.

"Let's get moving, King! We need to save my parents."

The Ender King scratched his chin and finished chewing his steak. After he swallowed, he said, "Why would Spike kidnap your parents? I guess I can understand him taking Herobrine, given the possibility to manipulate his power for something else, but your parents are just nobodies."

I dropped my spoon into my mushroom stew. It made a loud clattering sound. "My parents are not nobodies. You take that back."

The Ender King said, "I don't mean that they are losers, just that they don't have any sort of powers that might be worth manipulating. Neither do you. I don't understand Spike's obsession with you or your family."

I had to admit, the Ender King had a point. We are just of family of villagers. Sure, my great-great gramps, Cornelius, had done something pretty awesome when he killed all those zombies, and I had co-invented surfing, but it wasn't like we were heroes who had saved the world from the Apocalypse or something. And, my family certainly did not have any magical powers like Herobrine. *Did they?*

"Spike has been haunting my dreams. He wants to control me for some reason, but I don't know why,"

I said. "I feel like I need to confront him or he is just going to keep doing this to me and my family." I slammed my fist down on the table in frustration.

The Ender King nodded his head. "I understand your need for revenge or closure, but this could be a trap. We need to be very careful once we enter the Nether."

"I get it, King. But I'm ready," I said slamming my fist into my hand.

As I did that, Solar barked his approval, and then returned to eating a large piece of steak I had put in the bowl for him.

"I hope you *are* ready. This isn't going to be like riding waves, Jimmy. We can't go surfing in lava barrels down there, brah."

Solar growled at this attempted sarcastic insult.

"Dude, King, stop with this passive aggressive nonsense," I said.

Then the King laughed. "I'm sorry, but I was just trying to emphasize how serious this is. You've never seen a real war. We may not come back from this."

I nodded curtly. I understood the risks. "This is personal, King. I just want to rescue my parents, and if we get to kill Spike along the way, so much the better." I grinned.

The King wiped his mouth with a napkin and pushed his chair back from the table. He stood up and looked at me, his purple eyes glowing inside his pitch black head. He asked, "Are you ready to do this thing?"

I stood and nodded. Solar barked.

The King looked at both of us and smiled at us with a determined smile. "In that case, it's time to armor up."

At that instant, an ender soldier entered the room carrying a large chest. He placed the chest on the floor and then opened it. Inside, I saw numerous pieces of diamond armor and diamond weaponry. I found a suit of diamond armor that was about my size and put it on. It felt surprisingly light. I felt invincible. I dug around for a diamond sword, grabbed it, slashed it through the air a few times to test its weight, and then tucked it into my inventory.

"The dog too," ordered the Ender King.

I looked over at Solar who was sitting there with his tongue hanging out and looking stupid. I searched inside the chest and found a helmet that looked like it might fit the dog. I put it on Solar's head and he seemed to like it.

"Do you think there is any armor in there that will fit a dog?" I asked.

"There should be," said the Ender King. "You'd be surprised how many types of armor there are if you just pay attention."

I wasn't sure what he meant by that — *another passive aggressive insult?* — but I dug around in the chest and sure enough found some more armor that was the size of a dog. I put it on Solar. It looked pretty dominant, and the layer of diamond armor reduced his stench, so if you were a few paces away from him, you couldn't smell him.

Double-sided armor, I thought to myself with a grin.

We were ready.

I looked at the Ender King and set my gaze. I didn't say anything but just nodded my head with confidence.

Solar howled.

The Ender King approached us, touched us on our shoulders, and we teleported away.

Day 41 – One Hour Later

The King, five ender soldiers, Solar, and I had been walking around the Nether for about an hour. We hadn't seen any mobs other than a single magma cube. The cube was happily bouncing when we turned a corner. It caught sight of us, shrieked, and then jumped into a puddle of lava. It was very weird.

"Where is everyone?" I asked. "It's like the Nether's a dead zone."

The King rubbed his chin with his scrawny little hand and said, "I agree. It's quiet ... too quiet."

I laughed. "I've always wanted to have a reason to say that."

The King's arm shot out and covered my mouth to silence me. "Well, you have a reason now. Is your life complete? Do you want to die?"

I reached up and pushed the King's hand away. "Dude, you need to *chill*. I'm just trying to lighten the situation a little bit. It's pretty tense down here."

Solar barked his approval with my statement.

"Yes, Jimmy, it is tense because there is tension. The tension is that someone is going to die, and it might be us if we're not careful," said the King.

I knew the King was right, but I was getting sick of all the stress vibes I was feeling from everybody. I wanted to go surfing. I wanted to wash the stress away by getting a few barrels. But I knew that wasn't going to happen. I guess I did need to pay more attention.

We continued along the corridor in the Nether looking for signs of life. Looking for a clue. Looking for something that would help us find my parents or Spike or Herobrine or, maybe, all of them at once.

A few minutes later we were suddenly surrounded by three ghasts meowing angrily. I pulled out my diamond sword and was about to strike at one of the ghasts when the King put his hand on mine and said, "No, don't. They're not hostile right now, only making us wait."

I lowered my sword but didn't put it away. I didn't trust ghasts, but then again, I'd never really met any.

One of the ghasts said in a high-pitched voice, "Follow us. Our king wishes to see you."

We followed the lead ghast while the two other ghasts continued behind us to make sure that we didn't run away. After a few twists and turns we ended up in a very large chamber. It was filled with all sorts of statues, artwork, and valuable metals. It was the Ghast King's reception hall.

As we walked in, the Ghast King floated up from his throne and said, "Ender King! Dawg, that was a sick air at the last surf contest. I had no choice but to give you a perfect 10 from the judge's booth."

In response to the complement, the Ender King teleported next to the Ghast King and they did some bro stuff. The Ender King bumped chests with the Ghast King. The Ender King tried to fist bump, but the Ghast King frowned because he did not have any hands. They said a few things to each other that I couldn't hear, and then things got serious again.

The Ender King informed the Ghast King why we were there. The Ghast King expressed his condolences at the kidnapping of my parents and his astonishment at the kidnapping of Herobrine.

"Do you have any idea where they might be?" I asked, desperation in my voice.

The Ghast King meowed and then said, "I haven't heard anything about where they could be, but Clayton controlled the entire northern quadrant of the Nether before Notch put an end to his slaving days. If Spike is behind all this, I would assume they are hiding somewhere in the northern quadrant."

"Northern quadrant?" I asked.

The Ender King nodded his head. "The Nether divided into four quadrants. Most people in the Overworld don't know that. I think only the nether mobs refer to the Nether by quadrant. It's one of those local knowledge type of things."

I rolled my eyes. "So, anyway, which way is ... hurrr ... north?" I asked.

The Ghast King turned around and spit a fireball in one direction. "That way."

I found it interesting that the Ghast King had to shoot a fireball in order to point in a direction. It must be kind of lame not to have any hands or arms. He always had to spit a fireball just to indicate a direction. I guess that was why Ghasts lived in the Nether. If they lived in the Overworld, they would constantly be starting fires when they were telling people where to go. It would be a giant, ashy desert up there. All the forests would have burned long ago.

"Thank you, my good friend," said the Ender King. "I'm in your debt."

The Ghast King smiled and said, "There is no debt to pay. If you make Clayton and Spike leave the Nether permanently, that will more than repay any debt you could have ever owed me."

"Thank you," said the Ender King.

The Ender King then looked at his small crew and said, "Let's go, men."

Day 41 – Sometime Later

The Ender King and I were walking behind the five ender soldiers. Solar was walking directly behind us, bringing up the rear. I was unable to tell for how long we had been walking much less how long we'd been in the Nether. I supposed it was probably nighttime in the Overworld right now. When you don't see the sun or the moon, it's hard to know how much time has passed.

We still had not seen another soul since we left the Ghast King's reception chamber. Honestly, it was creepy. I knew there had to be more life in the Nether. A few times in the last couple of hours I thought I'd felt eyes watching me, but saw nothing.

Suddenly, my stomach growled. I realized I was starving. I looked behind me at my dog and realized I hadn't fed him in hours either.

"King, can we stop and eat something?" The King, putting his hand on his skinny abdomen, agreed. He called for a halt and a one hour break to eat and rest.

I reached into my inventory and pulled out a piece of steak and tossed it to Solar. He ate it quickly and then curled up and went to sleep. I ate some bread and some cookies.

The Ender King looked at what I was eating and said, "That doesn't look like a very healthy meal. You should eat some fruits and vegetables."

"Who are you, my mom?" I said. But just as the words came out of my mouth, I started to cry. My mom had been kidnapped. There was nothing I could do about it, except wander around the Nether, hoping to find her.

She might even be....

I refused to let myself think such a horrible thought. I knew I'd find her. I had to find her. I would save her and my dad.

I wiped the tears from my eyes and set my jaw resolutely. Spike would not win this one.

"Actually, maybe you're right," I said. I reached in to my inventory and found an old carrot near the bottom. It didn't taste very good, but it was a vegetable.

After we had all eaten, we rested. One of the ender soldiers volunteered to stand guard.

I was surprised how easily I fell asleep, despite my diamond armor now itching like crazy. When I had first put it on, I thought it was extremely comfortable but having had to wear it for eight hours, or whatever, straight, it had become super itchy. I wanted to take it off, but I knew I had to wear it in order to protect myself from surprises and enemies.

I slept soundly until I heard a scream. It was a scream of profound pain and terror. When I woke up, I sat bolt upright and saw suddenly there was a stream of lava flowing toward us. It was burning one of the ender soldiers alive! I watched as he took his final breath and burst into a puff of smoke.

The other ender soldiers were quickly grabbing rock blocks to try to cover the seams from which the lava was pouring. Fortunately, they were able to soon seal the hole, but they were exhausted. They slumped down against the wall and rested.

I looked at the Ender King and said, "That was close."

The Ender King nodded. "I can't believe that was just a natural lava flow. Something's happening."

Before I could ask the Ender King what he thought might be happening, a group of one hundred magma cubes hopped down from above us and began to attack. They were jumping on top of the resting ender soldiers, whose health bars were decreasing rapidly. I whipped out my diamond sword and began chopping the magma cubes as fast as I could.

The Ender King was doing the same. Each of us killed at least twenty magma cubes before they turned away from the resting ender soldiers and started to turn on us.

Two more of the ender soldiers had died, leaving only two remaining out of the five we had started with. As the magma cubes attacked us, those two soldiers were able to pull out their swords and chop at the magma cubes.

Solar was surprisingly dominant during the fight. He was jumping on the magma cubes and biting them repeatedly, crushing their hard bodies in his vise-like jaws. Many flashed red and burst into puffs of smoke in between his teeth.

As I watched Solar's wrath, I felt a magma cube jump on my foot. It landed so hard, I thought my foot was broken. After testing it gingerly, I realized I could still walk on it. I gritted my teeth and slashed my sword at the cube, killing it.

I looked over to the King and said, "There's too many of them. But I have an idea." I pointed at the seam from which the lava had come earlier, and then I pointed to another discolored area at the top of the chamber from which it appeared water was slowly seeping.

The Ender King grinned his understanding and said, "I agree. Let's do it."

The Ender King grabbed me, and we teleported to the lava seam. The two of us took our swords and slashed against the repaired lava, letting it flow again.

The magma cubes laughed and said, "You think lava can hurt us? Are you noobs or something?"

The Ender King then teleported back to where Solar was, touched Solar and teleported to a small ledge near the discolored portion of the ceiling. The Ender King's remaining two soldiers teleported to the ledge as well.

We watched as the wide, quick lava flow engulfed the magma cubes who remained unharmed. But then, the Ender King and I pulled pickaxes from our inventories and smashed them against the ceiling of the chamber, unleashing a massive flow of water which plunged on to the lava. The lava hardened almost instantaneously, trapping the magma cubes inside, killing them.

Somehow, one of the magma cubes had survived. It was hopping up the side of the chamber toward us.

"I've got this one," I said with a determined voice. I held my diamond sword ready to slash the magma cube when it came within an arm's length. But the magma cube stopped just out of reach of my sword. I suddenly saw its eyes turn a bright, glowing red, and the same possessed voice that had inhabited the bat near my kitchen window said, "Turn back now or your parents will die."

I was not going to let this possessed magma cube / messenger of Spike tell me what to do. No one was going to control me!

I reached down and picked up a rock and threw it at the magma cube, killing it.

But, before it vanished in a puff of smoke, it grinned at me and whispered, "You'll be sorry."

Day 41 – Moments Later

"Is that what the bat sounded like at your house?" asked the Ender King, very concerned.

I nodded my head. "Exactly the same voice. I think it's probably Spike."

"Probably," said the King, rubbing his chin. "That was pretty impressive that you killed it after the threat it made. That's something a King would've done."

I actually felt very emotional when the King gave me such an amazing and profound compliment. On the one hand, it was the first time he'd ever truly respected me and said so aloud. On the other hand, I knew the decisions made by royalty got people killed.

Had my decision to kill the magma cube rather than heed its warning condemned my parents to death? I hoped not. We needed to find out as soon as possible.

"King, do you think we need a few more of your ender soldiers down here? I mean … hurrr … three of them are dead now."

The Ender King looked at the two remaining soldiers, both of whom had sustained injuries in the battle with the magma cubes.

"Jimmy, we certainly could use more soldiers, but there's no way to get them down here. We are deep in the northern quadrant of the Nether. There's no way to communicate with them other than to teleport all the way back ourselves. Unless we come across one of those DOTS contraptions by chance, the four of us and your filthy mutt will have to be the ones to complete this mission."

I felt a lump in my throat.

I swallowed hard.

Twice.

The lump did not go away.

The weight of what we had to do and what would happen if we didn't accomplish our goal had finally fallen solidly on my shoulders. My knees buckled and I fell to the ground.

I looked up at the sky, or rather the ceiling of the underground chamber in which we found ourselves. So, I guess, hurrr, what I was really doing was looking up towards where I thought the sky should be, but instead I saw the filthy, stinking, dank underbelly of the Overworld.

As I stared at the filthy, stinking, dank underbelly, I shook my fist at it and yelled, "Notch, why have you forsaken us? It is our hour of need and you're nowhere near!" Then I let my head fall down and I shed a few silent tears.

The Ender King walked over and put his tiny hand on my diamond-armor-covered shoulder and said, "Notch has not forsaken us. The task is ours, not his. If he is needed, he will be here."

I snapped my head around and glared at the Ender King. "Do you really believe that? The only time I've ever seen Notch in my entire life was when he wanted to create a surf contest. Yeah, sure, it averted a huge war, but it seems that all Notch wants to do is … hurrr … show up for the good times, and then he ignores us during the bad times."

Solar walked up to me and sat down. He licked my face. If his tongue wasn't so nasty and his breath weren't so horrific – it smelled like a husk or a zombie – I might have appreciated the gesture. Solar then whimpered and sat down next to me.

I reached out my hand and patted Solar's diamond helmet, which mercifully prevented my hand from touching his dank, stinky fur, and said, "It's okay boy. We can handle this, even if Notch doesn't care."

Solar looked at me again. I felt his eyes penetrating into my soul. It was like he was reading my mind. I knew dogs could sometimes sense what villagers or players were thinking, but this seemed almost as though he were engaging in some sort of telepathy. It didn't really matter because I had no idea what he was trying to tell me or what information he might be trying to take out of my mind. It started to get a little creepy, so I broke eye contact and stood up.

"Okay, so now that I've ignored Spike's threats to kill my parents, we need to find them as quickly as possible. If this is the ragtag group that we have to do it with, so be it," I said with a determined edge in my voice.

Then the King looked at me proudly. "Let's do it!"

* * *

For the next ten or fifteen minutes we continued into the northern quadrant of the Nether. We occasionally saw the outlines of shadows moving or the dim glow of a blaze passing in the distance down a corridor. We heard the grunting sounds of a zombie pigman or the rhythmic sound of a magma cube hopping in the distance.

We didn't confront anything head-on.

It was as if the nether mobs were purposefully avoiding us or else entirely oblivious to our presence.

We didn't pursue any of them. We didn't take any of them captive or ask them questions. What was the point? They would have said nothing, or else they might have been possessed by Spike and said something horrible to me.

We continued to look for my parents, for Herobrine, and for Spike or anything that might help us achieve our goal of locating my parents and freeing Herobrine.

But, we found nothing that made sense. However, we did come to something that was nostalgic, but not in a good way.

As we passed down a long, wide corridor, we heard the clomping of horses hooves.

I looked over at the Ender King and whispered, "What's a horse doing down in the Nether?"

The Ender King glanced sideways at me and said, "Someone must have brought it here. It's not natural."

We slowly moved in the direction of the hoof beats. We took slow, quiet steps, careful not to alert the horse or its rider. It took us about a minute before we reached a junction in the corridor. It sounded like the horse was just around the corner. The Ender King poked his head around and once he saw what was there, he pulled his head back, but his normally black skin tone had turned a pale shade of gray!

"What is it, King?" I whispered, not really sure if I wanted to know the answer.

He shook his head. "I think it's that same group of zombie horsemen that rode through your village. There are three horses and dozens, maybe hundreds of spiders just around the corner."

"That sounds like them," I whispered. Then, I had a lightning bolt of inspiration. "That zombie you killed. Remember, he talked about his patron wanting him to … hurrr … drive the herd of spiders through Zombie Bane and make sure I saw it? It must've been Spike! We have to talk to them."

"I don't think talking is what's going to happen. We will have to kill them. *All* of them."

I shook my head. "How can we do that? Those one hundred magma cubes almost took us out. Now we are talking about taking on three zombies and a few dozen spiders? Do we even have a chance?" I was on the verge of shrieking, but somehow was able to keep my voice to a whisper.

Then the King looked over to one of his soldiers and said, "Micah, bring out the weapon."

Micah reached into his inventory and brought out a large obsidian cube. It was about four times larger than a normal sized obsidian block. He took it and placed it at the feet of the Ender King.

"Are you kidding me? A giant rock?" I said, disgusted.

The Ender King shushed me. "Be quiet. This seemingly normal rock, as you put it, is filled with enough TNT to make 20 TNT boxes. We ignite it and then toss it into the middle of the spiders. It should take care of most of them. We can mop up the rest ourselves."

"I'm sorry I doubted you," I said, my jaw hanging slack at the thought of this incredible and compact weapon.

The two ender soldiers held the bomb on either side. The Ender King ignited a torch and lit the fuse. The ender soldiers swung the bomb back and forth a couple of times to build up some momentum, and then they jumped into the corridor and tossed the bomb into the herd of spiders.

The soldiers then jumped back behind the wall in order to avoid the blast wave and yelled, "Fire in the hole!"

The Ender King and I dove behind a rock. Solar followed. One of the zombie horsemen galloped around the corner with a sword drawn looking for someone to kill, oblivious to what was about to happen.

At that moment the bomb went off.

The sound was deafening. The wall shook. Chunks of rock fell from above. There was dust and smoke everywhere.

The zombie horseman was blown off his horse and landed in a heap in front of me. He looked at me, surprised, but only for a moment because I swung my diamond sword at him with all my fury and chopped his head off. His horse was mortally wounded during the explosion and within a brief moment followed its master into the afterlife.

The few remaining spiders who had survived the devastating explosion came running into the chamber where we quickly dispatched them. Only one of them managed to get a bite in on one of the wounded ender soldiers. It didn't do much damage.

After the smoke and dust settled, we entered the chamber where the herd of spiders had been. There were no survivors.

One of the ender soldiers said, "Look, your Majesty. At the far end of the chamber. There seems to be a door."

We all looked in the direction indicated by the soldier. It was, indeed, a door.

"Maybe that's why the herd was here," I suggested. "Guarding the door."

The Ender King nodded his head and said, "There must be something important in there."

It was then that I realized my parents might be in that room. I gripped my sword tightly and ran across the room as fast as I could. I had to get in there. I had to see what they were hiding, even if it was the worst.

I slammed against the door, but it wouldn't open. I looked around and found a long iron bar and shoved it into the door between the doorframe and the door itself. I pulled on it, trying to use the leverage to pop the door open. After a few seconds, the door was beginning to move, but I needed a little more strength.

One of the ender soldiers joined me and helped me pull on the bar. We started pulling on it rhythmically. Once. Twice. And then on the third try, the door burst open.

Day 41 – Seconds Later

When I looked inside the door I saw what I had hoped I would see: My parents!

My parents were both tied to chairs, their mouths gagged, but otherwise they appeared to be unharmed. I rushed over to them and hugged them both. We all started crying tears of joy.

I let go of them, pulled out my diamond sword and cut the ropes that held them to the chairs. I removed their gags and my mom said, "You came for us, Jimmy!" And then she continued to sob.

My dad, who was still crying, put his hands on the sides of my head and looked at me in the eyes and said, "I'm proud of you, son. You saved us."

I couldn't say anything. I was overcome with emotion. I started to cry even harder. That's when Solar came over. He licked my parents' faces and my face. His breath was still nasty, but none of us cared.

Through my tears, I saw that someone else was tied to a chair in the corner. I blinked my eyes a few times to clear the tears and that's when I saw who it was.

"Mr. Blaze?!?"

The Ender King was already across the room, untying Mr. Blaze. I looked back at my parents. "Was Mr. Blaze here the whole time too?"

My parents nodded. My dad said, "Yes, hurrr, he was already here when they kidnapped us. In fact, they were in the middle of torturing him when we arrived."

"Who kidnapped you? Who was torturing Mr. Blaze?"

"We were kidnapped by several spiders. It was horrible. They tied us up in their disgusting webs and carried us in their pincers. We thought they were going to eat us," said my mom, shivering with fear, tears streaming down her cheeks.

"But they took us here," said my dad. "It was Spike. He was here whipping Mr. Blaze with a rope. He was asking Mr. Blaze for information about the Rainbow Creeper's whereabouts."

I looked over Mr. Blaze. "How would you know where the Rainbow Creeper was?"

Mr. Blaze was rubbing his wrists, trying to get circulation back into his hands now that the Ender King had freed him from his bonds. Mr. Blaze shrugged. "I wouldn't. Spike was insane. He kept asked me questions to which I could never know the answers. I think he just wanted to whip me satisfy his own insanity."

The Ender King cleared his throat and interrupted, saying, "I need to ask you all something. Did you hear any mention of Herobrine or his whereabouts? We think he's been captured by Spike."

My parents and Mr. Blaze let out a collective gasp.

"How could a mere mortal villager, even one as insane as Spike, capture Herobrine?" asked my mom. "He's practically a God."

Then the King shook his head sadly. "I have no idea. All I know is we need to find Herobrine before Spike completes whatever horrific plan he has. Have you heard anything?" he asked again, this time sounding a bit desperate.

They all shook their heads.

"The only thing I heard Spike say was that Herobrine wasn't going to be a problem anymore.

Spike himself said that between whippings," said Mr. Blaze. "If they did capture Herobrine, I assume he would be in the Nether somewhere, probably close by."

The Ender King nodded his head. "That is my suspicion too. In the Overworld, I can usually sense Herobrine's general location, but not here in the Nether." The King looked forlorn. "We will have to continue our search the hard way."

"How can you sense Herobrine's location?" asked my dad.

"That's none of your concern," said the Ender King.

My dad looked upset about being brushed off like that, but he didn't pursue it.

"My ender soldiers will teleport you back to the Overworld. You need some rest after your ordeal."

"Okay. Come on Jimmy. Let's go," said my mom, reaching out her hand to me.

I shook my head. "No, Mom, I'm staying. The King and I have unfinished business with Spike."

The King looked at me. "Jimmy, now that your parents have been rescued, I will not allow you stay with me unless your parents consent. Since they have not, you must go with them."

"Actually, he can stay," said my dad. "And … hurrr … I'm coming with you."

My mom snapped her head and glared at my dad. "Billy! You can't do this to me! I can't lose both of you!"

"Cynthia, this is a critical moment in history. I need to be as brave as my son. As brave as my grandfather, Cornelius. Hurrr, the battle is in my blood!"

My mom shook her head and started to cry. She repeated, this time in a whisper, "I can't lose both of you."

"You aren't going to lose us," said my dad. "I can feel it."

Did my dad have some kind of vibe sensor that allowed him to predict the future? I wished I could do that with my vibes.

"Fine. Do what you want," said my mom angrily. "But if Jimmy dies, you better die too because I won't want you back!"

Wow! That was super intense. I had never see my mom that upset and dominant.

My father nodded his head in understanding.

"Take her back," said the Ender King to one of his soldiers. "And then return as quickly as possible."

"Are you going back too, Mr. Blaze?" I asked.

"No way," he said, slamming a fist into an open hand. "It's personal now. I want to find Spike just as much as you."

"Then it's settled," said the Ender King. "Let's go find Spike and Herobrine."

Day 41 – Thirty Minutes Later

We were heading in a northerly direction, hoping to find some sort of clue as to the whereabouts of Herobrine or Spike. But it seemed a hopeless, monumental task. The corridors of the Nether seemed to branch every ten or twenty blocks, turning into a labyrinth. Spike literally could have been on the other side of the wall or he could have been a two-hour walk away.

"This is ridiculous," I said throwing my diamond sword on the ground like a petulant toddler villager. "We're never going to find Spike at this pace! For all we know, he's just right behind us letting us walk in front of him."

The Ender King sighed. "You're right. Even if I brought my entire Ender Army down here, it would probably still take weeks to search every room. We would need enough soldiers to leave one behind in each room after it was cleared to make sure Spike didn't sneak in."

It was then that Mr. Blaze spoke up, completely changing the subject. "Where did you get this ... hurrr ... dog, Jimmy?"

"He was wandering through the town. Later, he saved my life from a possessed bat. Ever since then, he's been at my side."

Mr. Blaze looked at the dog curiously as if he wanted to say something more about the dog, but then thought better of it. Instead, he asked, "How's his sense of smell?"

I shrugged. "How should I know? All I know is that he himself smells disgusting."

Mr. Blaze ignored my comment and said, "Most dogs can track a scent. If we had something of Herobrine's, maybe the dog could lead us to him."

I had to admit, it was a brilliant idea. But where could we get something of Herobrine's? I suppose one of the ender soldiers could have teleported to his palace and grabbed something, but who knows how long that would take and whether the ender soldier could find us again in the labyrinth of the Nether.

"Great idea, Mr. Blaze. Do you have something of Herobrine's we could use?" asked my dad.

Mr. Blaze chuckled but then his face quickly shifted to a look of dark disappointment. "Of course not. Why would I?"

Mr. Blaze's response seemed a little more defensive than it probably should have been. Maybe he was just going a little insane from having been trapped in the Nether for a couple of days and being tortured by Spike, but it did seem a bit odd.

At that moment, I remembered. "I think I might have something," I said sheepishly, my face turning red.

The Ender King looked at me with a shocked expression. "What do you mean? How would you have anything of Herobrine's?"

I scratched my hair under my diamond helmet and said nervously, "Hurrr, I may have taken a souvenir the first time we visited his palace."

"Stealing? You stole something?" asked my dad, clearly upset.

I probably could have argued about the definition of stealing, but decided this was neither the time nor the place. "Yes, Dad, I guess I did. But it's gonna help us out now."

My dad shook his head. "The ends do not justify the means, Jimmy."

Whatever that means....

I ignored my dad and reached in to my inventory and pulled out a small, square object. It was a portrait of Herobrine, painted by an unknown artist. It was very small, which is why I had taken it in the first place. I had assumed Herobrine would never miss it. Now that everyone knew about my shameful crime, I was horribly embarrassed. But, the past is the past.

I held the small portrait out to Solar who took a sniff of it. He then barked, alerted and started trotting down the corridor as we followed closely behind.

Day 41 – One Hour Later

We followed Solar up and down various passageways, into dead ends, back over the same path, and seemingly around in circles. It didn't seem like it was working.

I put my hand on Solar's back and said, "Do you know what you're doing, Boy? Seems like you don't."

The dog looked at me as if to say, "Shut up, kid." It was actually quite shocking. I swear I saw a humanoid face in place of Solar's dog face for just a second, as if there were a person living inside of my pet dog.

I shook my head. I couldn't have seen that. I must have been imagining it. People give too much personality to dogs anyway. They're just animals after all. Aren't they?

A few minutes later, Solar stopped in his tracks and his back grew very straight and stiff. He was staring straight ahead. We all stopped too.

The Ender King whispered, "Be very quiet."

The Ender King took a few steps forward and peeked around the corner. Then he came back.

"There is a large, thick door being guarded by three zombie pigmen. There must be something important in there."

I grinned viciously, sliding my finger along the edge of my diamond sword. "Let's go."

"Not yet," said the Ender King. "We need a plan. I'm sure we can kill those three zombie pigmen without much difficulty, but what if there's an army behind that door, or lurking just around the corner. We need to figure out the contingencies."

The King was right. So we sat down and hashed out a plan. It took us about five minutes.

Day 41 – Executing the Plan

Our plan in place, we moved in for the attack.

One of the ender soldiers picked up a large piece of netherrack and tossed it into a corner of the chamber. The three zombie pigmen guarding the door looked over at it. One of the zombie pigmen, who must have been in charge, pointed to the pigmen standing to his right and said, "You two check it out. I'll stand guard."

The two zombie pigmen slowly moved towards the source of the noise. When they moved away from the door, the second ender soldier threw his sword at the remaining zombie pigman standing in front of the door. The sword spun through the air, end over end, before finding its target, stabbing the pigman in the heart. The zombie pigman screamed for a brief instant, then disappeared in a puff of smoke.

The other two zombie pigmen heard the sound of their commander being killed and rushed back. When they arrived at the door, they looked toward the opening to the passageway and saw an ender soldier standing there. As they rushed towards the soldier, he teleported away. It was at that moment that the Ender King and I stepped from behind our concealed positions and stabbed both of them with our swords, killing them.

I looked at the Ender King and said, "That was too easy."

The Ender King nodded. "It was either too easy or there's nothing in that room."

One of the ender soldiers walked toward the door. When he put his hand on it to open it, a blaze suddenly zoomed out from a hidden alcove and attacked him! The ender soldier was engulfed in fire and quickly burned to death. It was horrible to see, hear, and especially to smell.

Nas. Ty.

The other ender soldier rushed in and attacked the blaze with his diamond sword. The blaze was beginning to flash red. I snuck behind the blaze and slashed at its back. Our combined effort was enough, and the blaze perished.

I looked around, expecting something else, and I got something else.

A wall on the other side of the room suddenly slid away, revealing a large chamber from which poured forth at least a dozen husks.

I looked at the Ender King in shock, "What the heck are husks doing in the Nether?"

"I have no idea. We just need to kill them," said the Ender King, all business as usual, cool as a cucumber, as cold-blooded as a snake, serene in the face of near certain death.

As the husks rushed toward us, the Ender King pulled out a TNT box, lit the fuse, and tossed the box at the husks before grabbing me and teleporting us to safety.

When the TNT exploded, it killed more than half of the husks instantly. Of the remaining husks, another half of them were seriously injured, not posing much of a threat. The few husks who remained in battle condition, closed in on the Ender King and me.

It was then that my father, Mr. Blaze and Solar emerged from their hiding places and struck the husks from behind. My father channeled his inner zombie killer, chopping at the back of two husks with his borrowed diamond sword. Solar bit the ankles of the remaining two husks, whom Mr. Blaze then pushed to the ground where they writhed in pain.

With the husks distracted, the Ender King teleported between all four of the husks in what seemed like less than a second, quickly stabbing each of them in the heart and ending the battle.

We all stood there, breathing hard, waiting for the next horrible trap, but nothing came. We looked around the room. And still nothing came. We looked up into the ceiling, assuming there would be spiders or bats lurking, waiting to attack us. But we saw nothing.

"Is that it?" I asked hopefully.

The Ender King nodded. "I think so. That was less difficult than I had anticipated. It just doesn't feel right. It was too easy."

"I agree," said Mr. Blaze.

"Too easy!" said my dad, wiping sweat from his forehead. "We almost died!"

"Mr. Slade, this was nothing. It *was* too easy. But we have no choice now. We have to open that door," said the Ender King.

"Allow me the honor, sire," said the remaining ender soldier.

"The honor is yours, Bubba," said the Ender King.

The ender soldier walked up to the door and turned the handle. To my surprise, it wasn't locked. He pushed the door open and walked inside. Again to my surprise he was not attacked. He simply turned around with a shocked expression on his face and said, "Y'all better get in here and look at this."

The Ender King walked in first, and I followed closely behind. My dad and Solar coming in last.

What I saw shocked me to the core.

There, across the room was Herobrine, tied to a wood plank, somehow unable to break free of the enchanted rope holding him fast. Entity 303 stood next to him, lashing him with a rope, seemingly unconcerned about our entrance into the room. Herobrine screamed in pain every time the rope crashed against his skin. Entity 303 gave no sympathy.

"Tell me the secret! Where is the creation stone?" shouted Entity 303, anger and frustration foremost in his voice. "I've read your ancient diaries after I stole them. I know you know the location of the stone!"

"Never!" said Herobrine in between breaths of agony. "I'll never tell you!"

"Tell me so I can rule the three realms of Minecraft!" insisted Entity 303 with menace, punctuating his words with the lash to Herobrine's face.

When he had finished screaming, Herobrine yelled, "No!"

As I watched the exchange between two of the most powerful creatures in all of Minecraft, I saw something else I thought I would never see.

I looked over at Solar who had started to glow. Initially, it was a dim glow, like a torch burning in a cave hundreds of feet away, but then it got brighter and brighter. Eventually it turned into an amber light and then a bright yellow light and finally a blinding white light, forcing me to look away. When the light dimmed and I was able to turn back around I could not believe what I saw.

It was Notch!

"Entity 303, you have violated my law. Prepare to be punished," said Notch.

Entity 303 laughed and said, "You can't do anything to me anymore, Notch. You think you're so powerful, but you have no idea what true power is."

"And you have no idea what you are talking about," said Notch calmly as he snapped his fingers. Somehow, suddenly an obsidian cage appeared around Entity 303, sealing him inside.

But, despite being captured, he continued to laugh. "You think this flimsy cage can stop me? Prepare to be amazed."

At that moment there was a whooshing sound and Mr. Blaze transformed into a real Blaze, but three times the size of a normal blaze!

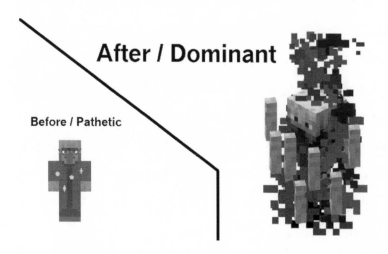

After / Dominant

Before / Pathetic

He laughed a deep, guttural laugh as he moved to the side revealing Spike standing behind him.

Where in the name of Notch did he come from?

Spike looked as though he was confused momentarily but then walked over to Entity 303's cage and pounded away at it with some sort of enchanted pickaxe, destroying it quickly.

I dropped to my knees, cowering in awe and fear of what I was seeing. My dad did the same. The Ender King stood his ground but looked scared. Even Notch seem to have a slight look of concern on his face

"How dare you contradict my law!" screamed Notch. "I was only going to banish you, but now I will have to destroy you forever."

Notch walked toward Entity 303, preparing to unleash power the likes of which I could only imagine. Entity 303 stood his ground, not showing the slightest bit of concern.

Notch began to move his hands in some sort of ancient pattern, a glowing ball of flame appearing in front of him. The ball was getting larger and larger, and I could feel the heat coming from it and the power vibrating throughout the chamber.

I began to back away. Something unspeakable was about to happen. I grabbed my dad's hand and pulled him with me. "Dad, we need to get behind something. This is going to be insane." My dad followed me as we ducked behind a large rock.

Now Notch had his hands above his head, spinning the giant ball of power, preparing to uncreate a part of his creation.

But just as he was getting ready to unleash the ultimate destructive power in the universe, he screamed in agony and the ball disappeared.

I looked up from behind my rock and saw that Spike and Mr. Blaze had surrounded and captured Notch using a rainbow colored rope of some kind! That's when I realized it was the same rope that had bound Herobrine to the wooden plank.

"No!" I shouted. "What's happening Solar ... hurrr ... I mean, Notch?"

"Run, Jimmy! Get away as fast as you can!" ordered Notch.

"No, I'll save you!" I yelled. I jumped up to go save him, but my dad's hand restrained me.

"Notch told us to get away. This is serious," said my dad.

It was then that the Ender King teleported to our location and grabbed both of us. "Notch is right," he said. "I know what's happening, and we have to leave now."

But it was too late, Entity 303 moved his hands quickly and aimed them in a chopping motion at a nearby wall, opening a vein of lava which poured toward us.

The Ender King suddenly screamed. "He's blocked my teleportation abilities! We're going to burn!"

I looked around for an exit. Something to climb. Something to cut through or jump over, but I saw nothing.

I looked behind me and saw lava rushing towards us. It looked like a wave. If only I could... And then I had an idea.

"Everyone take off your armor. We can surf this thing."

Everyone looked at me as if I had just escaped from an insane asylum, but then realized the brilliance of my idea.

"Your pathetic surfing can't save you, Jimmy Slade," said Mr. Blaze, still in his blaze form, ominously. "Your life is over, and we've won!"

"Not if I can help it, you savage!" I yelled.

We all removed our diamond armor and just as the lava flow reached us, we tossed our armor onto the lava and stood upon it.

As we rode the lava wave away, Mr. Blaze howled with anger, but Entity 303 just laughed and said, "Enjoy your fun, weaklings. Soon I will have the creation stone and you will bow to me for all eternity."

And with those words ringing in our ears, the lava flow took us out of the chamber and along another corridor. We were not pursued.

A few moments later, the Ender King said, "I think I can teleport now." The single remaining ender soldier nodded. "I agree, sire."

The King reached out and grabbed my dad and me and then we disappeared.

Day 42 – Dawn

The Ender King had to teleport two or three times inside the Nether before he reached a location where he could teleport back to his reception hall in Zombie Bane. When we arrived, we could see the first rays of dawn bleeding across the sky. We had been in the Nether the entire night.

When we arrived in the reception hall, I collapsed on the ground. My mind had stopped working. I could not think about anything. I couldn't even think about Notch or Entity 303. I was simply blank, a shell, maybe even a ... hurrr ... a husk.

Even the Ender King just stood there, shaken to his core. Unable to process what we had just witnessed and experienced.

Finally, after a few minutes of breathing, my brain started to work again. I looked over at the Ender King and said, "What's the creation stone?"

The Ender King looked at me with the most serious expression I'd ever seen on his face, which is saying something since he was always overly serious to begin with. He always looked like he was bored or upset. But now, I could tell that the fate of the world depended on our response to the unholy alliance of Entity 303 and Mr. Blaze.

The Ender King took a deep breath and then said, "The creation stone is a legend. It is said to have existed before Existence. It is said to have existed before Notch. In fact, some say the creation stone actually created Notch. As it floated through the formless nothingness before creation, it encountered a vapor or mist or dust, no one knows for sure. But when the creation stone touched it, Notch was formed. So they say, anyway. At that point Notch created the three realms of Minecraft – the Overworld, the Nether and the End – because the creation stone had touched him and given him the desire to create as well."

"So, what does Entity 303 want with it and why is Mr. Blaze involved?" I asked.

The Ender King took another deep breath and said, "I've no idea, but it cannot be good. Everything that can create can destroy. You saw yourself. Notch was going to take away Entity 303's very existence and even his ability to respawn. If you had the thing that created everything, you could destroy anything."

I couldn't believe this. Entity 303 was going to hold the three realms of Minecraft hostage to his threat of utter destruction. He would be able to do whatever he wanted, whenever he wanted, and no one could say anything against him. If someone spoke up, he would be destroyed. That is *if* Herobrine revealed the location of the creation stone.

I looked over at my dad who was sitting in a padded chair completely shaken. I looked back at the Ender King who didn't look much better. I had to ask. "Can we do anything to stop it?"

"Did you see the ropes they were using to restrain Notch?" asked the Ender King.

"I did. They were multi-colored, weren't they? I've never seen ropes like that."

The Ender King nodded. "That is because those ropes were made from skin flayed from the body of the Rainbow Creeper."

I gasped. "They've already killed the Rainbow Creeper!" I said, completely distraught.

The Ender King shook his head. "No. It is said that there was a time when the Rainbow Creeper allowed his followers to cut his skin off in thin layers in order to make powerful restraints which could even keep the most vicious prisoners from escaping. Somehow Entity 303 must have found those ancient ropes."

I slammed my fist onto the ground. "How do you know? Maybe the Rainbow Creeper is working with them."

"No," said the Ender King, "the Rainbow Creeper works with no one. Which is what is going to make this so difficult."

I looked at the Ender King confused. "Make what difficult?"

The Ender King sighed. "The only way we can rescue Notch is to work with the one remaining God of the three realms: the Rainbow Creeper."

Day 42 – Morning

I was still trying to process what I had seen. What the Ender King had told me. The creation stone! And, Notch himself had been captured by Entity 303, with the help of Mr. Blaze and Spike.

When we arrived home earlier, my father and I told my mother what happened. She broke down and cried. She was worried that the end of the world was coming. So was I.

At breakfast, I was in a bad mood. My mom hadn't cooked anything because she was still crying about the apocalypse. I had a piece of stale bread and three glasses of water. As I felt the water rehydrate the bread in my stomach, filling my empty stomach sack with something that approximated a meal, I let out a long, deep sigh and then let my head slowly fall to the table.

As I was sitting there, wallowing in my misery, my dad put his hand on my shoulder. "Jimmy, the Ender King will figure something out."

I sat up and looked at my dad. "Really? You think that he will be able to contact the Rainbow Creeper? That being that no one has seen in hundreds of years? A being that probably doesn't even exist?"

My dad pulled out a chair and sat down at the kitchen table. "Had you seen Notch before he appeared a few weeks ago? You believed in him, didn't you?"

"Of course I did! Everyone believes in Notch. The Rainbow Creeper is just some weird fairytale, I think."

My dad shook his head. "You yourself have seen the Rainbow Creeper in your dreams, have you not? Just because you haven't seen something in real life doesn't mean it doesn't exist."

"I suppose," I said not really believing my words.

My dad smiled. "Besides, the Ender King himself believes in the Rainbow Creeper. That should tell you something. And what about the rainbow colored flesh ropes we saw in the Nether? Those were from the Rainbow Creeper's own skin."

I rolled my eyes. "Maybe. But it could've just been some bizarre magical rope that Mr. Blaze had learned about from all those occult books he has in his bookstore. For all I know, it's fabric dye and some splash potions of harming soaked in spider webs."

"And, for all you know, it's actually the flayed skin of the Rainbow Creeper," said my dad.

"I don't know what to believe anymore, Dad. All I know is that the surf contest can't happen anymore. If Notch is gone, no one can judge it. And besides, what's the point? Notch was the one who created the contest to help stop war. If Notch is gone and Entity 303 and Spike intend to move forward with their plans for world domination or war or whatever, no surf contest is going to stop that."

"I wouldn't assume the worst just yet," said my dad. "Notch has some amazing abilities, and he may just get out of this yet. After all, who would've thought he could have disguised himself as a dog."

I looked at my dad. He was right. "Yeah, I guess he pretended to be a dog so he could get close to Entity 303 and Spike without them noticing. Too bad his plan didn't work out. Too bad he didn't know about Mr. Blaze."

"You go practice for the surf contest," said my dad. "You should assume it is going forward, otherwise, the evil people win. Remember, yesterday the King said he needed the morning to figure some things out. You should just try to forget about all this and go surfing."

I smiled, looking happy even though I didn't really feel it. "Maybe you're right, Dad. Plus, I can tell Emma about what happened. She'll be very interested to hear it."

My dad punched me softly in the shoulder. "That's the spirit, son. Go get pitted."

I smiled because my dad was the ultimate kook. Like, just because he knew a few surf words didn't mean he wasn't a total dork. Anyway, he was still a cool guy.

*　*　*

It took me about 10 minutes to get over to Emma's house. When she saw me coming up the walkway toward her front door, she ran out and gave me a long strong hug.

"Jimmy, you're back! Did you save your parents? Did you rescue Herobrine?"

If you had asked me a few days ago if anyone would ever ask me those questions, I would have told you that you were insane. Now ... hurrr ... I'm not sure I even know what sanity is.

I sighed. "My parents are fine, but..." I couldn't finish it. I broke down in tears.

Emma could tell it was serious. She led me over to the stairs in front of the door to her house and we sat down. She waited for me to finish crying. Once I had gathered my composure, I told her everything that happened, including about the Ender King's plan to contact the Rainbow Creeper.

Emma's mouth hung open in shock. "How? How is any of this possible? Notch being kidnapped? Herobrine in bondage? Spike in league with Mr. Blaze? I don't even know what to think. I don't even think I can comprehend this."

I stood up and said, "I know. I don't want to think about it anymore. Can we just go surfing?"

"I suppose. I was going to meet Princess Tina at the practice facility in about half an hour. Do you think her father will let her come?"

I shrugged. "I don't know. Maybe he will, with some soldiers to guard her."

Emma drew in a sharp breath and said, "Is the surf contest even going to happen? Without Notch?"

I shook my head. "I doubt it. It will be strange if Clayton's team shows up. What will we tell them?"

"Do you think Clayton knows? Isn't he in league with Spike."

"I don't know. I didn't see Clayton in the Nether this time. Maybe Spike is doing this on his own. Maybe Clayton has no idea what's going on."

Emma and I left her house and walked to the surf practice area. Tina was already there with her companions Rihanna and Ariana. There were also five ender soldiers standing guard.

We talked with Tina about everything that happened. Her dad already told her. She couldn't get over it either.

"My dad told me I should still practice for the contest. He thought that if he could somehow rescue Notch in the next couple of days, the contest could go forward."

"You really believe that?" I asked.

She shrugged her skinny black shoulders and said, "I don't know. But it's worth a shot."

"Oh, Jimmy, I forgot to tell you. We found a new recruit for the surf team. We didn't know if you'd be back. His name is Justin. He's pretty good. In fact, he is out there surfing right now," said Emma pointing into the water.

I looked out and saw Justin ripping. I recognized him as one of the local villager kids, but he was a couple years younger than me, so I had never spoken with him before. "Well, maybe if the King is still off on his mission or something, he can take the King's place."

Emma slapped me on the shoulder, smiled and said, "Cheer up, Jimmy! It will all work out."

I could tell she really didn't believe the part about it all working out, but she did want me to cheer up. "Well, if I can get a few sick pits, that will cheer me up, at least for a little while."

* * *

We surfed for about two hours before the warm square sun had nearly reached the middle of the sky. It was time for us to dry off and head back to the Ender King's palace to discuss his plans. The ender soldiers teleported us all there. My father was there as well, seeing as how he was so involved in all this.

I looked at the Ender King and said, "So, King, what's the plan?"

"I fear the plan is rather thin, Jimmy, like me," said the Ender King. "I've consulted my staff as well as various wise men and hermits who live in the End, but none of them knows how to contact the Rainbow Creeper."

I took a deep breath and said morosely, "So that's it then? Notch is gone, and we have no way to get him back?"

"I didn't say that," said the King confidently. "But I will have to ask you to talk to Claire. She's told you she was part of the Rainbow Creeper religion, right? Maybe she knows how to contact the Rainbow Creeper or will know someone who does."

I shook my head. "But, she says Spike knows what she thinks and can control her if he is close enough. I can't just teleport over to Capitol City and talk to her right now!"

Then the King nodded gravely. "I fully understand that. We'll have to wait until her surf team arrives for the surf contest. We have to keep this a secret. We can't let anyone know the surf contest is unlikely to happen or that Notch has been kidnapped."

I looked over at Emma. "Have you told anyone what I told you?"

She shook her head.

"I haven't told anyone either, except the people in this room, Daddy," said Tina.

The Ender King looked at my father and asked, "What about you, Billy Slade?"

"The only person I've told is my wife. She is sitting at home crying constantly. She hasn't told anyone."

The Ender King nodded his head. "Good. I'll send one of the queen's ladies in waiting to teleport your wife back here so that no one will know why she is crying. We must keep this a secret."

"So, what do we do now? Just wait?!?" I said, upset.

The Ender King looked at me and nodded. "We wait and we surf."

Day 42 – Midmorning

Claire, Clayton and the rest of their surf team arrived about 10:00 in the morning. I could tell they had arrived because it sounded like half of Capitol City had arrived with them. Groups of dozens and hundreds of Capitol City residents were marching through the streets of Zombie Bane chanting their love for their surf team, demanding a victory in revenge for the loss last week. Little did they know, they may not even get that chance.

I assumed Claire would visit Biff's house when she arrived in town. Therefore, Emma and I had made sure to arrive at Biff's house a few minutes before Claire. We were sitting on the porch, chatting with Biff (who didn't know anything about the drama with Notch or Entity 303 or Spike), when Claire came strolling up the path toward Biff's house.

Emma and I shouted to her and waved when she came in to view. By her expression, I could tell Claire was startled by our presence.

"Hi, guys, hurrr, what are you doing here?" asked Claire nervously.

I sensed good vibes coming from her. I didn't think she was being possessed by Spike. After all, Spike had other things on his mind.

I looked Claire in the eyes, raised an eyebrow and said, "Can we speak freely?"

Claire looked each of us in the eyes and nodded wordlessly.

At that moment, Emma said, "Hey, Biff, hurrr, I have this idea for a new type of standup paddle board. Want me to show it to you?"

Biff, not being the sharpest tack in the bag or the heaviest hammer in the sack or the brightest torch in the cave, said, "Yeah, I'd love to see it." He had no idea Emma was trying to get rid of him so that Claire and I could talk privately.

"In that case, let's go in your room. I need to draw pictures of it so you can truly understand how awesome it is." Biff smiled and trotted away with Emma following behind him. As she walked into the house, Emma looked over her shoulder and gave us a thumbs up.

I walked up to Claire, standing as close to her as I could without seeming creepy and whispered, "It's about the Rainbow Creeper. I need to arrange a meeting with it."

Claire clutched her chest as if she was having a heart attack. Her mouth moved up and down but no sound came out. After a few seconds she finally was able to utter a single word, "Why?"

I quickly explained what Spike and Mr. Blaze had done. Her mouth continued to twitch up and down, barely able to utter a word.

"Can you help me, or not? Emma can't keep Biff away forever. He doesn't know anything, and I'd like to keep it that way."

Claire had regained some more composure and said, "I only know where we attend Rainbow Creeper worship services. I've never met the Rainbow Creeper myself, but the priest might know. It's in Creeper Junction."

"Well, it's a good thing that the Ender King can teleport since we couldn't take the DOTS without arousing suspicion."

Claire looked at me with a strange expression on her face, which was a mixture of admiration and fear, awe and hatred and said, "I guess you're right."

After that, Claire gave me all the information I needed.

Day 42 – Afternoon

Emma and I went to speak with the Ender King. We told him what Claire had told me. He wanted to go immediately although he realized that it was important not to be seen. Therefore, we decided to go after dark.

Claire told us the location of the Rainbow Creeper temple in Creeper Junction. I asked, but she refused to come with us. She was afraid that Spike might be able to track her movements somehow and our plan would be given away.

Claire had given us enough information so that the Ender King could teleport within a block or two of the temple. She left Biff's to return to surf practice with Clayton's team so that no one would suspect anything. A little while later, the Ender King, Emma, Tina, and I showed up for our surf practice.

Clayton and his team were leaving the pool when Clayton came over to us. "What happened to Laird?"

"He had to attend the funeral of one of his friends," I said.

Clayton scratched his head, confused. "What's a funeral?"

It was then that I realized that most Minecraft villagers would have no idea what a funeral is. When creatures die in Minecraft, they disappear into a puff of smoke, with nothing left to bury. Even the drops they leave behind tend to be useful, so no one would think just to put them in the ground.

"It's what humans do when they die. They have a ceremony to remember the human's life, then they bury the remains," I said.

"You mean, they don't just disappear into puffs of smoke?"

I shrugged my shoulders. "No, they don't. I know it's pretty weird but that's how their world works."

Clayton nodded his head. "Interesting. I heard if they punch a tree in their world, they will break their hands. Sounds like humans are pretty wimpy."

"Whatever," I said.

"I'm sorry that Laird's friend died, but I'm glad Laird won't be here. Now we should be able to beat you guys without any problem."

That's when Tina stood up straighter and put her tiny hands on her tiny hips and said, "What about me? I'm replacing Laird. I rip."

Clayton laughed hysterically. "I doubt that. And your father's freaky teleportation air show won't help this time. During the last contest it was a new thing and no one had seen it before, so the judges totally over-scored him. This time, we're going to crush you guys."

It was my turn to laugh. "Somehow, I doubt that."

Clayton shrugged his shoulders and said, "Tell yourself whatever you need to in order to sleep well tonight. But this is gonna be a massacre."

When he used that word, I looked at him very closely, scrutinizing him. *Did he mean a bloody massacre or just mean that his team was going to score more points than ours?* I could not be sure, but I wasn't feeling any evil vibes coming from him. Just his normal stupid mean idiot vibes. I decided I would let it go. I took the lack of evil vibes to mean that, Clayton didn't know what Entity 303, Spike and Mr. Blaze had done to Notch.

"That's enough you two," said the Ender King. "It is our turn to start surfing now. You need to clear out of the practice area."

Clayton smiled a fake smile and then looked over at his team and said, "Let's go, guys."

I noticed that Clayton had the same team members. No changes for him. We barely beat his team the last time, so maybe Clayton was right about the upcoming massacre.

Day 42 – After Dark

We surfed for a couple of hours. It was fun, but I couldn't stop thinking about the Rainbow Creeper. After we finished surfing, we went back to the Ender King's reception chamber and had dinner and waited for nightfall.

Once it got dark, Emma, the Ender King, my dad and I teleported to the location provided by Claire. We materialized in a rabbits warren of narrow streets and alleyways, barely wide enough for one villager to pass through. If we ran into anyone, they were sure to notice we were out of place. Fortunately, we saw no one. Well, no villagers, anyway.

As we navigated the narrow streets, trying to find our way to the temple, we turned one corner and saw a zombie standing there moaning and drooling all over itself. In a surprise move, my dad withdrew an iron sword from his inventory and stabbed the zombie in his head, killing it instantly.

"Way to go, Dad," I whispered. He smiled.

"Come on, I think it's only a couple more doors down," said the Ender King.

He was right. Claire described the front door of the house we were looking for as having three vertical lines and three horizontal lines, each of which would be a different color of the rainbow. This is what we saw:

Not very subtle....

Anyway, just as Claire had taught us, we knocked on the door in a certain pattern: three long, two short, two long, three short, one long, one short and one long. We stood there, hoping Claire hadn't just steered us wrong or that Spike actually possessed her and his minions waited inside to kill us.

The door slowly opened. Inside stood a flaxen haired witch, just as Claire said there would be. Other than her quite attractive hair, the witch was extremely ugly. She peered at us with her one good eye, the other eye having been destroyed by the slash of a knife or a sword many years ago, then asked with a creaky gravelly voice, "What do you want?"

I looked at the Ender King, who was hiding in the shadows for approval to speak. I could just make out his purple eyes blinking twice, which I took to be a go ahead sign.

"We need to come in and talk to you about ... hurrr ... the Rainbow Creeper."

The witch's one good eye opened wide and she had tried to slam the door in my face, but at that instant the Ender King teleported between her and the door, preventing her from shutting it, eliciting a terrified scream from the witch. Fortunately, the Ender King slapped his hand across her mouth in less than a second, stifling the scream and preventing us from being discovered.

We pushed our way into the room and shut the door behind us.

The witch stared at the enderman in front of her, apparently not concerned about the legend that to stare one in the eyes was to invite an attack and perhaps death. Instead, she said, "Mumble mumble mumble."

The Ender King looked at her and realized his hand was preventing her from articulating any meaningful sounds. He said, "I'm going to remove my hand, but if you scream, it's coming back."

The witch nodded her understanding, and after the Ender King slowly removed his hand, she said, "Rainbow Creeper? I don't know what you're talking about."

I approached the witch and said, "Don't worry, we know all about it. Claire Dretsky told us to come here."

The witch had great fear in her eyes and said, "Priestess Claire?"

Priestess?

"What you mean, priestess?"

The witch looked confused and said, "Claire Dretsky. She's one of the Rainbow Creeper's priestesses."

"Does that mean she talks to the Rainbow Creeper?" Emma asked, incredulous.

The witch shook her head. "Oh no. Only the head monk is allowed to speak with the Rainbow Creeper. The priests and priestesses just help with the ceremonies."

"And who might the head monk be?" I asked.

The witch chuckled. "I'm not going to tell you that. Priestess Claire is nowhere near the top of the hierarchy. But I will tell you anything else you want to know."

At this point, the Ender King took over. "Do you know who I am?"

The witch shook her head negatively. "Should I?"

"I am the Ender King," he said, straightening his back so that he stood as tall as possible.

The witch let out a gasp of shock and then went silent.

The King continued. "I need to speak with the Rainbow Creeper about a matter of some exceptional urgency. I'm not sure how much I should reveal to you, but I will tell you that the fate of the three realms of Minecraft depends on whether or not I am able to speak with the Rainbow Creeper. And moreover, whether the Rainbow Creeper is willing to help avert catastrophe."

"And so you want me to relay your message?" the witch asked.

"In part. I want to setup a meeting with the Rainbow Creeper itself. This matter is absolutely that important."

The witch looked extremely concerned. "I've never heard of the Rainbow Creeper meeting with anyone other than the head monk and maybe Notch once or twice. Assuming those stories are even true."

"Indeed. Tell the Rainbow Creeper that we saw ropes made from its flayed skin being used for nefarious purposes. We need to discuss how to punish those responsible."

The witch was shocked. "You've seen the missing ropes? Those were stolen over a decade ago." Then the witch clapped her hands over her mouth, realizing she had said too much.

The Ender King squinted his eyes and looked into the witch's one good eye and said in his most serious voice, "I need to meet with the Rainbow Creeper as soon as possible. Tonight would be ideal, but I understand it may take longer to contact a god."

The witch looked at all of us and then said, "I can promise nothing other than to relay your message to the head monk. Whatever she decides, I shall obey. Where can I contact you?"

"I'm staying in Zombie Bane until tomorrow. After that, I shall be in the End for at least a day. Or, you may contact Jimmy here directly."

The witch nodded her head. "I understand. After you leave, I will contact the head monk as quickly as possible."

And with that cold comfort, the Ender King teleported us back to his chamber and then had ender soldiers teleport us back to our houses so we could try to get a few hours of sleep before the surf contest started tomorrow morning. If it started at all.

Day 43 – Morning

I woke up with a lump in my throat. Today was the day of the second surf contest, and I had no idea whether Notch was going to be able to free himself. Well, I had an idea, and my idea was that he would not be able to free himself and that the world would finally know that he had been kidnapped.

Yesterday, I discussed with the Ender King our strategy if Notch did not show up. His answer, "I'll think of something."

After I got up, I fixed my hair, put on by board shorts and then my robe. I walked downstairs and had breakfast with my dad. My mom was still in the care of the Ender King's servants.

We had a somber breakfast, of bread, watermelon, and cookies.

"I don't think Mom would be too happy if she knew what you were giving me for breakfast," I tried to joke with my dad.

He looked at me with a smile and said, "She wouldn't mind, under the circumstances."

I didn't have anything to say in response to that.

I grabbed my surfboard and started walking to the Ender King's palace. My dad told me he would be at the Surf 'n Snack in time for the contest to start.

"I hope Notch can make it," said my dad without much hope in his voice.

I sighed. "Me too, because if he doesn't, it's going to get real."

* * *

I walked toward the Ender King's palace feeling glum. Not only had I lost Notch, but my dog too. I missed Solar. If we could figure some way out of this mess and restore the balance of power in the three realms of Minecraft, I was going to get myself a dog. I had plenty of emeralds from the Surf 'n Snack and could easily afford it. I'm sure my parents wouldn't mind.

When I got inside the Ender King's palace, Emma was already there. Tina, the Ender King, Emma and I stood, each holding a surfboard and looking each other in the eyes. We didn't have to say anything. We knew what was likely to happen, and we are ready for it. The Ender King put his hand on my shoulder. Tina put her hand on Emma's shoulder and we all teleported to the surf contest.

When we arrived, Justin was waiting for us.

"Do I get to surf?" asked Justin anxiously.

I shook my head. "Not this time, unless one of us gets hurt."

Justin looked sad. "Okay. Maybe next time."

I smiled. "Maybe."

The crowd was already extremely loud. Groups from Zombie Bane and from Capitol City were chanting for their teams.

Flags were waving.

Someone created a Zombie Bane flag which was a picture of a zombie with a slash through it, in honor of my great-grandfather, and the name of our town. I could only imagine the number of reproductions of that flag that would be sold in Zombie Bane souvenir shops from this day forward.

I looked over and saw Clayton's team consisting of Clayton, Claire, Mateo, the zombie pigman, and John-John. They looked ready. But they would not have a chance if Notch didn't show up in the next ten minutes.

I tried to catch Claire's eye so that I could wink at her or something to let her know that we made contact with her Rainbow Creeper connection. But she refused to look over at us. I didn't know if she was just trying to protect herself or if maybe Spike was controlling her.

Normally I would have been stretching in order to get ready to surf, but I figured what was the point? Notch wasn't going to show up, and then the Ender King was going to have to tell the entire crowd what happened. It would cause panic and pandemonium. I hoped a riot wouldn't break out. People were going to run for their lives. I'm sure the rates of depression and anxiety would spike, as people began to realize that Notch was not powerful enough to protect even himself.

But then a miracle happened, Notch appeared floating in the air just as he had done at the contest in Capitol City!!!

He looked over the crowd as they applauded and screamed his name. He smiled.

I looked over at the Ender King and asked quietly, "Is that really Notch?"

Ender King squinted his eyes and then said, "It sure looks like him. Maybe he escaped? Just be on your guard in case it's a trick."

I nodded my head in understanding, but I didn't want it to be a trick. I wanted it to be the one true Notch, having escaped his evil captors.

Just as he had at the first surf contest, Notch announced the guest judges first.

"Welcome to the second of three surf contests to decide who will have the bragging rights between Clayton Dretsky and the Ender King. Our first guest judge needs no introduction. His dry disgusting skin and his ability to go about in sunlight mean he can only be, the Husk King."

Notch snapped his fingers and the Husk King appeared on the sand in between the two surf teams. He put his hands in the air and pumped his fist. The crowd, not knowing what to do and not really wanting to applaud for the King of the mobs who had killed so many villagers, politely applauded. Only the zombie pigman on Clayton's team truly hooted and hollered in appreciation of the Husk King's appearance.

"Thank you Notch for this chance to be a judge of the surf contest," said the Husk King in a formal tone. "I know that many of you in the audience are not fans of husks, and that is okay. Notch made us for a reason, and that's all that matters to me." And with that, the Husk King walked over to the judging platform.

The Husk King finished with his speech, Notch returned to his introductions. "Our next guest judge may surprise you, but I think you'll be amazed. Without further ado I give you... The Silverfish Queen!."

Notch snapped his fingers and the Silverfish Queen appeared on the sand in between the two surf teams.

The crowd let out a collective, "Eeww. Gross."

"Don't be rude!" commanded Notch, admonishing the crowd.

The crowd politely applauded and the Silverfish Queen spoke, "I understand your revulsion for me. Silverfish do creep around and look pretty gross. But, remember, we are entitled to exist too. We are part of creation. So, next time you see a silverfish, instead of trying to squish it, say hello."

The crowd sat in stunned silence while the Silverfish Queen scurried over to the judges' table

The introductions concluded, Notch floated over to the judges' table and then proceeded to announce the rules for this particular contest.

"The rules for this contest are much the same as the first contest, except I'm going to ban teleportation, since it potentially gives an unfair advantage to the Ender King's team, especially now that I see there are two ender people on the team. Other than that, the only other rule change is that one of the four rides required for each contestant will need to be on a longboard. I know that riding a shortboard is good for radical turns, aerials, and getting pitted, but I want to see some style, some steeziness, if possible, on the longboard. That way, we can see if you are a well-rounded surfer or just a one-dimensional shredder."

I looked over at the Ender King. "You should do that maneuver where you lie down on the longboard like a corpse. That's pretty cool."

The Ender King nodded his agreement.

"By the way, King," I asked. "Do you still think that's the real Notch?"

The King nodded confidently. "Yes, I do believe it is. I don't get a sense that he's being controlled by Entity 303 or anyone else. He must've gotten away. We will ask him after the contest."

I smiled happily.

*　*　*

From the beginning, the surf contest was a one-sided affair. Clayton's team had been preparing all week as if they were going to be in a surf contest, while my team had barely prepared at all, and we were short Laird who had been replaced by Tina. Tina was good, but nowhere near as good as Laird, who'd been a professional surfer for twenty years.

After the first round, it was still close, but after that, our lack of preparation showed. Although the Ender King had the highest individual scores of any surfer in the entire contest, Clayton's team crushed us. There's no other way to put it. It was humiliating.

After the contest was over, Clayton walked up to me and thumped his chest and said, "That's how it should be. Next time, wherever that contest is, we will crush you again."

I rolled my eyes. "You have no idea what we've been dealing with do you? If you did, you would not be acting like this."

Claire overheard what I said. I could see the color drain from her face and she blinked her eyes as if she were in shock.

What's wrong with her?

It was then that Notch floated back into the sky and said, "As promised, the third contest will be at a mystery location. I will tell you right now that it will be an island in the middle of the ocean where you will get a sneak peek at the Update Aquatic. And, I have created natural waves."

Everyone gasped. Natural waves? No wave machine needed? What would it be like?

We had to get Laird back. He was used to surfing powerful natural waves. None of us were.

"Yes, natural waves," continued Notch. "I will give each team the coordinates of the island one day before the contest. I will also ask that the Ender King and his people teleport Clayton's team to the island so they can get there on time."

The Ender King bowed his head and said, "Of course, Notch. Consider it done."

And with that Notch said, "Well then, I guess I will be going. But before I do..."

It was then that something entirely unexpected happened. Clouds suddenly rolled in, darkening the sky in a matter of seconds, and it started to rain. There was thunder and lightning and then Notch put his arms out to his sides and his eyes turned a glowing red and he said in a deep, hollow voice which was not his own, "You people are fools. I have complete control of Notch. You will never have your stupid contest. Prepare for the reign of Spike."

And as the villagers in the crowd screamed and cried and pulled their hair in agony and despair, Notch simply disappeared and Spike appeared in his place laughing at everyone.

When Spike appeared, Clayton and Claire's eyes suddenly turned a glowing red and they began to laugh with the same rhythm as Spike. It was then that Spike snapped his fingers and Clayton, Claire, and Spike all disappeared.

I looked at Emma and Tina and the Ender King, tears streaming down my face.

"Now what?" I said, assuming the answer would be that the world was going to end.

The Ender King was about to say something when a strange figure materialized next to us. It was a decrepit old villager woman not much taller than a six-year-old kid. She had wrinkled clothes and a strange hat pushed to one side. She had wrapped herself in a quilt that had all the colors of the rainbow on it but had many holes in it, as if it were hundreds of years old and not very well cared for.

And then she opened her mouth and with a cracky squeaky voice she said, "I understand you wish to speak with me. I am the head monk of the Rainbow Creeper."

END of Surfer Villager 8

Book 9

Day 43 – Morning (continued)

As I stood there staring at the strange little old lady who had identified herself as the head monk of the Rainbow Creeper, I took a trip back into my brain. I must have looked strange, probably with a glazed, dead–inside expression just for a few moments while I reviewed everything that had happened to me in the past few weeks.

I needed this moment of solitude in order to prepare for what was coming, what I knew would be one of the most difficult and stressful periods of my life. Here is what I thought about....

I had co–invented surfing in Minecraft with Emma. I had been enslaved in the Nether by Clayton Dretsky and escaped. I had helped find Herobrine and asked him for ideas to stop the war between the Ender King and the Dretsky family. I'd watched the Almighty — or so I thought — Notch announce the surf contest to prevent that same war. I had been tortured in my dreams by Entity 303 and had seen what I thought was the Rainbow Creeper. I had adopted a pet dog wandering the streets which turned out to be Notch in disguise. I had traveled to the Nether to free my parents and rescue Herobrine. I had seen Notch captured by Entity 303, only to miraculously — so it seemed at the time — escape to judge the second surf contest. And, just a few moment ago, I had seen Entity 303 control Spike, Clayton, and Claire and kidnap Notch.

Thinking through the events in which I had been involved made my head spin. It was like something from the early mythology of the Overworld. Amazing, stupendous, epic, but not really believable.

And now, I was looking at this strange little old lady who claimed to have direct contact with the Rainbow Creeper, a deity about which I had only recently learned. It was almost too much. I could actually feel my brain sweating as it began to overheat.

When I snapped out of my trance, I saw the Ender King standing next to the head monk and saying, "Thank you for answering our call. I'll get to the point: We're hoping the Rainbow Creeper will help us defeat

Spike and Entity 303 and rescue Herobrine and restore Notch to power."

The old lady laughed and said sarcastically, "Oh, is that all?"

The Ender King sighed. "I realize it's a big ask, but the Rainbow Creeper is the only supernatural being remaining who is not controlled by Entity 303, and I'm pretty sure we need supernatural powers to get us out of this mess."

"Well, based on what you are asking, I would agree the Supernatural is in order," said the old lady with a wink of her eye. "So, what do you think the Rainbow Creeper can do to assist you?"

I walked over to the two of them as they were chatting. "Look, lady, we need the Rainbow Creeper's help right now. ASAP. Pronto! If we don't get it ... hurrr ... well, Entity 303 has already corrupted Spike and is going to use Notch and Herobrine to get the creation stone and take over the three realms of Minecraft. The Rainbow Creeper will be destroyed." I crossed my arms over my chest. *That ought to wake her up to the terrible reality we all faced.*

The old lady laughed. "I don't think you understand what the Rainbow Creeper is, young man. The Rainbow Creeper cannot be destroyed."

Now it was my turn to laugh. "Well, just the other day I didn't think Notch could transform into a dog or be captured, but I've seen both of those things now. So I don't think you really know who your Rainbow Creeper is."

The old lady scowled at me and raised her hands above her head and shouted, "Silence!"

Normally, when someone who is only about three feet tall tells me to be quiet, I ignore them, mainly because it means they are a little kid trying to act all tough.

But there was something about this old lady that really made me listen to her. I actually felt **intimidated**, like when the Ender King would swell to several times his normal size and stare down at me. But in this case, of course, she was staring up at me through her wrinkled, scrunched up angry face. Her face was so purple with rage that she reminded me of a chorus fruit.

I nervously scratched my hair and pulled on the collar of my robe. "Hurrr ... sorry. But, you see what I mean."

The old lady shook her head in disgust. "The Rainbow Creeper is more than you can imagine, but I'm not going to get into that right now. The Rainbow Creeper has been watching Entity 303 slowly gain power over the past few years. The Rainbow Creeper had been relying upon Notch to keep Entity 303 in check, but somehow Entity 303 was able to acquire those old rainbow-colored ropes made from the Rainbow Creeper's own skin ... that was a game changer — no lie. With those, Entity 303 can control any being in Minecraft."

I gasped. "Even Notch and Herobrine?"

"*Any* being."

At this point, Emma, who had been standing to the side of the Ender King, interjected, "How do those ropes work anyway? They seem to defy all laws of nature."

The old lady chuckled. "Of course they defy the laws of nature. The Rainbow Creeper is not of nature."

Not of nature?!? Where did it come from then? What else is there?

The old lady did not explain any further, but left this strange mystery hanging in the air. I looked at Emma and opened my eyes wide and then rolled them slightly to express my dismay at the fact that this old lady wouldn't tell us more. Emma looked shocked. As a scientist, she was always looking for facts and data; I could tell the uncertainty disturbed her greatly.

The old woman continued. "Look, you may not know this but Entity 303 can exist in all three realms of Minecraft at the same time. But, when he is split into three parts, he is much less powerful, more like a ghost, a shy, passive mob, or a dream, but he can still influence events in the realms. When he joins all three of his bodies together in a single realm — the Overworld, for instance — he is as powerful as anyone other than perhaps Notch and the Rainbow Creeper. But now that he has the ropes, he is the most powerful creature in all of Minecraft other than the Rainbow Creeper."

The Ender King put both of his hands on his head and moaned in distress. "Will the Rainbow Creeper help us then? Without its help, we are doomed."

The old woman nodded. "Truly, the Rainbow Creeper is merciful, and I come bearing advice from the Rainbow Creeper. If you follow this advice and have a little luck, you should be able to defeat Entity 303."

"Well, spill then," I said. "We don't have all day." I needed this old lady to hurry up and get to the point. Seriously, guys, these people who have to monologue before getting to the point bug me.

The old woman looked at me angrily and then threw a tiny pebble at me. When the pebble hit my skin it inflicted a massive amount of pain but only for a brief moment. I collapsed to the ground and screamed in agony. "What have you done to me?"

"I wanted to show you but a small portion of the Rainbow Creeper's power. That pebble is made from the Rainbow Creeper's dead skin. As the skin falls off, the followers of the Rainbow Creeper followers collect it and turn it into weapons. You are a rude child and deservedly punished."

"That's child abuse, you hag!" said Emma, taking a step toward the head monk. "You should be ashamed of yourself."

The old woman shrugged. "I'm old school when it comes to stuff like that."

By now my pain subsided and I stood up and pointed my finger at the old lady. "I'm not old–school. If you do that again, I'm coming after you, even if you are an old lady."

The old woman began to growl at me but the Ender King stepped in between us and put his hands up. "This is not helping anyone. Head monk, stop inflicting pain on anyone who isn't evil. Jimmy, stop being so rude."

The head monk lowered her head in shame and said, "I'm sorry. I did not have a good childhood. I didn't mean to continue the cycle of violence."

I sighed and said, "I'm sorry. I was being a bit rude, but I just want to find my friends and ... hurrr ... this sounds crazy, but ... save the world."

At this point the head monk insisted that we go somewhere more private. The Ender King, Emma,

Princess Tina, and I followed the head monk to a private corner of the Surf 'n Snack. It was easy to find privacy as most of the crowd had run away in terror when Spike had appeared.

"I will tell you the steps you need to take to rescue Herobrine and Notch and to free the Dretsky family from Entity 303's control. You must find and free each of the people Entity 303 has imprisoned. In addition to Herobrine and Notch, he has imprisoned Claire Dretsky as leverage against Clayton and Spike. He knows they will be forced to obey him because they want to protect their sister."

I couldn't believe the audacity of Entity 303, holding Claire hostage so that he could keep Clayton and Spike doing his bidding.

"Are you saying that Spike might be able to break free of Entity 303's control if Claire were free?" I asked.

The old woman shook her head. "No, but the ongoing fear of harm to his sister makes it easier for Entity 303 to control Spike's mind, freeing up his energy to control Notch."

The head monk then reached into her tattered cloak and pulled out three splash potions. The liquid inside appeared to be all the colors of the rainbow, with actual gradients and separations between the colors inside the bottle. Somehow they didn't mix together and form an inky black potion.

The old woman handed the three potion bottles to the Ender King. "This is the rarest potion in all of Minecraft. It is the ***potion of sanity***. When you throw it on a person, they have thirty seconds of pure clarity where they can see the world for what it truly is no matter what situation they're in. When you find

Herobrine, Claire, and Notch, you must toss this potion on them because it will allow them to break free of Entity 303's control and, once they see the world for what it is, they will never be subject to his control again."

What did she mean by that? How does seeing the world for what it truly is allow you to be free from the control of others? Even from someone as powerful as Entity 303?

"Once we free them, can we capture Entity 303?" I asked.

The head monk looked at me curiously. "Do you want to capture Entity 303? Does it matter?"

I shrugged. "I don't know. Obviously, I want to free Claire and Notch and Herobrine, but shouldn't we capture Entity 303 once it's all done?"

"That's up to you," said the old lady. "The Rainbow Creeper has now given you the power to free your friends. The rest is in your hands."

"I would think the Rainbow Creeper would be more involved in the world of Minecraft. After all, without Minecraft, the Rainbow Creeper wouldn't exist." I said, starting to get angry again.

The old woman looked at me and smiled. "That's where you are wrong. Did I not already tell you the Rainbow Creeper is not of nature? The Rainbow Creeper stays here because it enjoys the creeper form and the blocky world. It is not of Minecraft."

I was shocked. I looked over at Emma. She was totally shook. Even the Ender King seemed a little twitchy.

"What do you mean? How could the Rainbow Creeper not be 'of Minecraft'? Minecraft didn't exist until Notch created it." I said.

"It is true that Notch created Minecraft when he touched the creation stone, but the Rainbow Creeper preexisted that moment," the head monk paused and looked like she was thinking of continuing, but then said, "That's a story for another time."

I balled my right hand into a fist and shook it at the old lady. "Netherrack," I cursed, "you're going to tell me that story right now!"

The old woman pulled out a little pebble and held it in her hand I could tell she was contemplating throwing it at me again. She put it back into her pocket and insisted in a calm, level voice, "No. It is a story for another time."

At this point, Emma intervened. "Look, head monk, I would really like to hear you explain the origins of the Rainbow Creeper, but I guess I can let that pass. However, where can we find Notch, Herobrine, and Claire? They've all disappeared. We have no idea where to look."

Leave it to Emma to be practical and ask how to start our quest. I wish I would think of things like that.

The head monk nodded her head and then was silent for a moment. She closed her eyes and made little circles by touching the tips of each thumb and middle finger together. She started chanting a little bit and then, after about twenty seconds stopped chanting and opened her eyes.

"I can tell you this. Herobrine is being held at the bottom of a stronghold tied to a chair. The chair is on a cobblestone platform surrounded by lava and there is a small tube through which air goes in and out of the area and through which his captor lowers food and drink to him. Claire is imprisoned on an end island inside an end ship. Notch ... well ... find the other two and you'll know how to find Notch."

I was about to ask her if she knew where the stronghold was when she simply vanished into thin air.

I screamed. "What is that supposed to mean?!? How does that nonsense help us find them?"

"I think it will be enough," said the Ender King. "There are not that many strongholds in the Overworld, and the Ender Army has mapped all of the known ones. We can quickly scout them for evidence of Herobrine's presence. Plus, if I'm inside a stronghold with Herobrine, I should be able to sense his presence."

Emma nodded. "Yeah, and then since strongholds always have end portals, we can go to the End once we find Herobrine and then we can locate Claire. And then, if the head monk was right, once we find Claire, we will know how to find Notch."

"Maybe," said the Ender King. "Or, maybe we will need a rest. There is no telling how long this might take. Still, I admire your optimism."

I sighed. This was crazy. I should be surfing right now and counting all the emeralds I was making from the Surf 'n Snack. Instead, I was going on a wild goose chase. But it was a goose chase that had to end with me catching the goose or else Entity 303 would take over the world of Minecraft and Claire, Herobrine and Notch would probably be …. I couldn't think it. It was too horrific to contemplate.

I looked back toward the remnants of the contest crowd, most of whom had dispersed when Notch was kidnapped and everyone freaked out. I saw my dad awaiting some distance off. I walked over to him and told him everything that the head monk had told us just now.

"Dad, I have to go on this mission. I have to finish what I started."

My dad took a deep breath and then nodded. "I shouldn't let you go," he said. "Your mother wouldn't want me to let you go, but I understand why you must. The blood of Cornelius, Bane of Zombies, runs through your veins. Do our family name proud son."

I felt tears forming in my eyes. I didn't realize how much it would mean to me to have my dad give me his permission and tell me he was proud that I was a member of the family.

I swallowed a couple times to avoid my voice cracking when I replied and said, "Thanks, Dad. I will."

After I received my dad's blessing I walked back toward the Ender King. It was then I noticed Emma had walked off and was speaking with her parents. They looked frantic and upset. Emma was gesticulating here and there and occasionally turned around and pointed at me or the Ender King. I could not hear what she was saying.

After about two minutes of argument, her parents both hugged her tightly and then said some words to her, hugged her again, and then watched with tears in their eyes as she walked back toward our group.

As Emma approached, I could see that she had been crying. "What's wrong?" I asked.

Emma sniffed and ran her hand across her nose before answering. "I told them I wanted to come with you to rescue Herobrine and Claire and Notch. They wouldn't let me go ... hurrr ... at first. But I convinced them that this expedition might need someone who can think in a scientific way, and let's face it, you and the ender folk aren't much for science."

I'd chuckled slightly and said, "So, that convinced them? Science?"

Emma shrugged and then added, "Well ... hurrr ... that and I told them that you were super dominant and could take care of me."

I could feel the flush in my cheeks from the embarrassment. "Really? You think I can take care of you?" I was flattered. I had never had anyone tell me that I was able to take care of them. And now Emma, my best friend, was telling me that. It made me feel very proud.

Emma laughed and then slapped me on my shoulder. "I can take care of myself, obviously, like when I saved you from being a slave in the Nether. I just told my parents that because they believe in all that old–school chivalry stuff."

I could feel my cheeks getting even redder from even more embarrassment.

Did Emma really mean that I could take care of her and she was just covering it up, or did she really mean that I was an idiot and she had just figured out what to tell her parents so that she could come on this trip with us?

I had no idea. Instead, I forced a chuckle and said, "Cool."

"Come on, Jimmy," said Emma with a smile, "Let's go see what the Ender King wants to do next."

The two of us walked over to the Ender King and Tina, who had been standing near the water's edge while Emma and I spoke with our parents. I took the lead speaking, mainly because I wanted to distract myself from the embarrassing conversation I just had with Emma. "So, King, what up? How it be? What next, dawg?"

The King scowled at me and my idiomatic expressions and then said, "First, we will return to my palace. I shall dispatch my soldiers to search the known strongholds. Then we'll decide what to do."

And with that, the Ender King reached out and touched my shoulder and Emma's shoulder and the three of us, along with Princess Tina, teleported back to the Ender King's palace in downtown Zombie Bane.

Day 43 – Moments Later

When we arrived at the palace, Laird, to our surprise, was standing in the reception hall!

When he saw us he flashed a brilliant smile, gave us a shaka and said, "I just got back from the funeral. I'm still sad, but I wanted to find out how the contest went."

We all had sad expressions on our faces which gave him a hint of how the contest went.

"So you lost?" He seemed genuinely surprised.

I shook my head. "Well, yeah, we did lose, but ... hurrr ... that's not the real issue."

By the way I said it, Laird could tell I was being serious. Laird lost the smile he been wearing and asked, "How bad is it?"

I quickly explained the events of the last week and how we were now on a quest for Herobrine, Claire, and Notch.

Laird shook his head sadly and said, "I didn't think anything could be sadder than the funeral of a friend, but this might just be. And even though I live in a different world and I am not of Minecraft, I feel great sadness."

That was weird. Laird mentioned that he was "not of Minecraft," just like the head monk had said about the Rainbow Creeper.

The Rainbow Creeper couldn't be a player in disguise, could it?

"So, is there going to be a third contest?" asked Laird.

I shrugged. "I doubt it. But I wish there would be. Notch said it was going to be on an island in the middle of the ocean and there would be naturally generated waves."

Laird sank to his knees and raised his eyes to the sky and said, "Hallelujah!" Then he stood up and said, "Gosh, it makes me sad that Notch was actually going to create powerful natural waves, and now that he is gone, it probably won't happen. I really hope you do find him because natural waves in Minecraft would be amazing."

I agreed with him and suggested that he check back with us in a few days. If we'd found Notch by then, the contest might be going forward, but if we hadn't, then maybe the world of Minecraft wouldn't even exist.

"Indeed, Laird, when you do return, be prepared to leave at a moment's notice. If the world of Minecraft begins to collapse and its existence begins to end, you will want to escape back to the human world, otherwise, who knows what will happen to you," warned the Ender King.

The Ender King's warning made everything far too real for me. The fact that he acknowledged that the world of Minecraft might actually end was too much for me to bear. I slumped into a nearby chair and began to sob.

Laird came over and put his hand on my shoulder and said, "You can do it, Jimmy. You can find them. I believe in you guys." Laird removed his hand from my shoulder and scratched his head. "Still, I guess I had best take the King's advice and go back to the human world. When I do come back, I'll be ready to leave as quickly as a possible, but also be ready to fight or surf, if necessary."

And with that, Laird shimmered and then disappeared, leaving Minecraft and returning to his world.

With Laird gone, the Ender King told us he was going to go talk with his soldiers in order to send them to reconnoiter all the known strongholds for any evidence of Herobrine's location. Emma, Tina and I acknowledged this, and he left the room.

The three of us sat in silence for several minutes, lost in our own thoughts, making peace with our souls and the thought of the ultimate destruction of Minecraft or, *at best*, a Minecraft where Entity 303 controlled everything.

When the King returned a few minutes later, he said, "We should know in a few hours if my soldiers have found a possible location for Herobrine. In the meanwhile, we should rest."

Day 43 – Five Minutes Later

After about five minutes of sitting in the Ender King's reception hall, I got bored. And I said so. "King, I'm bored."

The King looked at me with his purple eyes and rolled them. "What is it with you kids today? You're always bored."

I shrugged. "I don't know. I didn't used to get bored. But I've had so much insane stimulation, what with surfing and being enslaved and rescuing my parents and seeing Notch kidnapped. Just sitting around is kind of ... hurrr ... boring."

"So, you think it'll be a couple hours before the ender soldiers get back from searching the strongholds?" asked Emma.

The Ender King nodded his perfectly cubic black head and said, "Give or take. Strongholds are pretty complex structures and it will take my soldiers a while to perform even a cursory search through all the passages and rooms."

"In that case, do you mind if Jimmy and I go explore Mr. Blaze's bookstore?" asked Emma.

An icy chill ran down my spine. Why hadn't we thought of this earlier? Mr. Blaze was clearly an ally of Entity 303 and Spike, either by choice or because he was compelled to do so.

"Yeah, we should do that," I said, slamming my fist down on the nearby table to emphasize my point. "There might be clues in his bookstore."

"I want to go too!" said Princess Tina.

The Ender King regarded us and then said, "That's a good idea. Tina, you can go but I will send an ender soldier with you. I don't think your ladies in waiting, Arianna and Rihanna, are strong enough should Entity 303 or Spike appear while you're at the bookstore."

Tina smiled. "Okay. Whatever you say, Daddy."

An ender soldier suddenly materialized in the room, somehow he had been summoned by the Ender King. The ender soldier saluted and said, "Yes, my King?"

"Liam, I want you to protect Tina with your life. If you can protect Emma and Jimmy also, please do, but Tina is your number one priority."

The ender soldier clicked his tiny black heels together and saluted again, acknowledging his understanding of the task.

I looked over at Emma and whispered, "I guess we see how it is now, don't we?"

Emma shrugged.

Tina walked over and said, "Shall we go?"

The two of us nodded and Tina put her hand on Emma's shoulder and the soldier put his hand on my shoulder and we teleported to the front of Mr. Blaze's bookstore.

Because we had kept most of the story of what happened in the Nether secret from the public, no one outside our small circle knew that Mr. Blaze was a traitor. Therefore, his bookstore remained open. In fact, the teenage villager whom we had met the last time we visited the store was sitting behind the emerald register selling books. We walked up to him and I said, "What up? How it be?"

He looked at us and said, "Oh, it's you guys." Then, he noticed Tina and the soldier and looked very uneasy. "And ... hurrr ... you have two enders with you?"

"Yeah, they're cool. Don't worry about it," I said.

The teenage villager didn't seem convinced that he shouldn't worry about two ender folk in his book shop. Although he didn't challenge their presence, he refused to look them in the face.

"Have you seen Mr. Blaze around?" I asked, knowing that he hadn't.

The teenager shook his head and said, "I haven't seen him for a few days. I keep coming to work because I assume he just went on vacation or something and forgot to tell me. It's kinda weird though. He's never done that before."

"Gone on vacation or forgotten to tell you?" asked Emma.

"Either. He's a super–organized workaholic."

I nodded and scrunched my brow as if I were equally as concerned as the teenaged clerk. And then I said, "Hey, when we were here before, Mr. Blaze showed us some books he had in his private library. There is something in one of them I wanted to look at again. Do you think I could get in there real quick?"

The teenager looked nervous and said, "I don't know. That's his private area. I'm only allowed to go in there when he calls me."

It was Emma's turn to try. She leaned forward in a conspiratorial manner and said in a whisper, "Look, see that ender girl over there? She's actually the Ender King's daughter." The teenager's eyes got wide with a combination of amazement and trepidation. "He sent us over here to look for something. Something *very* important. Maybe even a clue to help us find out what happened to Notch this morning at the surf contest. You wouldn't want to prevent that, would you?"

The teenager started sweating and pulled on the collar of his robe to let some air in to try to cool down. He glanced quickly at the two enders standing in his book shop. He leaned toward Emma and whispered, "That was crazy about Notch. But, say, if she's the Ender Princess, who's the tall one?"

"That's her bodyguard. The Ender King told him to kill anyone who got in her way," said Emma, like it was no big deal.

At this point the teenage villager's face turned bright red and then immediately became a pale white.

It looked as though he was going to vomit. But he didn't. Instead he reached under the desk and fumbled for a key, handed it to Emma and said, "Go ahead. But if Mr. Blaze gets upset, I'll tell him the Ender King made me do it."

Emma took the key and smiled. "I'm sure Mr. Blaze will understand."

The four of us walked over to the door to Mr. Blaze's private office. Emma put the key in and opened the door. For a moment, I had a sick feeling that when we opened the door Mr. Blaze would be in there, waiting for us, doing something evil...

But he was not.

We walked into the office and shut the door behind us so that the teenage villager working at the front desk couldn't see what we were doing.

We started by looking around the room for anything obviously evil, but of course it looked just like an office. Just like it did the last time we were in there.

I looked at the locked glass cabinet that held the old books and from which Mr. Blaze had retrieved his book about Evokers. It seemed like that had been years ago.

I pointed at the cabinet and said, "If there is anything helpful, I bet it's in there."

Emma nodded and looked at the keychain. "There's only one key here and the door is locked on that cabinet. How will we get in?"

"Try the key anyway," I suggested.

Emma walked over and stuck the key in the keyhole. The key slid into the keyhole without any problem, getting my hopes up that it might work. Emma tried turning it a couple of times, but it just jiggled back and forth inside the lock, not opening it.

"Netherrack," I cursed under my breath.

"Do you really think there is useful information in there?" asked Tina.

Emma and I both nodded our heads and Emma said, "Yes. It's where he stores all his occult books."

"In that case, Muscles, open it up," Tina ordered her bodyguard.

The ender soldier did as he was told. He walked over to the locked cabinet, put his hands on each of the doors and then, using his long, skinny arms like levers, he pried the doors open in less than a second.

We now had free access to the occult collection of Mr. Blaze.

We all reached in and grabbed a book.

I grabbed a book called *Fantastic Mobs and Where to Find Them*. When I opened it up, expecting a summary of different types of "fantastic" mobs, the title page didn't match the cover. Instead, the title page said the book was entitled *Transmogrification of Mobs: Myth or Reality? A Visual Guide with Recipes.*

I held the book up and said, "Guys, check this out. This is a book about transmogrification!"

Emma's eyes got wide. "That's amazing and it might explain everything."

I looked down at the floor sheepishly and said, "Really? So ... hurrr ... what is transmogrification?"

"You didn't know?!?" asked Tina. "Why did you get so excited?"

I shrugged. "It is a long word, I guess?"

Emma slapped her head and then said, "Transmogrification is changing something from one form into another. So if this is about the transmogrification of mobs, that would mean you could change one type of mob into another type of mob."

"Like a chicken into a wolf?" I asked.

Emma rolled her eyes and said, "I suppose. Or maybe a villager into a blaze or vice versa."

I was offended. "Villagers aren't mobs! We are NPCs!"

"Don't be so attached to labels," said Emma. "We all come from the same source: Notch or the creation stone, if you believe the stone exists."

"Yeah, Jimmy, are you saying you're better than me or my dad?" asked Tina, her purple eyes shining with barely controlled rage. "Endermen are mobs."

I realized I had made a stupid mistake. "No, that's not what I meant. I just was kind of thinking of zombies and evil animal mobs, not you. I realize that the labels and divisions don't really make any sense."

Tina shot a death stare at me for a few more seconds and then relented. "Okay. Just don't make that same mistake again."

I handed the book to Emma and she flipped through it. After about a minute, she said, "Look. There's all sorts of techniques for turning blazes in the every kind of mob. The only transmogrification missing is converting them into villagers." She paused and tapped her lips with her right index finger. "Maybe Mr. Blaze figured out how to change himself into a blaze. I don't think a blaze would have turned itself into villager."

"Why not?" asked Tina.

"Well, hurrr, mainly because a blaze probably couldn't read this book without catching it on fire and destroying it."

"This is crazy!" I said.

"Yes, it is," responded Emma calmly, like a been–there, done–that know–it–all. "There's some writing in the margins that I can't decipher, but I would guess it is Mr. Blaze's handwriting and that it contained the extra information he discovered to change himself into a blaze."

I was totally shocked and blown away. Why would but Mr. Blaze want to become a blaze? Other than the fact of his last name, which was somewhat unfortunate and incredibly coincidental, I could not understand the desire to become a blaze. Maybe I'd find out someday, maybe not.

At that moment Tina gasped.

I looked over and saw her reading a different book. "What is it?"

"This book, it's called *Entity 303: A Misunderstood Life*." Tina held up the book and we could see the cover showed Entity 303 sitting on a rock with tears streaming down his face. "The author. It's written by a Señor Fuego, which is Spanish for ... Mr. Blaze!"

We were all shocked. Even the ender soldier betrayed a hint of emotion behind his disciplined military façade.

"Wait. How do you know Spanish?" I asked.

Tina shrugged. "Players enter Minecraft from all around the human world. I think I actually can speak just about every human language. Can't you?"

I searched my mind and concluded that no, I could not. But, I said nothing. Just shrugged.

"Anyway," continued Tina, "I flipped through the book and it reads as if Entity 303 is the greatest creation who ever lived. It also talks about conversations the author had with Entity 303 and how Entity 303 has a plan to take over the world." Tina paused for a moment and took a deep breath before continuing. "And, from what I can tell, it reads like a playbook for everything that has happened to all of us over the last few days!"

Gulp! I was shocked. *A playbook? Were we being manipulated this entire time?!?*

"Let me see that book," I demanded, sticking my hand out.

Tina handed me the book and I flipped through it. It was handwritten, more like a diary than an actual published book.

Tina was right. It mentioned, in general outline, all the events we had lived through in the past few weeks, though there was nothing in it about surfing or the Update Aquatic, which obviously was an overlay to the basic story.

I was flabbergasted. "How could Entity 303 have set all this up? How could he have foreseen so many events?"

"Does it really surprise you, Jimmy?" asked Emma. "If the mythology is true, Entity 303 is a single–minded creature that lives only to disrupt the world of Minecraft. He has probably been thinking about this plan for years, maybe hundreds or even thousands of years. However long he's existed. I just wonder why Mr. Blaze got involved with him in the first place?"

Then I had an idea. If this was a playbook of what happened, I needed to read it to find out what was to come.

I looked through the pages until I came to the part about kidnapping Notch and then read what was on the final four pages.

"Guys, this is terrible. Entity 303 does plan to enslave the world of Minecraft for one hundred years in order to make everyone suffer. And then, when he is satisfied with the world's suffering, he plans to destroy everything with the creation stone!"

Everyone gasped, groaned, and shook their heads in disbelief.

"Well, tell us, how is he planning to do it?!?" asked Tina. "Let's get ahead of this and stop it!"

I sighed. "That's the problem. All the pages that tell how he plans to do it are almost entirely illegible. It's like someone poured water on them and left only the conclusion I just explained. It is impossible to know how Entity 303 plans to get there."

Emma grabbed the book from my hands and flipped the pages, verifying what I'd said. She threw the book on the ground and kicked it across the room. "Netherrack," she swore.

I had never heard her swear before. This had finally gotten to her. It was too much.

Tina straightened her back and, acting like the princess she truly was, said, "We need to return to my father. He must be advised of this dreadful information immediately."

Emma and I set our jaws and gritted our teeth.

"Agreed," I said, retrieving the book Emma had just kicked and placing it in to my inventory along with the transmogrification guide.

And with that, we teleported back to the palace.

Day 43 – Moments Later

When we reappeared in the King's reception hall, the King was sitting on his throne, tapping his fingers impatiently on the armrest awaiting the return of his ender soldiers.

Tina ran up to her father and squealed, "Daddy! Daddy! We found something amazing!"

The King looked at his daughter and raised an eyebrow — at least I think he raised an eyebrow, it was difficult to be certain because his eyebrows blended so well with his skin — and asked, "Oh really? Tell me."

The three of us proceeded to tell him the story of how we had discovered the books about transmogrification as well as what appeared to be Mr. Blaze's handwritten summary of Entity 303's long–term plan to conquer and then destroy the world of Minecraft. The entire time the ender soldier who had accompanied us was nodding his head, indicating that we were telling the truth and that he had witnessed it.

When we had finished telling our tale, I asked, "So, King, what do you think? Was Mr. Blaze just some kind of deranged groupie of Entity 303 who gave over his life to him or has he been manipulated by Entity 303 to become his slave or is it something else?"

The King yawned and shrugged and said, "This entire pursuit is making me weary. All I wanted to do was destroy Clayton Dretsky for killing my people and stealing the resources of the End, but now, if Entity 303 gets his way, I may be presiding over the final kingship of the End. I just want this to be over."

Could this be true? Could the Ender King be giving up? Could this adult be unwilling to sacrifice to save the world for the children? If he gave up, what chance did we have?

We all stood around, an awkward silence slowly enveloping us, threatening to choke the life out of the room. I was trying desperately to think of something to say to break the silence, but nothing was coming to mind. I was becoming desperate and nervous. The weight of the silence became so heavy that I was about to scream when an ender soldier materialized in the middle of the reception hall.

In fact, the fool was standing on the dining table! I laughed.

The Ender King sat up straight in his throne when the ender soldier appeared. "General, you have returned. What is your report?" He paused and smirked. "But first, get down from the table, man!"

The general stood at attention and then jumped off the table. "My apologies, my King. I was in such a hurry to get here that I miscalculated my teleportation jump. Anyway, we have searched all three known strongholds from top to bottom and can find no area which would seem to be housing Herobrine. I'm sorry, but we have failed you."

"Was the head monk lying?!?" I shouted with rage and stomping my right foot hard on the floor.

The general snapped his head at me, I could tell he thought I was rude. The Ender King shook his head. "I don't think so. I just think that Entity 303 has hidden Herobrine so cleverly the merely inspecting the rooms over the course of a couple of hours is not enough to find him. We will have to go to each stronghold and search it like we are looking for a needle in a haystack."

"Aargh," I groaned. "That's going to take forever."

"Where's your sense of adventure, Jimmy?" asked Emma. "Who knows what we might find in the libraries and storage chests within each stronghold. Think of the knowledge!"

I squinted my eyes at Emma and sighed. "How can you be so optimistic at a time like this? Who cares if we find a bunch of enchanted books or whatever is inside those stupid chests. We are looking for Herobrine. We have to stop Entity 303!" I yelled, pulling my hair at the same time.

Emma wagged her finger at me like she was an old lady who thought she knew better than me. "That's what I mean. If Herobrine is hidden so cleverly, we will have to find clues. Probably hidden in chests or something."

"Emma's right, Jimmy," said Tina. "You need to chill."

I probably would have yelled at Tina and Emma if the Ender King had not been there, but I knew that if I yelled at them, especially Tina, the Ender King would be very upset. So, I refrained. "Okay, so now I'm going to have to look through dozens of chests and try to find some weird clue that some freak left behind to help me locate another freak? Sounds like a great way to spend the next five weeks of my life."

"Enough!" shouted the Ender King. "It will not take five weeks, and besides, even if it did, isn't five weeks of your life worth saving the entire creation of Minecraft?"

I scoffed. "Ah, weren't you about to give up a few minutes ago?"

The Ender King swelled to five times his normal size and yelled, "I was just tired. I *never* give up!"

I was ashamed.

Of course five weeks of my insignificant life was worth saving Minecraft. Even if I thought every mob and NPC and player in Minecraft was an idiot, I still valued my life and the lives of my family and friends. And I truly valued surfing. It was magical and majestic. I didn't want that to end.

"I'm sorry. I wasn't thinking … hurrr … as usual."

The Ender King's stony face softened, and he returned to his normal size and then smiled at me. "That's okay. We are all under a lot of stress. Look, we need to prepare. Tina, go to your room and collect your supplies. You are old enough to be on this mission with me."

Tina smiled a huge smile, ran to her father and kissed him on the cheek. "Thank you! Thank you!" she said before disappearing, apparently teleporting to her room.

When she had gone, the Ender King turned to the ender soldier who had accompanied us to Mr. Blaze's bookstore. "Liam, take Emma and Jimmy to their houses so they may pack their things and stuff their inventories full of food." *Stuff our inventories? Who says that?* "Stay with each of them while they do that and then return as quickly as possible."

"What are your orders for me, Your Highness?" said the general to the king.

"Prepare one hundred of your finest men. We will start by exploring the closest stronghold and then move further away to each successive stronghold as needed. With any luck, we will find Herobrine in the first stronghold, but you must be prepared for several days of exploration if we do not."

The general snapped to attention, saluted, and said, "Yes, my King. We shall be prepared within the hour."

Day 43 – One Hour Later

Once we were all ready, we teleported as a group to the closest stronghold. In addition to the general, the 100 ender soldiers, and the Ender King, and Tina, it was just Emma and me. We felt out of place surrounded by the tall, lanky, obsidian–colored creatures, but we were all in this together. If the head monk were to be believed, we had to find Herobrine if we wanted to ever find Claire or rescue Notch. We couldn't fail; the consequences were far too great.

As we approached the entrance to the stronghold, I saw that it was being guarded by two ender soldiers. When we got closer, they saluted.

"At ease, men" said the Ender King. "Have you seen anyone attempting to enter the stronghold since you searched it?"

"No, Your Highness, no one has come in through the main entrance, anyway," said the first soldier.

"That's correct," said the other, "I have seen no one. Several other soldiers have been teleporting periodically over the surface of the stronghold and have not seen any new holes dug by any players attempting to locate the stronghold."

The Ender King nodded his head and said, "Excellent. Remain here on guard while we enter the stronghold. If anyone approaches who you cannot convince to leave, one of you should teleport to find me while the other should prevent that person from entering. Use all necessary force."

The ender soldiers clicked their heels together and saluted as the Ender King walked past them into the stronghold.

Emma and I followed the Ender King and Tina with the mass of one hundred soldiers directly behind us. I had never been inside of a stronghold before. I was excited and scared at the same time.

"Emma, have you ever been inside a stronghold before?" Tina asked. "I haven't."

She shook her head. "No, but I've read a lot about them. They are labyrinthine in their construction and typically contain prison cells, libraries, random chests with various items, and silverfish spawners and ... hurrr ... even an end portal!"

I rolled my eyes. "Everybody knows that."

Emma squinted her eyes at me, slightly angry. "Well, Jimmy, I didn't see you paying very good attention in geography class last year, so I wasn't sure if you knew anything about strongholds. I thought I'd give you a quick summary."

She was right. I hadn't paid much attention in geography class. Now that I'd been all across the Overworld and parts of the Nether, it probably would have served me well to have paid attention.

Stay in school, kids.

I laughed. "I suppose I deserved that."

The Ender King looked back at us and shushed us. "Stop talking so loudly. We may need the element of surprise."

The King was right, as usual. Emma, Tina, and I followed in silence for a few moments until we entered a fairly large chamber.

When everyone had gathered inside the chamber, the Ender King said clearly, but quietly, "I want this stronghold explored from top to bottom. I want every room checked and double checked. If it takes all day, then it takes all day. I know that the initial scouts found nothing, but Entity 303 is *extremely* clever. And, for that matter, so is Herobrine. If Herobrine had been held captive here, he may have left clue. Look for anything out of the ordinary."

The ender soldiers shouted with one voice, "Hoo—rah!"

The ender general turned to his men and said, "Form up into squads of two to search the stronghold. If anything is discovered, one of the members of the squad should teleport back to this central room and find me. I will wait here. The other members of the squad should stand guard and protect the clue with his life." The Ender general paused to look over his men with a determined expression. "Any questions?"

There were no questions. These were highly trained ender soldiers who knew what they were doing. A simple reconnaissance mission was something they could handle with ease. Without further instructions. They weren't babies.

"In that case, get to work," ordered the general.

The ender soldiers quickly dispersed from the room, some walking and others teleporting.

"Yo, King?" I asked. "How the heck will they know if they have searched all the rooms?"

The Ender King shook his head and looked at me like I was an ignorant toddler. "They have maps. Didn't I tell you we mapped all the strongholds?"

I could feel my face flushing with embarrassment. "Oh, yeah. Of course, I remember. Hurrr, can I get a map?"

"You won't need a map," said the Ender King. "You and Emma are coming with me and Tina."

I tried to act all cool. "That'll work, bruv."

Emma laughed at me. "Jimmy, you have to stop trying to act so cool and chill. You are a terrible actor. Why can't you just be your non–chill, non–cool self?"

Ouch.

I looked at Emma with a cold stare and said in an aggressive voice with a sharp tone, "Dang. Mom much?"

Emma shook her head. "What? Are you trying to be an edge lord now?"

The Ender King reached out his long arms and put a hand on each of our shoulders and shook us. "Kids, seriously? Get your heads in the game! The time for petty differences and bickering about teenage

341

façades is over," said the Ender King in a low, firm voice. "Look where you are. It. Is. On!"

He was right, again, as usual, *again.*

I looked over at Emma and said, "Sorry. I'm kind of a kook sometimes."

She shrugged. "I guess it's mutual. Although, I'm way less of kook than you, ya feel?"

She was right, of course. *Again.*

It was difficult hanging with people who were always right. I was going to get an inferiority complex.

"Okay, now that that is settled, follow me," said the King.

We entered one of the corridors at the side of the large chamber to begin our quest. The King led the way. Emma, Tina, and I followed, walking side–by–side. It was very dark inside the corridor, and we each had to ignite a torch in order to see where we were going.

The corridor was very long and had narrow side passageways to break up the wall. We walked for about two minutes without seeing anything other than stone walls and a few torches.

"Who do you think put these torches on these walls?" I asked.

"Jimmy, torches spontaneously spawn inside strongholds. Hurrr, probably no one put those torches here," whispered Emma.

I nodded.

Yep, I should have paid better attention in geography class.

"This way. I see a strong light ahead," said the King, snuffing out his torch. We followed suit and put out our torches.

The King moved slowly forward, and we followed closely behind. When we got to the source of the light, I saw it was a small opening, like a window. We looked through it and saw another large chamber below. Two ender soldiers were inside, investigating the room.

The Ender King turned to us and said, "I guess that area is taken care of for now. Let's continue down the passageway." Then, the King reignited his torch, and we continued.

Again, the passage stretched on for a long time without any breaks in the stone walls. It was starting to get a little creepy. I was starting to feel claustrophobic. I was beginning to sweat.

Don't lose it, Jimmy.

The walls seemed to be closing in on me.

Don't lose it, Jimmy.

I was really worried about flipping out and screaming or curling up into a fetal position … you know, the typical freak out stuff. Thankfully, just as I thought I could endure no more, we approached a doorway.

We stopped and stared at the closed iron door in front of us.

The King looked at us and said, "I know ender soldiers previously searched this room during the brief reconnaissance mission. But, who knows what may be behind this door? Stay behind me, your weapons at the ready, and prepare for anything."

I pulled out my diamond sword, shield, and helmet. I *was* ready for anything.

Emma pulled out a bow and arrows and a helmet.

Tina had a diamond pickaxe, helmet and shield.

We tensed, ready for anything, prepared to defend ourselves and each other.

The Ender King approach the door slowly.

Quietly.

He reached out his tiny black hand.

And then … he smacked the door open.

We listened for sounds coming from the room, but heard nothing. We waited for a few moments, but still there was nothing but silence. A silence as still as death....

Finally, after about one minute, the King pulled another torch from his inventory, ignited it, and tossed it into the center of the room. It cast eerie shadows on the walls but didn't reveal anything. Or, anyone.

We entered the room and each removed several torches from our inventories, ignited them, and attached them to the walls so we could illuminate the room fully. It wasn't very large, maybe 10 blocks by 15 blocks. There were no windows and nothing in the room other than a chest.

Emma leaned over to me and whispered, "I bet there's some enchanted items in that chest."

I shrugged.

"Go ahead and look inside," said the Ender King.

Emma walked over and opened the chest. "There's a few books in here and a potion of some kind."

The Ender King noded. "Look through the books and see if there is anything noteworthy in them. Emma, you are more of a scholar than Jimmy and will certainly notice anything out of the ordinary," said the Ender King, offering me a backhanded insult.

I shook my head at the Ender King and said, "What the heck, man? Hurrr, I thought we were on the same team?"

The Ender King smiled. "Teammates can joke with each other, can't they Jimmy?"

I shrugged. "I suppose, but it still wasn't very nice. I'm sure I could notice something out of the ordinary."

"Perhaps, but let's let Emma handle this one."

"Well, then, what should I do?"

"Why don't you look at the walls to see if there any weird scratch marks or things out of place," said the Ender King.

"Okay. What are you going to do?" I asked.

"I'll search the walls too. But first, I want to look at that potion Emma found. Maybe it'll gives us a clue of some kind." The King looked at his daughter. "You help Emma."

"Sure thing," said Tina.

I watched as Emma and Tina began looking through the books. They seemed very intent on the contents of the books, but never seemed surprised. I doubted they would find anything, unless one of Herobrine's old diaries happened to be stuck in the chest.

The Ender King had picked up the potion and was swirling it around, holding a torch behind it so he could better see its coloration. It was sort of bluish in color. He pulled the stopper out of the potion bottle and sniffed it. That's when he pronounced, "It's either a potion of water breathing or a potion of night vision." The King tucked it into his inventory.

I nodded my head and then began looking at the walls. There didn't seem to be anything of note. I didn't see any etchings or discolorations or scratch marks. However, I noticed that the walls seemed to be almost alive. It was as if there were skin over the blocks. It was very curious. I decided to test what the walls were made of so I smacked the wall really hard with my fist.

That was a mistake.

Dozens of silverfish suddenly jumped off of the wall and onto my body. They were pinching my skin with their disgusting teeth and poking me with their hideous arthropod toes.

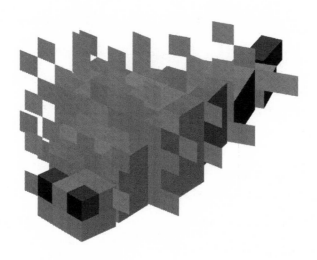

I screamed, "Get off me! Get off me!" I was pushing and punching at them, trying to kill them.

"Stop!" yelled the Ender King.

I looked over at him as I was still smacking the silverfish. "Me?"

"Yes," he insisted. "Don't you remember what the Silverfish Queen said just before the surf contest?"

It flashed into my brain.

Could that really work?

It was worth a try. So, even though I felt totally foolish, I said, "Hello, silverfish."

The silverfish suddenly stopped attacking, backed away from me, and gathered together in a group looking at me, confused.

After a few seconds, they replied as a group. "Hello to you, too."

I looked over in the direction of Emma and Tina and then back at the King. "It worked! Oh my Notch! It worked!"

The silverfish looked at me with a confused expression. One of them asked, "What worked?"

"Well, the Silverfish Queen told us that you all just want us to say 'hello' to you and I did."

"Yes," said one of them. "Everyone thinks we are disgusting and mean, but we are just misunderstood.

We go around cleaning up debris. Without silverfish, the world would be a very dirty place."

I supposed, they were right. But, I didn't really care. All I cared about was that they weren't trying to kill me anymore.

One of the silverfish continued, "When you hit the wall so hard, we thought you were attacking us. We're sorry."

I shrugged as I inspected my arms. "Just a few red marks. I didn't lose any hearts on my health bar, so it's all good."

That's when I glanced at the wall where the silverfish had been and my jaw hit the floor. (Not literally, of course. Another figure of speech that makes little sense when you think about it.) "Look!" I pointed at the wall.

The wall was read: *Go hang a salami. I'm a lasagna hog.*

"What could it mean?" Said Emma.

"I have no idea," said the Ender King. "What's a salami anyway?"

It was then that I realized what it was. It was a palindrome. I said so, "It's a palindrome."

The Ender King looked at me with a confused expression and said, "A palindrome?"

Emma nodded her head. "Oh my Notch! It *is* a palindrome! Yes, King, a palindrome is when an expression has the same letters forward and backward."

The Ender King rubbed his chin and said, "Interesting, I suppose."

"Yeah, my favorite palindrome is 'Madam, I'm Adam," I said.

"What can this palindrome mean? Do you think it's a clue from Herobrine?" asked Tina.

"Well, on the surface it clearly has a meaning, although it is a ridiculous one. But maybe it has some sort of other meaning," I said.

"Same forward as backward, eh?" said the Ender King, muttering to himself.

I stared at the palindrome. Emma and Tina stared at it too. Then, Emma said, "We haven't seen anything in the books in this chest that is related to this wording."

At that moment, the King snapped his fingers like he had discovered something. "I don't believe this. One of the other strongholds has the exact same map as this one only flipped backwards. Maybe what this palindrome means is that Herobrine was here but then he was taken to the other stronghold with the reverse orientation!"

I looked at the Ender King in shock. "That's just crazy enough that it might be true!"

"Okay, here is what we are going to do," said the King. "We will finish our thorough investigation of this stronghold. Then, instead of going to the second stronghold as was the plan, we will go straight to this reverse palindrome stronghold and see if we can surprise Entity 303 and find Herobrine."

"That sounds like a plan," I said.

"What's all this about Herobrine?" asked one of the silverfish, who seemed to be the leader of this group. I had almost forgotten they were there.

"He's been kidnapped and we need to find him in order to ... hurrr, anyway ... we just need to find him," I said. I did not want to reveal the fact that Notch had also been kidnapped and the Overworld might soon be enslaved for one hundred years before being utterly destroyed. "So, do you know anything about the kidnapping? About the palindrome?

They told us of that they remembered some activity in this room because they could hear screaming and heated conversation, but no silverfish were alive who had seen anything.

"What do you mean, no silverfish are alive that had seen anything?" asked the Ender King.

"Some of our friends had been in here, but when we came back into the room they had vanished. We think that whoever was using the room had killed them all and they disappeared into puffs of smoke," the silverfish leader said forlornly.

I reached out and rubbed the silverfish's head like it was a pet dog, but it felt scaly and disgusting and so I pulled my hand away ... a little too quickly. The silverfish noticed and shot me an evil glance. But I tried to soothe him by saying, "It's okay. I'm sure they've respawned into a better place."

The silverfish nodded its head sadly and said, "I hope you find whoever did this and bring them to justice."

I smiled grimly. "That's our plan."

The Ender King had watched this exchange curiously and said, "If all the silverfish who were in this room are dead, how did you know any of your kind were in here in the first place?"

The silverfish looked at the King like he was an idiot and said, "I told you. We heard noises."

The Ender King nodded and then said, "But, that does not explain how you knew any silverfish were in here." He paused for a moment and then asked slowly, "Do silverfish have a hive mind? I mean, can you communicate with silverfish a long way away without using words?"

The silverfish nodded and said proudly, "Sure. We can send signals back and forth through our combined mass, kind of like a network of information."

The Ender King rubbed his chin and thought for a moment and then snapped his fingers and said, "So, if I were to introduce you to a new group of silverfish, you could just touch one of them and ask questions and learn what they know?"

The silverfish leader smiled and said, "Of course. That's how silverfish make friends. We become friends instantly. It's very nice."

"In that case, would you like to come with us?" asked the Ender King. "We are going to another stronghold and it would sure help if we could get information quickly rather than having to sneak around for hours."

I was astonished. The Ender King was brilliant and silverfish were insane. The fact that a silverfish could touch another silverfish in a separate colony and learn what they were all thinking and communicate with them was amazing. I wished villagers could do that. Then maybe we'd all be a lot nicer to each other.

The silverfish reared up on its two back legs, puffed out its chest and said, "I'd be happy to come with you, King. When do we leave?"

"As soon as possible," said the King in a deep, serious voice.

Day 43 – One Hour Later

After we had completed our search of our designated room, the Ender King, Tina, Emma, and I, along with our new companion silverfish, returned to the rallying point where the ender general had remained during the search. Within another fifteen minutes, all of the ender soldiers had returned.

None reported finding any obvious clues, though they did find strange contraptions that they had never seen before. Oddly colored potions. Strangely colored blocks. Even some rainbow-colored gossamer fabric. It had all been collected and put into a chest.

"Take the chest to my palace in the End," the Ender King ordered one of his soldiers. "Tell my Chief of Science to begin a comprehensive study of everything. I shall expect a preliminary report when I return from locating Herobrine."

"Wow, a Chief of Science. Cool," whispered Emma.

The soldier holding the chest saluted and teleported away.

I looked over at Emma and said, "Do you think the fabric could be some of the Rainbow Creeper's skin?"

Emma nodded her head seriously. "I'm sure Entity 303 has been here with Herobrine. Probably Spike too. I would like to examine the strange contraptions though and see if I might be able to utilize their technology."

"I can't allow that," interrupted the Ender King. "They're all probably booby–trapped. If anyone goes back there and tries to move them, I'm sure something horrible will happen."

I could tell the scientist inside Emma didn't care about the risks, but she probably also knew the Ender King was right, so she didn't pursue it any further.

"Where to now, Your Highness?" asked the ender general.

"The children and I found a clue," said the Ender King.

Children?

The Ender King continued. "We believe that Entity 303 has taken Herobrine to the third stronghold on our map. That is our next destination."

"What leads you to believe Entity 303 has imprisoned Herobrine in the third stronghold?" asked the ender general.

"It was a curious clue. I don't have time to explain, but it seems fairly certain we will find him there, or ... what is left of him," said the Ender King in an ominous tone.

"I'm coming to help," said the silverfish standing proudly near the Ender King's feet.

The ender general had not noticed the silverfish had gotten so close to the King and raised one of his feet into the air in preparation for squishing it. The Ender King's long, black arm shot out and pushed the ender general's foot away. "He's not kidding, General. He is going to help us."

The ender general bowed deeply to the Ender King and said, "My apologies, Your Highness." He then looked at the silverfish and said, "My apologies to you as well, creature."

The silverfish scurried over toward the ender general's foot and patted it with one of his many revolting little legs. "It's okay. Just about everybody tries to do that when they first meet me."

The ender general looked down at the silverfish and said, "I like you silverfish. You have charisma. What's your name anyway?"

"My name is Skittles."

The ender general nodded his head, smirked for a brief instant, and said, "Skittles is a ... peculiar name, but it suits you."

The silverfish smiled and looked as though it was blushing. Its normally gray face turning a lighter gray, nearly white. "Thank you."

"Okay everyone, let's get ready to go," commanded the Ender King. "Everyone put any loose items back into your inventory and prepare for teleportation. We will stop by the second stronghold briefly and then onward to our destiny."

What a drama queen ... hurrr ... I mean, drama king!

When we arrived at the gates of the second stronghold, the Ender King explained to the guards there that we would not be exploring that stronghold for now. He left an additional ten ender soldiers there to increase the guard ... "just in case."

The Ender King explained to the guards, "We've already explored the first stronghold, and now we go to explore the third. It is vitally important that *no one* comes in or out of this second stronghold. Keeping this stronghold sealed is the only way we can ensure that our strategy and search is complete," explained the Ender King.

The soldiers guarding the main entrance to the stronghold saluted and snapped their arms down at their sides and said in unison, "Of course, Sire."

The King nodded his head quickly in appreciation of their military discipline. "I'm not sure how long our search of the third stronghold may take. If no one from our group has returned within twenty–four hours, send two of your men to check on us."

Again the two soldiers saluted and said, "Of course, Sire."

I rolled my eyes. All this military discipline stuff and chain of command stuff was getting annoying.

"Let's get on with it already," I whined.

The King looked at me like I was a mushroom growing on the back of a mooshroom, a pathetic fungus dependent entirely upon another creature. To say he gave me a vicious look would be an understatement.

"What?" I asked.

"Jimmy, you have no respect for authority or for organizational structure, do you?" asked the Ender King.

"What do you mean? I have plenty of respect."

Emma chuckled. "Sure you do. Hurrr. I've seen that respect for organizational structures every year in school since we were six years old."

I could feel my face turning red. "Are you saying that I don't like to follow rules? Especially stupid rules?"

Emma laughed again. "Something like that. But, you don't have to follow the ender army's rules. You're not an enderman, and you certainly are not a soldier."

I smiled at my freedom. "That's right. I call myself 'Free Will' Jimmy. No one tells me what to do."

The Ender King teleported next to my side quickly and grabbed both my shoulders with his hands and said with menace, "You'll do what I say or you can go home to your mommy. What'll it be?"

I'll admit it now, but I would not have admitted it then, but my knees were trembling. This was the first time I felt the King might actually try to kill me. At that moment, I really did want to go home to my mommy.

On the other hand, I was part of the greatest adventure in the history of Minecraft, and I didn't want that to end. Against every self–preservative fiber in my being, I managed to respond, "I want to stay. I'll follow your lead. But don't make me call you 'Sire'."

The Ender King stared at me for a moment applying additional pressure with his hands on my shoulders. He was making a point. He was more dominant than I. But then, he released his arms from my shoulders and laughed a bit. "Jimmy, you may not be much else, but you are a unique individual."

I guess he was finally understanding who I was. It only took him, what, three or four weeks?

"Yeah, cool King. Anyway, hurrr, let's get this show on the road."

The Ender King teleported to a stone outcropping a short distance away, giving him a vantage point above the entire assembled group. The silverfish was standing by his side, having been teleported by the King.

"That silverfish sure thinks he's cool, doesn't he?" I whispered to Emma.

She looked at me and rolled her eyes and said, "Are you actually jealous of a silverfish?"

My face flushed red and I said quickly ... probably too quickly, "Of course not. I just ... hurrr .... Nevermind."

Emma rolled her eyes again and then turned her head back to watch the Ender King deliver his instructions.

"Okay, everyone, it's time to go. On the count of three, let us all teleport to the third stronghold." He looked directly at us. "Emma, you can teleport with Tina. Jimmy, stand next to an ender soldier so he can teleport you."

Emma and I did as we were told. Tina put her hand on Emma's shoulder, and an ender soldier touched mine.

"One. Two. Three."

Day 43 – A Few Moments Later

As usual, when we arrived at the next stronghold, there were ender soldiers guarding the main entrance and several other soldiers teleporting here and there ensuring that no one entered the stronghold after the initial search the soldiers had conducted. The Ender King quickly spoke with the guards and confirmed no suspicious activity had been located inside or outside of the stronghold.

"Did you guys see any lava in there?" asked Emma.

This was a good question. I remembered the head monk had said Herobrine would be found in a small cage surrounded by lava, so if there weren't any lava pools in the stronghold, that might be a problem.

One of the soldiers nodded his head crisply and said, "Yes, miss, there's some lava in there, alrighty. I've never seen no stronghold without no lava."

The Ender King pulled out a map of the stronghold, unrolled it, and then held it in front of the soldier. "Tell me where you saw lava," he ordered.

The ender soldier pointed to several different locations on the map, including next to the small chamber which would have been the exact opposite chamber in which we had found the palindrome in the prior stronghold.

The Ender King cast a glance at me and said, "We will start there."

Tina, who was holding Skittles, asked, "Shouldn't we first talk to the silverfish who live in the stronghold?"

Skittles bowed his head in a symbol of obedience and said, "I'm happy to do it, King."

The Ender King nodded his head and then led us into the stronghold. It didn't take long before we found a silverfish scurrying along the ground.

So. Gross.

Sorry, but it's true.

Tina put Skittles on the ground and he trotted over to his fellow silverfish and said, "I need to access the Collective within this stronghold. Do you mind if I do it through you?"

The other silverfish looked around suspiciously at the King, Tina, Emma, and me and said, "What are they doing here? What's this all about?"

"They're looking for someone. They think he might be here and wanted to see if the Collective had any clues," explained Skittles.

The other silverfish remained somewhat suspicious but eventually shrugged all six of his shoulders and said, "Whatevs, bruv. Let's do this." He then held out one of his disgusting little legs.

Skittles approached more closely and then stuck out his own disgusting leg until the two disgusting legs touched. Both silverfishes' his eyes rolled back in their heads and they remained motionless with their little scaly legs touching each other for about fifteen seconds. Then, they both let out a deep sigh and collapsed to the ground for just a moment before shaking their heads and regaining consciousness.

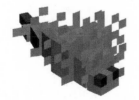 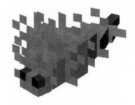

The new silverfish, having gained knowledge from Skittles during the encounter, said, "I can't believe what has happened! Could this really be the end of Minecraft?"

Skittles shrugged. "I hope not. But with the information you and the Collective just gave to me, I think it may help."

"Cool," said the other silverfish as he waved to Skittles and then scurried away to live the remainder of its strange little life collecting debris.

"So? What is it?!?" I asked.

Skittles approached us and Tina picked him up and held him so he would be closer to eye level. "Entity 303 has been here. The Collective recalls his presence and his extermination of the silverfish living within several of the rooms. However, it has been days since they have seen him."

Tina stroked Skittles's back. It was so disgusting to watch, I thought I might barf, but Tina didn't seem to mind. Skittles appreciated it. He probably never had any sort of contact with anything other than another disgusting silverfish.

"Can you tell us in which of the rooms the exterminations occurred?" asked the Ender King.

Skittles nodded sadly. "Of course I can. Just let me see your map and I will tell you."

The Ender King walked over to Skittles, unrolled the map and held it in front of him. Skittles pointed to four different rooms. Three of the rooms were the same areas where the Ender soldier had said there was lava, including the room that was the exact duplicate of where we had found the palindrome in the prior stronghold.

Then the King looked at all of us and then looked behind us at the mass of ender soldiers gathered at the main entrance of the stronghold.

"I have a plan," he said. "Follow me."

We walked back outside the stronghold. The Ender King left us and stood on top of a rock to address the gathered soldiers.

"Okay, men, I have a high level of confidence we are going to find Herobrine inside this stronghold. I need twenty–five of you to remain outside. Ten of you will guard this entrance and the other fifteen will teleport constantly over the full width of the stronghold. If you see any player or mob who looks as though he may be going into or is coming out of the stronghold, your orders are to detain them immediately. If they struggle or try to fight you, you may kill them. If you are unable to detain them, you may kill them. This is very serious, and we need to make sure that no one gets away."

The soldiers nodded solemnly. The kill command still ringing in their ears.

The ender general said, "First squad, you're lucky ones who get to guard the exterior. Deploy."

And with that, they instantly moved into position. They looked like a swarm of insects, only very large, very intelligent, very scary insects.

"Excellent," the Ender King continued. "The rest of you will form into four different groups. We have four rooms that need to be searched first. Each of the rooms must be entered cautiously, as it is possible Entity 303 may be in one of them, although our current intelligence information indicates that he is not within the stronghold at this time. Upon entering each room you must secure it and remain there. If you find Herobrine, do not attempt to free him as there may be booby traps. Contact me immediately."

The Ender King paused for a moment and then turned to his general, "Please come here so that I can show you which rooms we need to search."

The general took two steps over and examined the map. The Ender King pointed and said, "These four rooms need to be searched. You and your men should search these three while I will search this fourth room with Skittles, the children, and 5 soldiers. Got it?"

Children? Again?

The general wordlessly saluted and then said, "Squads three, four, and five, stay with me and I will give you your assignments. Squad two, pick five of your number to go with the Ender King and disperse the rest of the squad into the other squads.

I watched for fifteen or twenty seconds while the soldiers complied with their orders.

The Ender King then looked at us all solemnly. He was taking in the moment and we were taking it in too.

And then he said, "Let's do this. And, let's do this right. If we can't find Herobrine in that stronghold, this could be the end of everything we know. Nothing you have done in your life has ever been this important."

I could feel a tightness in my chest. I felt anxious and proud and scared and brave all at the same time.

He was right. This was our chance to make history. To *save* history. *To save Minecraft!*

The Ender King entered the stronghold and we followed immediately. The other three groups of soldiers followed behind us and then began to disperse into the labyrinth of the stronghold. We continued on.

I had to fight once again my claustrophobia as I had in the other stronghold, given that the map of the stronghold was an identical, mirror–image of the first.

We had to stay alert but saw nothing other than a few silverfish — Skittles said "Hi" to a few of them — and a few zombies here and there. One zombie attacked us, but one of the ender soldiers sliced his head off with little difficulty. The other zombies either didn't see us or they decided to ignore us.

"Doesn't this seem a little too easy to you?" I whispered to Emma and Tina. "I mean, if Herobrine is imprisoned in here somewhere and Entity 303 doesn't want him captured, why wouldn't he have all sorts of mobs attacking us?"

"Maybe Herobrine is not here? Or maybe Herobrine is just hidden so well that Entity 303 isn't worried about us finding him?" suggested Tina.

Emma was thinking and tapping her chin. "Or, hurrr, maybe he *does* want us to find Herobrine. Most of the plan for world domination had been smudged into illegibility in the book we found in Mr. Blaze's library. Maybe we are *supposed* to find him in order for Entity 303's plan to be realized."

Now my mind was reeling.

Should we *not* be finding Herobrine? Should we *not* be listening to the head monk? Was the head monk in on all of this? Was the Rainbow Creeper some fake creation of Entity 303 just to distract us and make us go along with the plan? I mean, I've only seen the Rainbow Creeper in dreams, and Claire may have been under Entity 303's control when she claimed to be a priestess.

Don't lose it, Jimmy!

I shook my head clear of these confusing and concerning thoughts. Even if Entity 303 were manipulating us right now, I couldn't allow myself to think about it. I had to move forward and hope for the best. I could not let my friends down. Unless I found clear, irrefutable evidence that we were being manipulated or controlled, I was not going to change my course.

At that moment the Ender King said, "Be quiet. Get down."

I crouched as quickly as I could. Something in the Ender King's voice told me that he believed something dangerous or horrific was coming.

Sweat began to form on my brow.

My blood pressure spiked.

My heartbeat quickened.

Next to me Emma crouched. I could feel the heat coming off her body as her muscles tensed and warmed up ready to respond to any adrenaline rush that her body sent her.

On the opposite side of Emma was Tina, her long black legs folded like a daddy longlegs to bring her as close to the ground as possible. She held Skittles close to her. Skittles was shivering with fear.

At this moment I was very jealous of the Ender Princess and her father. They could teleport away from danger if they had to. I didn't think they would abandon us, but if it got really bad ... who knows?

As we all crouched in tense silence, I began to hear the rhythmic sounds of ... of ... something walking toward us. It made a sharp noise against the cobblestone. It didn't sound like the shuffling of a zombie. I wasn't sure what it was. Maybe a spider or skeleton? It couldn't have been a slime because there was no squishing noise. It couldn't have been a blaze because they don't have feet.

As the seconds passed I became more and more anxious. I began to shiver uncontrollably. Emma noticed and put her hand on my shoulder and looked at me and shook her head. I nodded my understanding and tried to stop my shivering, but it was futile. I'd never been this scared in my life. When scary things have happened to me in the past, they have typically happened suddenly, not while I'm anticipating all the horrible things that could be.

I did not like this.

The sharp noises were coming closer and closer. I saw the Ender King grip his sword more tightly, and I did the same. There was a faint glow of a torch illuminating the room. We would be able to see what this horrible creature was when it entered and then we might have the element of surprise. At least that was something.

The sharp sounds of the rhythmic walking came closer and closer.

This was about to happen.

What could it be?

And then, coming around the corner was...

A llama?

I sighed with relief. And Tina chuckled a little bit and the Ender King shook his head in astonishment and then stood up. "Llama? What are you doing inside of a stronghold?"

The llama, looked over at the Ender King with its stupid eyes and said in a goofy high–pitched voice, "Looking for you."

The Ender King was surprised by this response and asked, "How did you know I was down here?"

The llama moved its mouth in such a way that I can only describe as a smile ... a sinister smile ... and said, "Entity 303 told me."

And then without warning the llama transmogrified into a husk that leapt at the Ender King and thrust a sword at his neck. But I was faster. I raised my sword vertically as fast as I could and it deflected the blow, such that the husk managed to land only a slicing blow on the Ender King's shoulder.

Tina screamed. "Daddy!"

The Ender King screamed in pain but was able to stab the husk in its stomach with his sword. The husk moaned in pain and growled before coming at the Ender King again.

I was still off balance from my prior strike and was unable to deflect the husk's second blow, but fortunately, Emma was able to reach out and slice the husk's sword–holding hand clean off. The sword clattered to the ground allowing me to recover my balance in time to slice the husk's head off. The husk disappeared into a puff of smoke dropping only a small piece of nasty smelling rotten flesh. I kicked it under a nearby rock.

Tina rushed over to her father and said, "Daddy, are you all right?"

The Ender King gritted his teeth and nodded his head. "I should be fine soon. I only lost 3 hearts from my health bar. I should be able to recover in no time."

I could tell Tina was relieved. We all were. Even Skittles walked up to the Ender King and placed one of his disgusting little feet on the Ender King's foot and said, "I'm glad you are okay."

I was standing up, my head on a swivel, looking for more adversaries or traps. But nothing came.

The five ender soldiers, who had been standing on the opposite side of the room when the husk appeared and had been taken by surprise, were likewise on high alert.

"This is disturbing," said the Ender King. "If Entity 303 knows we are here, does that mean he's already moved Herobrine somewhere else? If he has, it will be a serious blow to our chances of defeating him, Spike, and their minions."

I felt my stomach clench. *Was this it? Had Entity 303 so easily defeated us?*

"Or, maybe he just did this for laughs," suggested Emma seriously. "I mean, everything else that has happened has been part of his plan to take over the world right? So, maybe this is just his way of messing with us."

Tina looked at Emma. "Could he really be that diabolical? That clever?"

Emma shrugged her shoulders. "I'm not sure, but it seems like he has been so far."

At that moment I saw the Ender King's head snap to attention and he looked to the left. "I think I can feel him."

"What you mean, King?" I asked.

"I told you I can sense Herobrine if he's close. I think he might be that way," said the King as he pointed toward a nearby wall."

Skittles approached the wall and looked toward it. He stared at it for a few seconds and then walked back to our group and said, "He's not immediately behind that wall but there are a couple more walls that I cannot see through at this distance. Maybe he's beyond them."

I looked at the silverfish in astonishment. "You can ... hurrr ... see through walls?"

"Sure. We silverfish do it all the time, to look for debris to eat or players to attack."

I slapped my forehead. "That's ... hurrr ... amazing!"

Emma laughed. "You should've paid more attention in mob biology class. *Everybody* knows silverfish can see through walls."

"Really? Everyone? I didn't know. So, you are wrong," I said, trying to somehow recover from my embarrassment at not knowing things.

Emma punched my shoulder playfully. "Chill, Jimmy."

The Ender King stood up and rubbed his wounded shoulder, which had almost completely recovered. "Okay, we're going to head in that direction," he said, pointing.

The Ender King pulled out his map and showed us our present location. It looked like we could take one of two passageways to get to the area where the Ender King was sensing Herobrine's potential presence.

The Ender King continued, speaking to the five soldiers, "Okay, I along with the children and Skittles will take this passageway, and you soldiers take this other passageway. We should meet at the door to the chamber here," the Ender King pointed, "and then we will enter it together. If after about five minutes you haven't seen the other group arrive, enter the room yourself because something has happened to them."

We understood our tasks and nodded our heads sternly. I tucked my sword back in my inventory and dug around until I found a carrot for a snack. I was going to need a little energy if it came to a battle.

I pulled my sword back out of my inventory and tapped the point on the cobblestone to make a loud, dramatic metallic sound and said, "I'm ready."

The Ender King looked at me and my drama and rolled his eyes. "Yeah, I can tell."

Day 43 – Seconds Later

I watched as the five ender soldiers took the passageway to the left. Their military discipline and professional demeanor inspired me. But it did not change what was inside me. I was still super scared, mentally jousting with my outsized fear of death.

The Ender King watched his soldiers depart and then turned to face Emma, Tina, Skittles, and me. "Stick together. Who knows we may find. I expect Herobrine to be in that room ... or, at least, what's left of him."

My chest tightened. *Could it be possible that Herobrine was no more? Could Entity 303 have actually destroyed him?* After what I had witnessed with Notch's capture, I was sure he could.

The Ender King continued, "Skittles, keep scanning the walls. If you see anything unusual, let us know immediately."

Skittles, who was now standing on the floor and was no longer being held by Tina, raised one of his front legs and saluted the Ender King. "Yes, Your Highness."

The Ender King took a deep breath and then asked, "Any questions?"

"I have a question," said Emma. "What should we do if we encounter any more mobs? Even ones that seem friendly, like ... hurrr ... that llama?"

"Stay behind me. I am not trying to brag here, but I'm way more dominant than any of you. I will assess the situation and give commands. Obey them without question because your life will depend on it."

Good, I thought. *Let him take the lead. This is crazy.*

"Move out," ordered the Ender King as he began walking in front of us.

* * *

The next few minutes were uneventful, though very tense. Skittles walked immediately behind the Ender King, scanning the walls, but finding nothing.

Next in line was Emma, her bow and arrows at the ready. Behind her was Princess Tina, carrying her diamond pickaxe and seeming surprisingly relaxed for the situation.

I brought up the rear, looking over my shoulder every couple of seconds. I never actually heard any mobs, but I thought I did. I was nervous and jumpy. But, I knew I had to do this. My loyalty to Minecraft ... to my World ... overrode my fear of death.

As I continued walking down the corridor, I started to hear something that sounded vaguely like a single note of music or maybe a humming sound. "What is that?" I whispered to the group.

Everyone stopped walking and the Ender King took a few steps back towards me. "What?"

"Do you all hear that? That humming noise?"

Everyone stopped and was quiet for a moment. I could tell by their expressions that they were starting to hear it.

"I think ... hurrr ... I do hear it," said Emma. "It's almost like the sound of wind blowing through the grass."

"There isn't any grass down here though," I said.

"I hear it too," said Skittles. He paused momentarily and scanned the surrounding walls. "I don't see any source of the sound behind any of these walls."

The Ender King nodded his head. "Yes, this is very peculiar. Let's move on. It could be a trap."

As we resumed, the sound got louder and louder. Not so loud that it sounded like it was next to you, but it began to fill the air.

"I don't like this," I said. "Are there supposed to be loud humming sounds like this inside strongholds?"

The Ender King turned around with a worried expression on his face. "No, there aren't. We have no choice though. We need to continue toward the rendezvous point. Stay alert." That was one thing he didn't have to say. I was so alert, I thought I was going to pass out from the stress. The blood vessels in my skull were pounding.

With every step I took, the noise continued to increase. It felt like my body was vibrating to the frequency of the sound. It was just this one long, continuous, unending, unabated, ineluctable vibration coming from the fringes of being.

It was starting to drive me insane.

And then I blacked out.

Day Unknown – Time Unknown

When I regained consciousness I was in a bright white space.

I wasn't sure if it were a room or not.

I could not see any walls.

I could not see my friends.

I had no idea where I was or what time it was.

For all I knew, I had died and was in the afterlife, waiting to respawn.

I felt my brain screaming inside my skull. Then my mouth started to scream. I wasn't screaming any words or anything that made sense. Just primitive noises of fear, rage, and incomprehension emanating from the primal depths of my being.

Was this what it was like to be insane? Irredeemably insane?

Because of the brightness of the space and the apparent absence of walls, I couldn't tell if there were any entrances or exits to this place. I knew I was standing on something, but there was no ceiling. I was completely disoriented.

And then something happened.

Lines of color began to drip down the distant walls. Colors of the rainbow!

Was I in some kind of place controlled by the Rainbow Creeper?

I stood and watched as the lines of color continued to make their way down walls that must have been hundreds of blocks tall, until they reached the floor, creating a horizon at least 500 blocks away. The lines continued along the floor towards me.

I was frightened. I didn't know if the lines might harm me, and I was too terrified to move. It was like I was paralyzed. My screaming had stopped, and the rest of my body had stopped responding to my brain's commands to run.

The lines approached me with increasing speed and then suddenly stopped, just as they reached my feet. The tips of the lines circled around my feet, the colors running together and forming a black circle in which I now stood.

I stared at the black circle around my feet. I tried to step out of the circle onto the colorful lines and found that I still could not move. When I took a deep breath and tried to flex all my muscles to raise my foot out of the circle, it still didn't work.

What is going on?

The rainbow lines in the white room were weird enough but now I was trapped inside a tiny black circle?!?

Why is this happening to me? Why do I always have these weird dreams and visions? If this ... hurrr ... is a dream.

Suddenly the rainbow–colored stripes began to undulate. They moved faster and faster until they looked like ... hurrr ... well, waves. The rippling stripes did not break the way waves in the water did but just rippled back and forth around the room.

As I watched them, I began to feel dizzy. Like an idiot, I kept watching them, and began to feel nauseous. Just as I was about to barf, I closed my eyes and counted to ten. When I opened my eyes, the lines mercifully has stopped undulating, and I felt better.

The black circle was still down by my feet. I still couldn't move my feet out of the black circle. It was starting to feel kind of stupid. I was stuck here in this room with all these rainbow colors on the walls and floor, and I was standing inside a tiny white circle outlined with a black line and couldn't move.

"Entity 303! Spike! If you're doing this to me, get on with it. I'm getting bored!" I was trying my best to sound brave, but my voice cracked a few times and I probably sounded like a scared little toddler villager.

Of course, there was no response. Well, no audible response.

Instead, the walls of the room began to undulate again and began to close in upon me. I tried to move to run away somehow, but my legs would not respond. The stripes of colored rainbow continued to close in on me.

In just a few short seconds, the lines had enveloped me. They were still rippling and were just inches from my body. It was one of the most creepy things I had ever experienced and yet it looked so beautiful.

And then the lines collapsed upon me with a tremendous pressure. I felt as though I were being squished, like when you step on an apple and all the flesh squeezes out, leaving just a streak of goo on the ground. Except, I was the apple, not the foot.

I knew this was it for me. Entity 303, Spike, or whoever had won this battle. I could only hope I would respawn somewhere to continue the fight against them.

The pressure continued to increase, and I felt as though the lines were reaching in to my mouth and down into my chest until they wrapped around my heart.

For just a split second, I thought I understood the mystery of the universe. It was as though ....

And then, the pressure became too intense and it was over.

I was dead.

Day 43 – Moments Later

I shook my head and came to. The Ender King, Emma, and Tina were standing and looking at me. Skittles was standing on my chest rubbing my cheek with one of his disgusting feet. I pushed him away and screamed.

"Jimmy, we were so worried!" said Emma. "You suddenly passed out and then screamed for a few seconds and then went into some sort of coma or trance."

I pushed myself up on my elbows and said, "I did?"

Tina nodded. "You did. It was one of the most frightening things I've ever seen. Your eyes rolled back in your skull and then darted back and forth under your eyelids."

I pushed myself further up and leaned against the wall. I rubbed my head, trying to get rid of the dull throbbing sensation. I noticed the strange humming sound had disappeared. "The sound. It's gone."

The Ender King nodded. "It stopped the moment you passed out."

I told them what I had seen in my vision. Then I asked, "What do you think it means?"

"I bet it was Entity 303!" said Tina.

"Yeah, he was probably trying to distract you with the rainbow colors to make you think it was the Rainbow Creeper," said Emma.

"Maybe. But, there was this moment, at the end, where I thought I ... hurrr ... where I thought I had complete knowledge of everything that existed or ever would exist."

They all stared at me as if I had turned into a skeleton or a squid.

"Did you hit your head when you passed out?" asked the Ender King.

I scowled at him. "No."

"Well, then, maybe it was the Rainbow Creeper after all," he said.

"Maybe the meaning of your vision will reveal itself," suggested Skittles, a tiny, scaly sage.

I nodded my head. "It always seems to. That's what I'm afraid of."

I pulled a carrot from my inventory and ate it quickly. Then, I pulled a cookie out and ate it too. I took a deep breath and stood up. "I'm ready to go. How much farther do you think it is?"

The Ender King looked at his map and said, "Not far. Two minutes at the most."

I smiled. "I hope these are the most uneventful two minutes of my life."

The Ender King looked at me with sad, serious eyes and said, "I do too, Jimmy. I do too."

* * *

The amazing thing was, they did turn out to be uneventful.

Sure, I was tense and scared the entire time. I sweated more in those two minutes than I had sweated in my entire life, of course, it was from nervousness rather than exertion. I probably took several years off my life with the stress I endured during those two minutes. Every little breath of wind or echoing sound of a distant zombie or spider made me nearly jump out of my skin but we made it without any issue.

(Okay, guys, I have to stop here and talk about that expression "jump out of my skin." Honestly, who comes up with these idioms? How could anyone jump out of their skin? If you jumped out of your skin and managed to stay alive you would be a skeleton or maybe a skeleton with some internal organs exposed to the air? It doesn't make any sense. Basically, if someone actually had jumped out of his skin and survived, I am sure he would be known around the world. It would be the most significant historical event in the history of jumping. Everyone would know about it. Instead, it's just some expression that people say when they mean to say they are really scared. Anyway, back to my diary.)

Finally, our group had arrived at the door to the room in which we believed Herobrine was being kept. There were no mobs guarding the door. The five ender soldiers who had gone the other direction had not arrived yet. Therefore, as planned, we would wait for them for five minutes before opening the door.

We all set up in defensive positions, under the assumption there must be some sort of trap or a mob patrol that would pass by sooner or later and attack us. After we took our positions, we asked Skittles to use his powers to look through the wall into the room.

Skittles nodded his head, smiled, and then peered at the wall. He had a confused look on his face and then shook his head. He looked again squinting his eyes this time. Again, confusion.

"What is it, Skittles?" whispered Princess Tina.

"I don't know why, but I can't see through this wall," said Skittles with a worried voice.

"Are you sure?" asked the Ender King.

"I tried really hard. I used all my concentration. Normally, it's easy, like breathing, but I can't see through this wall at all."

The Ender King rubbed his chin. "That concerns me. My guess is there is some sort of trap inside that room. It must have an enchantment on it preventing Skittles from seeing through the wall. Let's wait for my soldiers to arrive and then we can come up with a plan of entry."

While we continued to wait, Skittles periodically tried to look through the wall but to no avail. I could tell he felt very sad and useless. And, he sort of was useless at this point. I mean, what good is a silverfish in battle against who knows what horrific things were inside? If he couldn't see through walls and give us some assistance, why was he even here?

And then I realized what a jerk I was being, even though I was only doing it in my thoughts and no one had heard me. I was a bully. At least I hoped no one had heard me. Actually, Skittles had contributed by giving us information from the Collective. And, he did seem like a pretty nice silverfish. I felt ashamed and resolved never to be mean to Skittles again, even if it were just in my head.

At that moment, the ender soldiers finally arrived, but there were only three of them. They looked bedraggled and exhausted. Two of the three were wounded.

"What happened, men?" asked the Ender King.

The one soldier who was not wounded said, "Your Highness, I don't know how it happened. We were about halfway here when suddenly a group of five zombies and eight spiders seemingly appeared out of nowhere and attacked us. The zombies came from behind and spiders came from in front of us. We were surrounded. They had the element of surprise. I'm sorry, but we lost two of our men."

The Ender King looked sad. "I know you did your best, son. I wonder why they attacked you and not us?"

The Ender soldier shrugged his shoulders and said, "I think it was just happenstance, Your Highness. It didn't seem like it was planned. We were just in the wrong place at the wrong time."

"Perhaps," said the Ender King, not entirely sure. "In any event, we need to get into this room. We need to come up with a plan. The silverfish can't see through the wall, so there must be some sort of enchantment on it. Who knows what could be inside."

* * *

It took us about five minutes to come up with a plan. It was mainly the soldiers and the Ender King who decided what to do, but the rest of us contributed ideas, most of which were determined to be lacking in military value.

Anyway, here's what we did.

One of the ender soldiers had a TNT block. The ender soldier put the block next to the door and we backed away. Another ender soldier shot a flaming arrow into the block and it exploded, destroying the door and opening the entrance to the room. We then waited in defensive positions while the smoke cleared, ready to defend ourselves from an army of hostile mobs we assumed was going to rush out of the room and attack us.

But, after thirty seconds, nothing had happened. I looked over at the King and said, "Should we go in?"

The King thought about it for a moment and then ordered his three soldiers to enter and report back. The soldiers cautiously approached the door. They peeked in and then, seeing the coast was clear I suppose, entered the room with their swords drawn. They were out of sight for ten or fifteen seconds until they came out and looked at us, expressions of amazement on their faces, and said, "You need to get in here and see this."

We entered the room and what I saw made my knees buckle and I collapsed to the floor. The room was painted with rainbow–colored lines and only a small white circle with a black stripe around it was unpainted in the center of the room.

"This ... this ... hurrr ... is what I saw when I passed out."

Everyone looked at me in shock. I continued, "*Exactly* like this."

The Ender King teleported quickly to my side and grabbed my shoulders and said, "Jimmy, think very carefully. There must have been something in that vision that was helpful. Herobrine must have been in here. Where do you think he's gone?"

I thought about it for a while. I hadn't gone anywhere in my vision. I just stood in that circle unable to move until I was crushed by the stripes.

And that's when I knew.

"The hole. He's down the hole."

One of the ender soldiers walked over to the white circle and stood on it. He jumped on it. But nothing moved. Another soldier bent down and tried to pry the hole open but it didn't work.

"Nothing's happening, kid," said one of the soldiers.

"It has to be that. In my vision I was standing on that circle and was nearly crushed to death by the rainbow stripes. I'm sure it pushes you down into that hole somehow."

The same ender soldier rolled his eyes. "Prove it then. Open this thing up for us."

"I will not have insubordination," said the Ender King. "Apologize to Jimmy for your tone."

I waved my hand. "It's cool, King. Everyone's just frustrated."

Skittles walked over to the white hole and peered at it. He let out a gasp of shock and said, "I can see through this! And I can see … Herobrine!"

"I was right!" I said in triumph. I looked at the ender soldier who had doubted me. "In your face, skinny man!"

The ender soldier lunged towards me, but the Ender King intervened. "Enough! Both of you!"

"What else can you see down there, Skittles?" asked the Princess Tina in an excited voice.

Skittles looked down through the hole again, squinted his eyes, and said, "Herobrine is tied to something, maybe a chair. It gets fuzzy pretty fast when I look around him but I think I see the glow of lava down there."

"That's what the head monk said. She said Herobrine would be somewhere with a tube for air and food and that room would be surrounded by lava," said Emma.

I nodded my head in agreement. "Skittles, do you think we could mine our way into that chamber without getting killed by the lava?"

Skittles looked down the hole again. "It's difficult to tell. I don't know if the lava might be running down the walls or if it's just on the floor level, like a lake."

"Let's try mining directly down," suggested one of the ender soldiers.

The Ender King looked at him and said, "Normally, I would say no. Everyone knows you shouldn't mine straight down, but in this case, we should probably try it."

The three ender soldiers removed pickaxes from their inventories and began to strike the white circle. It was impenetrable. They each took a few steps back and started mining down through the rainbow-colored floor. This time, their pickaxes were able to penetrate the floor as if it were regular stone. They slowly made their way down, checking carefully after the initial layers of block, to make sure they did not break through and fall into the lava pit.

But, they were not careful enough.

Without any warning, lava erupted up through the three nascent mineshafts in which the ender soldiers were standing. They were vaporized instantly. The lava, having accomplished its mission, receded back into the area where Herobrine remained.

The rest of us could do nothing but watch in horror. It took a few moments before anyone could speak. Finally, the Ender King said, "Their sacrifice was honorable. Their names shall be sung in our songs for all eternity." The King then bowed his head for a brief moment of silence before saying, "Skittles, can you go back to the circle and check on Herobrine?"

Skittles approached the circle cautiously, careful to walk as far from the mineshafts as possible, and looked down. "He's still there. He's looking around, probably as surprised as we were. But he seems to be okay."

I snuck over toward one of the shafts through which the lava had erupted earlier.

"Be careful, Jimmy," said Emma, clutching the front of her robe nervously.

I looked over my shoulder at her and said, "I'll be fine." Then, I got down on my hands and knees and crawled to the edge of the shaft. I peeked over and saw lava beneath me. I peeked further over in an attempt to see anything else that might give us a clue as to how to get down there.

Suddenly, the lava shot upward. My lizard brain took over, reacting before I had realized the danger, and I was able to pull my head out of the lava's path with no time to spare. The rising lava singed my hair and another drop of lava hit my arm. It was painful but not very damaging.

"This is crazy," said Tina. "We obviously can't get in there unless we can somehow figure out how to open that white hole."

I had to agree with Tina. This seemed very difficult, if not impossible. I tried to think back to what happened to me in that strange white room when the rainbow engulfed me. There had to be a message there. Someone, good or evil, was telling me how to open that hole.

But what? But how?

And that's when I had a crazy idea. I reached into my inventory and sheepishly removed my rainbow–colored robe that Claire Dretsky had given me so long ago.

Emma saw it and laughed. "Are you kidding me? You are carrying that stupid robe around with you?"

My face flushed red with embarrassment. I shrugged my shoulders and said, "I put it in my inventory a while ago and kinda forgot I had it," I lied. Actually, I knew it was in there. I carried it with me everywhere. I was always looking for an excuse to wear it. I hoped I was right that this was a good time for it ....

I pulled the rainbow–colored robe over my ugly brown robe and said, "I think the reason the hole won't open is that the rainbow is incomplete. When I was unconscious in that strange white room, the only way I got out was when the rainbow enveloped me and squished me back into the regular world. I'm thinking that if I stand on the hole and match the stripes on this robe to the stripes in the floor, something might happen."

Everyone stared at me in shock. Skittles was the first one to speak. "Jimmy, that's both the most ridiculous and most beautiful idea I've ever heard in my life. I hope it works."

I smiled at Skittles. The ugly, bottom–feeding, debris–cleaning bug was starting to grow on me. He wasn't so disgusting and foul after all.

I walked over and stood on the white hole. I looked down and arranged it so that the stripes on my robe matched each stripe on the floor. What shocked me was the fact that there weren't any stripes left over. My robe was a perfect match for the pattern in this room!

"A perfect match!" marveled Tina.

"Oh, no, I almost forgot," said the Ender King reaching into this inventory and removing the splash potion of sanity. "Here. Take this. When you get down there, you will need to throw it at Herobrine, like the head monk said."

I reached out and took the potion. "Thanks. I had forgotten about that," I said as I put the potion into my inventory.

I stood on the white hole assuming the passageway would open on its own, but it didn't. *Was I supposed to do something else? Was I supposed to sing a song or do a dance or drink a potion or something?*

I stood there wondering what was happening or rather what wasn't happening. And then I decided just to close my eyes and take a deep breath and wish for the hole to open.

The next thing I knew I was falling. It seemed as though I were falling for hours. It was dark. It was cold. Then, slowly, over the span of what seemed like minutes, it got brighter and warmer until I hit the ground. Thankfully, it was not a hard landing.

I shook my head and saw that I had landed on hard rock. I was slightly dazed but then shook my head again and regained my senses. I looked up and sitting in front of me, tied to a chair was Herobrine.

"I did it," I said excitedly as I thrust my fist into the air.

Herobrine looked down at me, rolled his eyes, and said, "Congratulations. Now get me out of here!" He paused and then added, "So I can kill you!" He leaned forward in his chair, trying to get to me, but he was tied to the chair by the rainbow–colored robes.

I backed away, removed the sanity potion from my inventory, and got ready to throw it at him.

"What is that?" he asked. Suddenly, his voice changed into the voice of Entity 303. "No, don't!!!"

I tossed the potion and it splashed all over Herobrine.

At first, nothing happened. Then, he screamed in agony as if he were being tortured. Then, he fell silent. His pupils dilated and he stared in silence into the distance. Tears formed in his eyes and he sobbed uncontrollably.

"It's so beautiful," he whispered right before he passed out.

I probably should have slapped him back to consciousness, but I needed a moment to assess the situation.

I stood up and looked up the passageway to the room above. It seemed impossibly far. Even though Skittles had seen Herobrine just a few blocks below the room above, it now seemed like the shaft stretched for almost an eternity up into the sky.

I walked over to Herobrine's unconscious form. "I hope that potion really worked," I muttered before slapping Herobrine a few times.

He slowly sat up and looked at me as if he were seeing me for the first time. "Jimmy? Is that you?"

"Yes, we came to save you from Entity 303."

Herobrine smiled. "Thank you. I thought I was done for." He paused. "That potion, what was it?"

"The head monk of the Rainbow Creeper called it a potion of sanity."

Herobrine nodded his head. "And so it is. So it is."

I sat there staring at him. He was changed for sure. The potion had done something to him. But, now was not the time to find out how it had altered his worldview. We needed to escape. Entity 303 knew I was here. He was able to possess Herobrine just a moment ago. I had to act quickly.

"H–man, do you know what the deal is with that shaft?" I asked. "I was just in a room a few feet above you and now it seems like we are miles below the surface of the Overworld."

"The ropes, kid. Untie the ropes," insisted Herobrine. "I'll tell you about the shaft later."

I was able to easily untie them, since their power of restraint appears only to affect the victim being restrained by them. I put the ropes in the pocket of my rainbow–colored robe and looked at Herobrine as he stood up from the chair and rubbed the feeling back into his wrists. "So, how do we get out of here?"

Herobrine sighed. "I was hoping you would know. Look around you. We are surrounded by lava and there is no obvious way to get up to that shaft."

I had to admit, I was perplexed. There was no hole for me to stand over or stripes to match to my robe, only a dark passageway leading upward and well out of reach.

I didn't know it then, but things were about to get much worse.

Into the room, from some unseen passage, came four blazes! They got on all sides of us and came towards us. Herobrine tried to conjure some magic but his powers failed him.

"Entity 303 did something to me," he said angrily. "I can think of clever things to do but I can't do any of them. I don't know if it's this room or if he somehow stripped me of all my powers. Give me a sword or something. It's our only chance."

Now I was completely panicked. I reached into my inventory and pulled out an iron sword and tossed it to Herobrine. I pulled out my diamond sword and got ready. If there were more surface area for us to stand on or if there were only one blaze, I would have been confident we could survive, but four blazes against two people was not fair odds.

One blaze attacked us all by himself. Herobrine slashed it and we both hacked as fast as we could and were able to defeat it.

For whatever reason, the other three blazes remained at a distance, watching it happen. Maybe they had given the first blaze the honor of the kill or maybe they did not like him and hoped he would die. It didn't really matter in the end. Now all three of the blazes came in unison towards us. This was it. It was over. Entity 303 had won.

I could feel anger and rage rising inside of me. Was I going to be killed by blazes surrounded by lava? Death in a hot place?!? If I had to die, I wanted to die in the cool water of the ocean. Not inside of an enchanted deathtrap created by Entity 303.

Then, I felt something strange inside of me. A small, soft voice whispered words to me. I could not understand the words, could not tell you what they said, but somehow I knew what to do.

I moved my hands in a certain pattern and felt the power of something coursing through my body. And then without warning dozens of evoker fangs emerged from the lava and — SNAP! — chewed the three blazes to death!

Herobrine looked at me with astonishment. "I didn't know you had evoking powers!"

I looked at my hands in shock. I looked up at Herobrine. "I don't have evoking powers. Or at least ... hurrr ... I didn't have any evoking powers until now." I was so confused.

Herobrine reached out and touched my rainbow-colored robe. "Where did you get this?"

"Claire Dretsky gave it to me a while ago."

Herobrine bit his lower lip thoughtfully and nodded his head. "I wonder if the power comes from the robe?"

"I've worn the robe a couple times before and never felt any evoking powers coming through my body."

"Maybe it only works when you're in danger? We will have to figure it out once we escape."

"Or maybe the power was given to me by the Rainbow Creeper when I was taken to the rainbow–colored room."

Could that be it? Had the Rainbow Creeper bestowed this power upon me?

"What are you talking about, boy?"

I shook my head. "Nevermind. We can talk about it later. We need to get out of here before any more mobs come our way."

That's when an idea popped into my head. "My robe was what got me down here, so maybe it's what's keeping me down here."

Herobrine furrowed his brow, confused.

I quickly pulled off my rainbow–colored robe, folded it, and tossed it back into my inventory. And sure enough, at that moment there was a whooshing sound, then complete darkness, and after what seemed like five minutes, we appeared in the room from which I had originally departed.

The Ender King, Princess Tina, Skittles, and Emma stared at us in astonishment.

"What happened. How did you get Herobrine? You were only ... hurrr ... gone for like five seconds," said Emma.

Herobrine put up a hand and said, "You guys can talk later. We need to get out of here before Entity 303 comes back. He left me a few hours ago, and he typically comes back every few hours to slap me around and laugh in my face."

"Yeah, and he spoke to me through Herobrine's body just before I threw the potion of sanity!"

"We leave immediately!" ordered the Ender King.

And with that, the King and his daughter teleported all of us out of the stronghold.

Day 43 – A Few Hours Later

After we had teleported to the relative safety of the surface of the Overworld and told the soldiers outside to stand down and go to the other strongholds and spread the word to return to the End, we returned Skittles to his home stronghold where he greeted his friends and, I am sure, shared his experiences with the Collective.

"Good–bye, everyone, it was a fun adventure," said Skittles.

"You should come to Zombie Bane. We can teach you how to surf," said Emma.

Skittles smiled. "Maybe I will."

We all smiled and waved to him and we teleported away to Zombie Bane. When we arrived back in our home village, we dropped Emma at her parents' house.

After that, we stopped by the Ender King's palace to drop off Princess Tina. Finally, the Ender King,

Herobrine, and I teleported back to Herobrine's fortress.

When Herobrine arrived and saw its demolished state, he shook his head. "I can't believe I let my guard down and let myself be taken." By this time, Herobrine's powers had returned, and he was quickly able to clean everything and put his palace in order using his magic.

As we sat in Herobrine's kitchen, waiting for him to bake some bread, we heard a knock on the door. Herobrine excused himself to answer the door. A few moments later he came back laughing and slapping the back of a villager who was about my age. The villager was laughing and slapping Herobrine's back. It was strange.

"King. Jimmy. I want to introduce one of my best friends, his name is John." John had brown hair and was about twelve or thirteen years old. I'd never seen him in Zombie Bane, so he must be from a different village.

"Yeah, Herobrine is the best," said John.

"John, do you recognize me?" asked the Ender King.

John stopped and stared at the King and said, "Sorry, man, you look like all the other endermen I've ever met."

The Ender King shook his head and said, "I rescued you and your parents one time from a zombie attack. I was in the Overworld on some business and when I saw you in trouble, I saved you. You were only about three years old though, so I guess it's no surprise you don't remember me." The King paused for effect and then said, "I am the Ender King."

"Wow, wait until my friends hear that the Ender King saved my life when I was a baby! It's weird enough that I'm friends with this guy," said John tilting his head toward Herobrine.

"How exactly did you to become friends?" I asked. *I mean, what are the odds that a villager would know Herobrine and the Ender King? I couldn't believe that I did.*

Herobrine said, "Oh, I was putting up signs and stripping all the leaves off trees one day, you know, just for fun. I saw John, who must have been about five years old at the time, out there following me around. I thought about maybe just killing him, like I do, but he seemed so curious and so nice. So I stopped to talk to him. He wasn't afraid of me or anything. He was the first villager I had ever met who wasn't scared, so I thought we should remain friends."

John nodded his head. "Yeah. I've never been afraid of anything. My mom says it's an imbalance in my brain chemistry, but I just think I'm super dominant."

I rolled my eyes, but had to respect a kid who wasn't afraid of Herobrine. I know I was afraid of Herobrine until I met him.

I looked over at the King and said, "Shouldn't we go after Claire? The head monk said she's in the End."

The Ender King sighed. "I suppose we should, but I'm very tired. Let's go back to Zombie Bane and get a good night's sleep. We can go after Claire tomorrow."

"Are you going to come with us, Herobrine?" I asked.

"I don't think so, Jimmy. I really need to recover. Having my powers stripped away and being imprisoned and tortured is not very conducive to adventuring. But, if you can figure where Notch is, come find me. I will help you rescue him."

"Suit yourself," I said as I stood up and looked at the King. "Shall we?"

The King nodded his head, put his hand on my shoulder, and we teleported back to Zombie Bane for a well-deserved rest.

End of Surfer Villager Book 9

Book 10

Day 44 – Morning

I thought I would have had a difficult time sleeping after the struggle to rescue Herobrine. I assumed that I would be thinking about the upcoming rescue mission to the End to free Claire Dretsky from the clutches of Spike and Entity 303. But I was so tired from the previous day's adventures, that I slept deeply, so deeply that I felt as though I had simply gotten into bed, closed my eyes, and then awakened. Sometimes when you sleep, especially when you have a fitful sleep, it seems like the night lasts forever. But for me, last night, it was as if night didn't even exist.

I got out of bed and stretched my tired muscles. I used to hear my dad say that his muscles hurt when he woke up in the morning and that I would understand someday when I was old like he was. Well, I am only twelve and a half years old, but I already understood.

It's not the years; it's the mileage.

I put on my robe and went downstairs to look for some breakfast. My plan was to eat something, say goodbye to my dad, and then pick up Emma on the way to the Ender King's Palace.

My dad was sitting at the table, waiting for me. He had a worried look on his face. "Jimmy, are you sure you have to go today?"

I walked over to the counter and grabbed a piece of fresh bread my dad had made that morning. I took a bite of it, chewed, and swallowed before I answered him. "Of course I do. The mission is not completed. If we don't rescue Claire, then we will never find out Notch's location. Hurrr, assuming the head monk of the Rainbow Creeper wasn't lying about the chain of events we had to follow."

My dad's expression remained serious. "As your father, I should not let you go. I think you're too young for all this. But, you've proven me wrong on that several times already."

I kept chewing my bread but didn't say anything in response.

"Anyway, I won't stop you from going. I admire your bravery. I just don't want you to respawn until you have reached a ripe old age."

Ripe old age? What a bizarre and slightly distasteful expression.

I felt emotional. I could see my dad's perspective. I knew that he didn't want to lose me in a battle or any other way for that matter. But this was a fight for the survival of all of Minecraft. For the freedom of every mob and NPC alive today. Entity 303 and Spike had to know that their behavior would not be tolerated. Even if every last citizen of Minecraft died fighting them, it would be better than living under the yoke of their slavery.

"Thank you for understanding, Dad." I took another bite of the bread and said, "This is really good bread. Thanks for making it. It is almost as good as Mom's."

My dad sighed. "When you go to the Ender King's palace this morning, don't let your mother see you. You know her psyche is still recovering and she remains under the care of the Ender King's servants."

I nodded. My heart hurt. I wanted to say goodbye to my mom before I left for the End just ... just in case the worst happened. "Okay, Dad."

My dad stood up and slid his chair away from the table. He walked over next to me and gave me a hug. It was like the hugs he gave me when I was four years old. He squeezed hard and held me for a long time. If the circumstances had been any other than what they were, I would have pushed him away and told him to leave me be. Told him that I wasn't a baby. But this hug was all good. It might be the last one I ever had....

My dad let go of me and backed away. He pulled out a box and handed it to me. "There is a bunch of food in there. Put the box in your inventory. I don't know what kind of food they have in the End. You don't want to be eating chorus fruit all day."

I smiled and tucked the box into my inventory. "Thanks, Dad." I stood there for a moment, looking around the kitchen. Wondering if I would ever see it again. I had already come so close to dying so many times, that I refused to take any moment of my life, no matter how small, for granted anymore. "I think I'll go get Emma now."

My dad nodded and said, "Good luck, son."

Day 44 – 10 Minutes Later

Even though I was in a hurry to get to the End and rescue Claire, I took my time walking to Emma's house. I enjoyed the feeling of the cobblestones and dirt under my feet. I admired the old trees that had been planted along the streets of my village. I even took some time to admire the souvenir shops that sold cheap memorabilia related to my great great grandfather's dominant actions that one night so long ago in Zombie Bane.

When I arrived at Emma's house, I walked up the steps to the front door and knocked. Within a few seconds, Mr. and Mrs. Watson answered it together.

"Good morning, Mr. and Mrs. Watson."

Mrs. Watson offered a weak smile and said nothing. Mr. Watson said, "Good morning, Jimmy. I suspect you're here to pick up Emma for your latest escapade."

Escapade? Dude, this was serious.

"That's right. Is she still allowed to come with me to the End?"

Mrs. Watson made a noise that indicated she didn't think Emma should go but remained otherwise silent.

Mr. Watson nodded his head and said, "We don't really want her to go, but we understand why she needs to. I expect you'll do your best to protect her?"

I stood up as straight as I could and puffed out my chest. "Of course I will, sir. I'm trying to protect all of Minecraft."

Mrs. Watson could stay silent no longer. She pointed a finger at my face, the flat tip of which was so close I could see her fingerprint, and said, "I don't care about all of Minecraft. I only care about my daughter. If you come back without her, I'm going to be very, very upset." As she finished her final words, she began to cry. Then, she ran up the stairs and into Emma's room. I assumed they were having a moment.

Mr. Watson looked up the stairs after his wife with sad eyes. He stared at the door to Emma's room for a few seconds before looking back at me. "Jimmy, this all has been really hard on my wife. And, truth be told, on me as well." Mr. Watson sighed deeply and then said, "I hope this is all worth it."

I wanted to scream at him. "Of course it's worth it! Don't you want to save the world?" But I didn't. I knew he was very emotional, and so I let him be how he needed to be.

You do you, Mr. Watson.

Mr. Watson indicated that I should sit down on the couch and wait for Emma. He went up the stairs and into her room as well. After about five minutes, Emma came down the stairs by herself. Her eyes were red from crying. "Let's go, Jimmy."

"Hurrr, don't you want to say goodbye to your parents?"

Emma sighed. "I already did. They said they wanted to remember me in my room and not going off on a quest." She paused for a moment and then said, "You know, hurrr, in case I never return."

My chest tightened briefly at the thought of Emma dying. I did not mind the thought of my own death, but the thought of my best friend dying made me anxious. "You. Will. Not. Die."

She shrugged. "You don't know that. And besides, I could fall into a pool of lava underneath the town if some stupid player dug a mine in the wrong spot, so I don't see how going on this quest is much different."

"That's a rather fatalistic way to look at life."

Emma looked at me with surprise on her face. "I didn't know you knew the word fatalistic?"

"I didn't either. I must have heard it somewhere."

We left Emma's house and walked down the road toward the Ender palace. We were about halfway there when we heard a familiar voice.

"Guys. Wait up. I'm coming too."

I turned around and said, "Biff, what are you doing here?"

"You are going to rescue Claire, right?"

"That's the plan," said Emma.

"Well, she is my cousin. I owe it to her to try to save her."

I suddenly felt bad for keeping Biff in the dark about who Claire really was. That she was a priestess for the Rainbow Creeper and that Emma had tricked Biff into looking at some fake mechanical ideas so that I could talk to Claire by herself about Spike and Clayton.

"Is it ... hurrr ... okay with your parents for you to come along?" I asked.

"Of course it is. They know how important family is." Biff thumped his chest with his fist to emphasize his point.

"You do realize this is extremely dangerous, right?" said Emma. "One of us or even all of us could be dead soon."

Biff did look a little worried, but he did not change his mind. "You guys have been risking your lives for days now. The least I can do is help rescue my own cousin."

I guess that was it then, Biff was coming with us. "Good to have you along, Biff. Who's going to run the SUP school while you are gone?"

"Oh, I hired some high school kid. I told him he could have ten percent of the emeralds that come in while I'm gone. He's already creating an advertising campaign so he can maximize his revenue."

I laughed at the greed of villagers and said, "Come on then. Let's get to the Ender King's Palace."

Day 44 – 5 Minutes Later

When we arrived at the Ender King's Palace in Zombie Bane, the ender soldiers guarding the entrance waved us through but stopped Biff to search him.

"He's okay," I said, assuming they would listen to me. "He's our friend."

The ender soldiers looked at me like they could care less what I thought and who my friends were. In the view of their cold, mysterious purple eyes, I was just a weak, ignorant villager to whom their king happened to take a liking. A pet.

They gave Biff a pat down and inspected his inventory. When they determined he was not a threat, they waved him through like a delivery boy.

Rude!

As we made our way to the Ender King's throne room, Biff marveled at the interior of the Ender palace. "This place is amazing! And this isn't even the

Ender King's normal Palace. It's just like a vacation house!"

"Yeah, it must be nice to be rich," said Emma.

We arrived at the door to the throne room and knocked. The door opened and there, framed by the opening, stood Princess Tina. She had a big smile on her face and squealed and hugged Emma. "Nice to see you again."

"You too," said Emma, though her squeal was not as high-pitched as Tina's.

After the princess had finished hugging Emma, she looked at me and smiled and said, "Hi, Jimmy!"

I smiled back and then pointed at Biff. "This is our friend, Biff. He runs the SUP School and Pool. But, more importantly, he's Claire's cousin. He wants to come with us to help rescue her."

The princess stuck out one of her tiny black hands and Biff took it and shook it in a greeting. "Nice to meet you, Princess."

"Likewise. I'm sorry that your cousin has been kidnapped."

Biff nodded his head sadly. "So am I. That's why I want to help get her back."

At that moment the Ender King walked in and noticed Biff. "Why is he here?" demanded the King.

Biff puffed out his chest and said, "I'm here to help rescue my cousin, Claire, Your Highness."

The Ender King considered this for a moment and then said, "If you want to come with us, that is fine. But you have to know the risks. There is a substantial likelihood you and your friends may die." The Ender King paused meaningfully, letting the weight of his words sink in, and then asked, "Do you still want to come with us?"

Biff set his jaw and clenched his lips. He nodded his head curtly and then said, "Of course, sir. I have to do this. Family above all else."

Formalities out of the way, the Ender King smiled briefly and said, "Welcome aboard, then, Biff. We're going to need all the help we can get. If the head monk is correct and Claire is imprisoned on an end ship, then we will need a lot of firepower to get through the end city and its nefarious dangers. And that's only what we know will be there. Who knows what sort of booby-traps or strange mobs Spike and Entity 303 have waiting for us."

I looked over at Biff as the Ender King was ranting about danger and saw beads of sweat forming on his forehead. I could tell he was reconsidering whether to come with us, but he remained steadfast.

The Ender King looked at me and asked, "So, have you figured out why you suddenly have evoking powers now? Have you done any tests?"

Biff's head swiveled around and he looked at me in shock. "You can evoke?!?"

I shrugged like it was no big deal. Like I was the coolest kid in town, even though deep in my heart, I knew I was just a derp. "Well, I evoked kind of by accident yesterday when we were rescuing Herobrine. I'm not even sure how it happened."

"That's amazing!" said Biff. "Evoker fangs, vexes, and everything?"

"It was just evoker fangs," I said. "Maybe it will be vexes next time."

"Try something, Jimmy. Let's see if you can do it again even though you haven't had any training," demanded the Ender King.

I took a deep breath and backed away from everyone. I brought into my mind the image of a vex and began moving my hands around in a random pattern. I was waiting for bubbles to appear and then the vexes to manifest ... but nothing happened. I tried again, this time trying to call evoker fangs up from the floor, but again I failed.

I looked at the Ender King and said, "Someone needs to teach me how to do this or else I guess it's just gonna happen randomly."

The Ender King clucked his tongue. "That's a shame. It would be really helpful to call some vexes to our aid or even evoker fangs if there is a large group of mobs attacking us. Maybe we can figure something out. I have an extensive library at my Palace in the End. I bet there's something we can reference."

"And, if we can't find anything in the End, when we get back, we can ... hurrr ... look through Mr. Blaze's bookstore again," said Emma.

"If we get back," I mumbled.

The Ender King clapped his two tiny black hands together and made a disproportionately loud noise which actually frightened me a bit. "Okay, kids, let's go to the End. Follow me to the portal room."

We were all very excited. None of us had been to the End before. I'd seen drawings of it and heard a few players talk about it. It sounded like a very mysterious and somewhat boring place, well boring scenery anyway. But we were not going there to be bored. We were going there to fight against the greatest evil in the history of Minecraft.

After a few twists and turns through the palace we arrived at the end portal room. Inside the portal room there were several ender soldiers standing guard by the portal. They all saluted the king and the princess as they entered. They looked at us suspiciously, their purple eyes questioning their king's wisdom, but said nothing.

"Okay," said the Ender King. "Stand on the edge of the portal on the end stones. When I count to three, everyone jump in at the same time. Make sure you're holding the hand of the person next to you so no one gets lost during the transit."

I suddenly felt nervous. "Is that possible? Could we get lost in the transit? Where would we go?"

The Ender King shrugged. "I have no idea. Endermen cannot get lost during a transit to the End. But I've heard others can. There are tales of people entering end portals and never coming out. I have no idea what happens to them."

A shiver ran up and down my spine at the thought of being lost in the murky darkness of space or ... wherever. Princess Tina was standing next to me so I reached out and grabbed her hand a little too roughly, so great was my fear of becoming lost.

Tina looked over at me and said, "Ouch! Not so hard."

"Sorry," I said sheepishly. "Your dad is freaking me out about this whole getting lost thing."

Tina smiled. "It's okay. I understand."

After everyone had linked hands, the Ender King counted to three, and we jumped.

Day 44 – Moments Later

There was a brief moment of darkness, a feeling of a deep, bone chilling cold and then we stepped out of an end portal located inside the Ender King's Palace in the End. I felt my feet touch down gently on stone.

When I opened my eyes I saw that there were several ender soldiers staring at us. At first, they looked surprised but then noticed the Ender King was with us. They saluted him immediately.

"At ease, men."

The soldiers relaxed a bit, put their arms by their sides, and then one of them said, "Welcome home, Your Highness."

The Ender King nodded to the soldier who had spoken to him. "Thank you, Mike. It is good to be home." The King paused and then said, "We are going to my war room. Send the Ender general at once." Mike saluted as the Ender King passed by him. The King motioned that we should follow.

c

We walked through the Ender Palace for a few minutes before arriving at the war room. The Palace itself was astonishingly large. Given that endermen are quite tall and skinny, the ceilings were high above my head, being that I was just an average-sized villager kid, after all. The doorways were also quite narrow, though I had no trouble fitting through them. Numerous paintings and maps were hung on walls. There were also a few statues here and there of famous endermen like kings and queens, princes and princesses.

The war room itself was a large rectangular windowless chamber. A large wooden table was in the center. Maps of the End, the Overworld, and the Nether were hung on the walls. Different battle plans had been drawn on them. I was astonished to see that there were plans for invasions of the Nether and the Overworld. But, even more astonishing was evidence that the Ender King had been planning for various attacks and battles within the End itself!

"Take a seat," said the Ender King.

We all found a place to sit and had just gotten comfortable when the ender general arrived. He didn't teleport in this time. He simply opened the door and walked in. He approached the King and the King whispered a few things to him. The general nodded gravely and then sat down.

I was getting impatient. I was drumming my fingers on the table. I couldn't take it anymore. "So what's the deal, King? When are we leaving to find Claire? The head monk said she was being held on an end ship."

The Ender King looked to me crossly. "Jimmy, when are you going to learn to be more polite?"

"What are you talking about? There is no time for manners. We need to rescue Claire before Spike kills her or drives her insane or ... hurrr ... something worse."

The Ender King shook his head. "Haven't you learned by now that I'm several steps ahead of you?"

"What are you talking about?"

The Ender King walked over to his map of the End. He pointed to some small chunks of rock on the edges of the map, surrounding a large island-shaped area. "Do you know what this is?"

I rolled my eyes. "Duh. It's a map of the End."

"You are correct. The large island in the center is where we are. This mountain here houses the ender dragon. But see these little areas surrounding the large island where we are?"

"My eyes work, you know," I said with all the snarkiness I could manage.

The ender general suddenly teleported to my side and pointed his tiny little black index finger right at my eyeball. "Behave. Or die." Then he teleported back to his seat.

I did not know why the endermen thought it was important to teach me manners. It was annoying. But, I will readily admit, the ender general easily could have killed me, so I decided I would stay silent for a minute.

"As Jimmy correctly, but rudely, pointed out, the head monk said that Claire was on an end ship. End ships only exist on end islands, floating above end cities. Therefore, she could be on any one of these islands," said the Ender King, pointing to the dozens of islands encircling the main island of the End.

The scope of our search suddenly dawned on me. "That could take weeks! Months!"

The Ender King chuckled. "It would only take that long if you can't transit between the islands very quickly or teleport into the end ships."

"Well, obviously none of us villagers can teleport. Are you going to do all the searching or something?"

The Ender King smirked and said, "Tell them, general."

The ender general stood up and walked over to the map where the Ender King had been standing. "You all will recall that after the second surf contest the head monk appeared and explained that Herobrine was imprisoned in a stronghold and that Claire was imprisoned in an end ship. Immediately thereafter, at the King's orders, my army began a search of all the end islands trying to locate Claire." The ender general paused and then a peculiar sad, defeated expression crossed his face. "We found her."

Biff stood up and pumped his fist in the air. "Awesome. I want to see my cousin."

Emma smiled broadly. "Wow! Something finally was easy for a change."

"Yeah, why didn't you just bring her to Zombie Bane instead of making us come here to this forsaken dimension?" I asked with bitterness in my voice.

The Ender King stood up and swelled to five times his normal size. "Silence!" He bellowed.

Let me tell you, when you see a 5x-normal-sized Ender King bellowing at you, you do what he says (and you try really hard not to pee your robe). We immediately became as silent as death.

The Ender King slowly returned to normal size, looked at the ender general, and said, "Continue."

The ender general let out a deep sigh. "We found her ... on the Island of the Savages."

"And?!? Let's go get her!" I demanded.

The ender general shook his head. "It's not that simple. The endermen on the Island of the Savages have never recognized the legitimacy of the Ender

King. If any of us set foot on the island, we will be killed immediately."

"So … hurrr … how do you know Claire is on that island if you haven't even been there?" asked Emma.

"We searched every other end ship in existence. We've looked under every nook and cranny and even torn some apart. She wasn't on them. The only other end ship in existence that we have not searched is on the Island of the Savages."

"Pardon me for saying this, Mr. Ender King, Sir, but I need to go get my cousin. I'll go without you if I have to," said Biff.

It was the Ender King's turn to talk. "Biff, I'm not going to stop you. In fact, the only way your cousin will ever be saved is if a group of non-endermen go there and rescue her."

I could see that Biff felt proud of himself. He had been right about what needed to happen. "Great. Can you take us there? Or at least get us close?"

"We can take you to a portal which will transport you to the island. They're called end gates and we know which one will transport you to the Island of the Savages. But first, we need to make sure you have as many weapons in your inventories as possible."

Day 44 – A Few Minutes Later

The Ender King and the ender general led us to the armory. When we walked in, I couldn't believe my eyes. There were weapons everywhere. On the wall. In chests. Piled in the corner. It was insane.

On the wall there were crossbows, crossbow bolts, bows, arrows, swords of all kinds, spears, shields, armor, bombs made from TNT, and strange redstone devices that I did not fully understand.

"Wow! If you had gone to war with the Dretsky clan, I think you might have won," I said, impressed.

The Ender King shook his head. "And we would have already accomplished that if it wasn't for certain people wanting to get certain ideas from Herobrine...," said the Ender King, his purple eyes boring into me.

I swallowed hard. I wondered if the King might finally snap and kill me like he had threatened to do so many times in the past. But he looked away from me and spread out his skinny long black arms and said, "Take whatever you think you'll need. I'd recommend some bombs. You'll also need some shields to help block the shulker bullets. You all know about shulkers, don't you?"

I had heard of shulkers but I really didn't know much about them. I knew they were some sort of bizarre, mysterious creature existing in the End and looked kind of like a weird box, but this was the first I had heard about bullets.

"Not really," said Biff.

The ender general explained. "Shulkers are creatures who appear to be a large block. They can be attached to floors, walls, ceilings, just about anywhere. When you get close to them, the block opens and you can see their bodies. They shoot a little bullet at you which you can block or hit with a sword or an arrow, but if the bullet hits you, it levitates you. Sometimes this is a good thing if you want to go up for some reason but other times it can be bad if there's no roof above you or you are too high above the ground when the levitation effect wears off. You could float away into oblivion or plummet to your death."

This wasn't making me feel very good. "That sounds very troubling. Thank you, Notch, for creating such a monstrosity. But, I'm sure there are not very many of these shulkers out there, are there?"

The ender general and the Ender King both laughed heartily. "Quite the contrary. There are numerous shulkers throughout end cities. If you want to get to the end ship you will have to fight your way up through the end city past probably dozens of shulkers."

I sighed and slumped my shoulders. "Well, at least we know what we are going to face."

"I'm not so sure you truly do understand," said the Ender King. "First, you will have to deal with the savage endermen. I'm sure they will not appreciate your presence on their island. There will be too many of them for you to defeat, so you will have to find some way to sneak past them without arousing their wrath."

Just great!

"And," continued the King, "we don't know what sort of traps or other mobs might be on the island as the result of the acts of Spike or Entity 303. You will recall they, along with Clayton, were building an army of nether mobs to invade the End before Notch ordered them to stop and participate in the surf contest instead. Who knows if they are on the island now?"

"Is there no way to find out the situation on that island?" asked Emma, concern in her voice. "Can you have some soldiers teleport out there quickly and do some reconnaissance?"

The Ender King shook his head. "My grandfather, who also had not been recognized as king by the savage endermen, once attempted something like that. Not only did the inhabitants of the Island of the Savages kill the two soldiers sent there to perform reconnaissance, but they sent ten of their own into the Ender Palace and killed everyone they could before they themselves were finally the killed."

"And so ... hurrr ... we are supposed to go there by ourselves, three young villager children, and defeat a horde of savage endermen, dozens of shulkers who are shooting bullets at us, Notch knows what sort and number of nether mobs, and maybe even Spike, Clayton, or Entity 303 himself, before we rescue Claire. Is that what you're saying?" I asked, practically hysterical.

The Ender King pursed his lips together and nodded his head up and down a few times before responding. "Yes, that's exactly what I'm saying."

"In that case, give me as many of those TNT bombs as you can."

It took us about five minutes to fill our inventories full of bombs and other weapons. It turned out the strange redstone devices I had seen earlier were items used by ender soldiers to communicate with each other across great distances.

"Can I speak with one of your scientists about how these work?" asked Emma. "I'd love to be able to build something like this myself."

The Ender King shook his head. "State secret."

Emma pursed her lips, obviously upset. But, she said no more.

The King ordered us to each take two of the communications devices. "You never know. They may come in handy," he said. "If you find Claire, call me. I would be willing to send over a couple of soldiers to help extract her from the end ship. I think if we teleported directly on to the end ship and got out of there really quickly, we might be able to do it without alerting the savages to our presence. It's a risk, but one I'm willing to take if you can find her."

"Thank you, King," I said.

"Yes," added Biff. "Thank you so much, Your Highness. I wish you could come with us, obviously you are a super dominant warrior and all that stuff, but I thank you for the help that you can give us."

"I wish Tina could come with us," said Emma. "But, I understand."

Tina, who had been silently watching us load our weapons, teleported to Emma's side and hugged her tightly. "Be careful. I like having you as a friend."

The Ender King looked at us with remorse. "If the only life I were putting at risk were my own, I would of course go with you. But if any of the savage endermen see me there, they will assume I have come to conquer them, and they will instantaneously send an invasion force to the main island of the End in retaliation. Tens of thousands of endermen would likely die if I did that. I simply cannot risk it."

"I get it," I said. "Hurrr, now show us to this end gate thingy and let's get on with it."

Day 44 – 5 Minutes Later

The Ender King, Princess Tina, and the ender general teleported us to the end gate which was connected to the Island of the Savages.

The gate itself was a great distance above the ground. I could have never gotten up to it by myself without building a one-block column on which I would've had to perch precariously before attempting to jump into the end gate. Fortunately, the ender folks said they could teleport us up there and toss us into the end gate.

"What do you mean, toss?" I asked, worried.

"Well, you have to jump inside the end gate. Normally, if an enderman wants to transport through one, he or she just teleports right up to it and jumps in. Since we are going to have to teleport you up in the air, we will have to teleport up in rapid succession and just toss you into the end gate so that you will all arrive on the Island of the Savages at approximately the same time."

"I'm not sure I like this," said Emma.

"Me either," said Biff.

"I'm sorry, kids, but I think that's the only way we can do this without sending you one by one. If you happen to materialize in the center of a bunch of savages, who knows what would happen."

"Are you telling me that this end gate doesn't go to a particular location? It's just random?" I asked incredulously.

The Ender King nodded his head. "Yes. You will appear somewhere on the island, but you might appear a great distance from the end city and the end ship. You may have to travel for quite some time before you even get there."

"This is stupid. Can't you afford some better technology?" I asked, angrily.

The Ender King looked at me like I was a bug he wanted to squish. "Look, Jimmy, you need to relax. If I had better technology, I would give it to you. The endermen did not create end gates, they were created at the time of the creation of the world. We learned to use them as best we can."

I crossed my arms in front of my chest and pouted. "I wish I could teleport. That would be such a better deal."

"Maybe think about it hard enough, you'll be able to," said Biff. "That's what my dad always says. Just put your mind to it."

I snapped my head around and squinted my eyes angrily at Biff. "That's the dumbest thing I've ever heard. How can I put my mind to wanting to teleport? It's a genetic gift. It's not something that you can just manifest. You have to be born with it."

Biff shrugged. "Maybe, maybe not."

I rolled my eyes and shook my head. *What an idiot.*

"I agree with Jimmy on this one, Biff," said Emma. "Scientists have tried for generations to create a teleportation machine, but no one has succeeded. I think it's a fool's errand."

"Anyway ... hurrr ... let's get this show on the road. I'm ready for you to throw me into the end gate and see what happens when I come on the other side," I said sarcastically.

The Ender King walked up to me and put his hand on my shoulder. The ender general put his hand on Biff's shoulder and Princess Tina put her hand on Emma's shoulder. Without saying a word, the Ender King teleported me to a location directly in front of the end gate opening and threw me inside. As I screamed in terror, I heard Biff right behind me screaming and then further in the distance Emma screaming. The Ender folk had done their job of getting us into the end gate at nearly the exact same time.

When I landed on the island, I found myself inside a forest of chorus fruit trees.

As Biff and then Emma appeared nearby, I scanned the area for savage endermen. I saw nothing. I looked over at Biff and Emma and waved at them silently to come toward me. When they were next to me, Biff whispered, "Do you see any of the savages?"

I shook my head and put my finger to my lips to tell him to be quiet. I pointed in various directions and into my eyes and outward from my face. They got the idea and took a few paces and went off in slightly different directions and did some reconnaissance. A few moments later we gathered back at the original point.

Emma whispered, "I don't see any endermen, savage or otherwise. I don't see anything except these chorus fruit trees. They continue for a great distance."

"Same here," said Biff. "Nothing's moving."

"It's pretty weird," I said. "The Ender King seemed so convinced that we would be surrounded by these aggressive savage endermen. I'm not seeing anything alive other than the chorus fruit trees."

"Did either of you see the end city? I didn't," said Emma.

Biff and I both shook our heads.

"How do we know which direction to go?" asked Biff.

I looked around and noticed a tall mountain to the south. I pointed at the mountain and said, "Let's get to the top of that mountain. If we can't see the end city from that vantage, we will just have to find another mountain."

They all agreed with my suggestion and we set off for the summit.

Day 44 – One Hour Later

As we made our way through the chorus fruit forest and up the foothills of the tall mountain, we saw nothing but end stone and chorus fruit trees. We picked some of the fruit and teleported short distances. This helped us make good time. Plus, it was kind of fun.

"Make sure you keep a few of those fruit in your inventory. We might need them to escape at some point," suggested Emma.

Although we had been on this island for one hour, we had seen nothing other than plants and rock. No endermen, no nether mobs from Spike's army, nothing. It was like there never been any beings alive on the island.

Spooky.

"Where do you think all the endermen went? Usually there are always packs of them milling about on other parts of the End," said Biff.

"It's as if they've been completely annihilated," said Emma ominously.

"You think they've all been murdered? Slaughtered?" I asked.

She shrugged. "I don't know. Maybe. I mean, look at this place. Look at how much chorus fruit there is. Didn't the Ender King tell us that was why Clayton wanted to invade and enslave endermen? To get chorus flowers and end stone? Why not start with the Island of the Savages where no other endermen are allowed to go?"

As I thought about Emma's words, I realized what a brilliant strategy it would have been. In fact, Clayton and Spike could have pretended to have been honoring the truce forged by Notch and participated in the surf contests, while at the same time exterminating the population of the Island of the Savages and obtaining all the resources they wanted!

I looked around and realized that the chorus fruit trees had become extremely dense. I'd heard chorus fruit were common on the end islands, but I'd never heard about jungles of them. "Do you think this forest is actually cultivated by the Dretsky family's slaves?"

Emma and Biff shrugged wordlessly.

With that dark thought in my mind, we continued up the mountain. We moved cautiously and quietly, but again saw nothing. We were not approached by any mobs of any kind.

"It's quiet. Too quiet," I said using a deep mysterious voice to make these words seem as ominous as possible.

Emma hit me on the arm. "Stop messing around, Jimmy. This is serious. We need to be alert."

I rolled my eyes. "Of course, I'm alert. The world needs more lerts."

This time Biff hit me on my other shoulder. While Emma had hit me lightly, Biff punched me as hard as he could. It didn't feel good. As I rubbed my shoulder, Biff said, "Shut up, dude. We need to find Claire as soon as possible. Stop goofing around."

I thought about saying something else goofy, now that both of my shoulders had been used up, but then I realized they could just hit my shoulders again. Therefore, I decided to remain silent.

About five minutes later we reached the summit of the mountain. We looked around and saw an end city some distance away to the west.

"Gee whiz, that looks like it's a long way. Probably take us a couple of days," said Emma.

"Maybe longer," I said, staring at the valley floor in shock.

Emma and Biff looked at me, and Emma said, "What do you mean?"

But I didn't need to answer her question. Biff and Emma saw where I was looking. They saw the shocked look on my face. They knew it was something bad. They both slowly turned their heads to look down into the valley where I had been staring.

They saw it too.

Hundreds of villagers picking chorus fruit, guarded by dozens of heavily-armed zombie pigmen.

Day 44 – Moments Later

"We need to free them!" said Biff.

As much as I agreed with Biff's sentiment, I couldn't agree it was a wise strategic move. "What about all those zombie pigmen? If we go in there and even one of them sees us, we're done for. There's too many of them."

"We can't leave our own kind enslaved by nether mobs. Enslaved by Spike and Clayton," said Biff.

"Biff, I agree with Jimmy," said Emma. "If we had some ender soldiers with us, we might be successful, but just the three of us ... hurrr ... we don't stand a chance."

"But we can't just leave them there to be worked to death!"

I put my hand on Biff's shoulder to console him. "Look, once we free Claire, we should be able to find out where Notch is being held. Once Notch is free, we can defeat Clayton and Spike ... hurrr ... I hope, anyway. If we can win that battle, then all the villagers will be freed."

Biff's eyes were starting to fill with water and tears as he realized that Emma and I were correct. I admired his spirit and desire to free those villagers, but he knew we were right. It would be a suicide mission.

Biff ran a finger across his nose to wipe away the boogers of sadness that had flowed freely and then said, "If we are going to leave them there, then how do we get to the end city? If we have to avoid this valley, it's going to add at least another day to our trip. What if Claire can't last that long?"

I hadn't really thought about that. The longer Claire remains imprisoned in the end ship, the more likely it would be that Entity 303 or Spike might torture her to death or corrupt her mind to an extent that she could not be saved. Still, I didn't think Spike, as evil as he had become, would let harm come to his own sister. But, Entity 303 didn't care about anyone.

I looked over at Emma and asked, "What do you think? Is there any way we can get through the valley without being seen? I'm not looking forward to walking up and down mountains for the next couple of days to get to the end city."

Emma surveyed the area for almost thirty seconds. When she was finished, she looked at Biff and me and said, "What is that down there? Underneath those trees to the left?"

Biff and I squinted to see what she was pointing at. Initially, I couldn't make much out. Then, I noticed what appeared to be movement. Lots of movement. And that's when I said, "I think it's a herd of cows."

"Exactly," said Emma. "And cows do not exist in the End, unless someone brought them here."

"Who would bring them here?" asked Biff, surprisingly clueless.

"Obviously it was the zombie pigmen. The cows must be here to provide food for them and their slaves," I explained.

Emma was nodding her head. "I was thinking that if we could sneak down into the valley without being seen and get to that herd of cows, we might be able to use them as cover while we move past the zombie pigmen and their slaves. My guess is there will only be one or two zombie pigmen guarding the cows, so we should be able to avoid being seen or take them out, if necessary."

I considered Emma's plan for a moment. It was a good one. It would save us at least one day's walk and had minimal risk. Still, if one of the zombie pigmen guarding the cows were able to sound an alarm, we would likely be done for.

"I'm willing to risk it," I said.

"I'm in," said Biff.

Emma smiled. "Good. Then it's agreed. I suggest we stay as far to the left of the herd as possible, and then move slowly once we start being able to hear the cows mooing. Anyone guarding the cows will stay fairly close to them, so we shouldn't have to worry about anyone spying from high up or anything like that."

I made a fist with my right hand and smacked it into the palm of my left hand. "Sounds like a good plan. But, before we get started, I want to have some apple pie." I reached into the food box my dad had given me before I left home and pulled out one of the apple pies that was in there. I quickly cut it into six slices with my diamond sword and held the pie plate out to Emma and Biff. "Help yourselves. Two slices each."

Their hands shot into the pie pan, grabbed a slice with each hand, and stuffed the pie in their mouths. Emma mumbled with her mouth full, "Your mom makes the best apple pie."

I smiled and said sadly, "Actually, my dad made it. My mom is still under the care of the Ender King's servants in Zombie Bane. She is still recovering from her shock."

Emma and Biff sadly nodded their heads.

"It is good pie, I'll have to agree," said Biff.

Day 44 – 10 Minutes Later

After finishing the first apple pie, I decided that if today were the day we were going to die, I wanted to die with a stomach full of pie, so I got the other one out, and we each had two more pieces. Unfortunately, because we had consumed so much pie and had become bloated, we had to sit down and rest until our stomachs could digest some of the pie. I rubbed my bloat for about ten minutes before I was ready to proceed with our plan. When Emma and Biff were ready, we began.

As we walked down the hill, we entered a very dense forest of chorus fruit. I had come to the conclusion that the zombie pigmen servants of Clayton and Spike had been planting these trees. They would move the villagers between groves of trees to harvest the fruit and the flowers before moving on. Once the trees had grown new flowers and fruit, the slaves would return for another harvest.

In fact, the portion of the forest through which we were walking right now appeared to have been recently harvested. There were small flower buds but no flowers or fruit on the trees. I took that as a good sign meaning that it was highly unlikely that any enemy mobs would be lurking in this sector of the forest.

My suspicion was partially correct. Certainly, there were no villagers and no nether mobs. However, when we had made it about halfway through the grove and nearly to the base of the mountain, I heard a sound. It sounded slightly like a scratching sound, like fingers against the dirt or a stick against stone. I froze in my tracks. Biff and Emma did the same.

I whispered to them, "Did you hear that?"

The both nodded their heads silently.

"Where did it come from?" I continued.

Biff pointed in one direction and Emma pointed in another. I wasn't sure where it had come from so I said, "Let's be quiet and see if it happens again."

We waited for about five seconds until we heard it again. *Scratch scratch*. We could tell where it was coming from now. We spread out and then moved in the direction of the noise. We had our swords drawn, ready to strike. We could not afford to be discovered. No matter what we came across we had to kill it. Quickly.

As we continued forward, we heard the noise again. I looked at Emma and Biff with concern in my eyes. They mirrored my feelings back to me. We knew this was going to be a pivotal moment in our quest.

We heard the noise again. We could tell we were very close. It seemed to be coming from behind a rock just in front of us. Emma went to the right and Biff went to the left while I indicated to them with hand gestures that I would climb on top of the rock and jump down.

When Biff and Emma were in position, I slowly crept up to the top of the rock. I didn't risk looking over to see what it was because once I looked all bets were off. I indicated to Emma and Biff on the count of three we should all spring our trap. I raised my hand and lifted one finger, then two, and finally three and then I jumped over the edge of the rock to the ground. Emma and Biff sprung from their locations to cut off sideways motion for whatever was making this noise.

To my surprise, it was a young ender boy savage who, quite frankly, didn't look any different than any other ender boys I had seen on the main End island *except* for his one strange blue eye.

The boy looked at us in shock with his small, purple and blue eyes. He dropped the stick he had been holding and scratching against the ground. His eyes looked back and forth, scared. It was like he had never seen anyone like us before. As I watched his chest fill with air, his mouth opened as if he were about to scream. It gave me no pleasure to do it, but I smacked him on the side of his head with the flat of my sword, knocking him out.

"Ooof!" he groaned as he fell to the ground.

We quickly tied his hands and feet and put a gag around his mouth. While he was still unconscious, I said, "Do you think this is one of those Savage Enders that the Ender King was talking about?"

"He doesn't look very savage to me. Just looks like a scared little kid," said Biff.

"Yeah, Jimmy, why did you ... hurrr ... have to hit him so hard?" asked Emma.

"He was going to scream. He would have alerted everyone." I said.

Emma didn't seem convinced, but I knew I had done the only thing I could, other than killing him. And I didn't want to kill anyone if I didn't have to.

"Let's mine a small cave and take him inside," suggested Emma. "We can seal the cave and light some torches and then we can talk to him. He might know something useful."

Biff and I agreed with her plan. We removed our pickaxes from our inventories and made a quick cave inside the end stone mountains. After we sealed the entrance, we took the gag off the young ender boy's mouth and threw some water on his face. He woke up sputtering and started to shout. "Help! Help!"

I put my hands in front of me and pressed them down toward the ground in a gesture to calm him. "Relax. We are not going to hurt you again. We just needed to stop you from screaming."

"What do you want?" he asked, blinking his multicolored eyes.

"What were you doing hiding behind the rock?" asked Emma. "We had not seen any other endermen on this entire island."

Tears formed in the boy's eyes and streamed down his face uncontrollably. After a few seconds, he was able to muster the strength to speak. "That's because I am the only enderman left on this entire island." He paused for a moment, sobbing, before saying, "Entity 303 and his army slaughtered the rest of my people."

The three of us stood there in shock. Our suspicion that all the endermen on the island had been killed had been confirmed by the last living survivor. "Are you sure they killed everyone else?" I asked.

The ender boy nodded his head sadly. "The only reason I escaped is that my mother threw me off the edge of the island onto a small piece of land that cannot be seen from above. The zombie pigmen who had been pursuing us must have thought I had fallen into the void and died." He paused and looked at me, rage flashing in his purple and blue eyes. "But I didn't."

"So ... hurrr ... why were you hiding behind the rock?" asked Biff.

The ender boy gritted his teeth. "Trying to figure out how to kill them. Kill them all."

An idea popped into my head and so I expressed it. "Say, is it true that the rest of the endermen in the End referred to you and your people as savages?"

The boy grunted. "*They* are the savages. We live in the traditional enderman way. The rest of them have abandoned all of our historical customs. But, yes, they call us savages."

I tapped my chin with my left index finger. "You know, I'm sure the Ender King would come here with his soldiers and we could kill all the zombie pigmen, if you wouldn't mind. I know he said he wouldn't set foot here because he didn't want to break the treaty."

The boy nodded. "They teach us about that treaty from the time we learn to read. I've heard about it for years. The Ender King is correct that he isn't supposed to break the treaty, but now...," his voice trailed off as he fully realized that he truly was the last of the Savage Enders alive.

"Well then, should we call them?" asked Emma.

The ender boy sat silently, contemplating. And after a few moments he said, "If he can kill all of these scum that killed my family, then yes. Call the King."

I nodded. "Before I do that, what is your name? I'm Jimmy, and this is Emma and Biff."

The boy smiled and said, "My name is Aurelius."

I had never heard of such a name. Actually, it seemed kind of weird. But, you can't blame a kid for having a weird name. I mean, the kid's parents were the ones who chose it. And, maybe the name isn't really all that weird, maybe it is just unfamiliar.

Anyway..., I said, "Cool" and then walked toward the wall of the cave. I pulled my pickaxe from my inventory and knocked a hole in the wall before stepping outside.

I reached into my inventory and pulled out one of the redstone communication devices we had been given before we left the main island. I removed the locking mechanism that secured the lid over the button to prevent the accidental pushing of it. I took a deep breath, held the device above my head, and pressed the button with my thumb.

Day 44 – 30 Seconds Later

After I pushed the button, the first ender soldier arrived in just under ten seconds. After thirty seconds had passed, I was staring into the fiery purple eyes of the Ender King who was surrounded by twenty-five of his best soldiers and the ender general.

"What has happened, Jimmy? Have you rescued Claire? I did not expect you to summon us so quickly, if at all," said the King.

"They're all dead, King. The savages. They're all dead," I said.

A look of astonishment passed across the Ender King's face. "What do you mean? The three of you killed them all?!?"

I sighed deeply. "No, it was Entity 303, Spike and Clayton. Their forces killed everyone. They are here exploiting the island's resources using their villager slaves."

The ender soldiers began to mutter amongst themselves. They were shocked that a single combined Overworld and Nether force could be sufficient to defeat an entire island of endermen. Though I did hear at least a couple of the soldiers whisper to each other they were glad the savages had been exterminated.

At that moment, Emma, Biff, and Aurelius walked out of the cave. When the ender soldiers saw the Savage, they immediately pulled their swords. The Ender King looked at me and said in horror, "You've destroyed the treaty! Now the savages will come and kill us!" The King reached out and with both hands grabbed me firmly by the throat. He began to squeeze.

"King, stop," I croaked. "He's the sole survivor. He saw it all happened."

The Ender King tossed me aside and walked over to Aurelius and looked at the young ender boy and said, "So, Savage, is this true?"

Aurelius stood tall and proud and looked up, directly into the King's eyes and said, "*You* are the Savage."

Emma jumped in between the King and Aurelius and said, "This isn't helping. King, all of Aurelius' people are dead. He is the last one. We found him just a short time ago."

The Ender King softened a bit and looked at the boy and said, "This is true? Are you the last?"

Aurelius nodded his head forlornly. He sighed and then said to the King, "I want revenge. I don't care about the stupid treaties my parents made with you or your parents. We need to come together as endermen to defeat this menace."

The Ender King nodded his approval. "Aurelius, is it?"

"Yes, it is."

"In that case, Aurelius, we are of a like mind. The Dretsky clan, in coordination with Entity 303 has broken the truce established by Notch. Their lives are now forfeit. Anyone who helps them has also forfeited his or her life."

I had never heard the Ender King say anything more ominous than what he said right then. It sounded like total war. Unless we could somehow find Notch and he could restore order, I wasn't sure how this could be solved.

Unless, somehow, the Rainbow Creeper could do something about it. But the Rainbow Creeper seemed to always stay on the sidelines, manifesting in a dream or alternate reality, but never engaging in the world of Minecraft. I had not lost my hope entirely on a real-world intervention by the Rainbow Creeper, but I would need to speak with Claire about it, if we found her ... hurrr ... no, **when** we found her.

"King, we need to tell you what's happening down in the valley. It looks like a force of zombie pigmen is holding dozens of villagers captive. They are harvesting chorus fruit and chorus flowers. We were going to sneak around to the end city to the west but then we stumbled upon Aurelius. Since he told us all the other endermen native to this island were dead, we assumed it would be okay to call you."

The Ender King looked at me with an understanding glint in his eye. "You did the right thing, Jimmy. Now that there is no treaty, we need to secure the entire End for all endermen."

The ender general approached the King and said, "I just teleported up to the nearby mountain and observed this valley of which Jimmy spoke. It looks like there are at least two dozen zombie pigmen down there. We could probably take them in direct combat, but I cannot guarantee that one or two might not escape and alert the Dretskys that we are here. This may compromise the safety of Claire Dretsky and Notch himself." The Ender general paused for a moment and then with a look of profound seriousness on his face said, "Maybe it's time to try ... the weapon."

The Ender King looked very concerned and asked, "How is that any better than direct combat?"

"Direct combat will give our mission away. They will run away to inform Spike and tell him that the Ender King knows where they are. But, if we use the weapon, they will be so scared and astonished, they will be unable to do anything other than die."

"But the weapon ... it has not been tested very well. What if we lose control?"

The ender general understood the King's concern. "If we lose control let's hope it is after all the zombie pigmen have died and we can step in and destroy it ourselves."

"What the heck are you guys talking about?" I asked. "What sort of weapon can you use but can get out of control? Don't weapons just do what their handlers ask of them? A sword will slash and a bomb will explode?"

The Ender King cast a sidelong glance at me and said, "Not this weapon. We think we have it under control now, but you never know."

Emma came closer and said, "What sort of weapon is this? Is it really safe to use?"

"We will find out," said the Ender King quietly. "We will find out."

Day 44 – 15 Minutes Later

The ender general dispatched several of the ender soldiers back to the main island of the End. They returned with two ender scientists and several large boxes.

I watched as one of the ender scientists busily assembled some sort of harness or horse bridle. It was made out of leather with metal buckles holding it together.

Biff and Emma were watching this display with me. Aurelius was talking with the ender general, debriefing him about the assault on the Island of the Savages by the Dretsky forces.

Biff said, "What are they doing? Do they have some sort of giant horse in those boxes?"

Emma squinted her eyes at the device. "I've never heard of a horse that large. Plus, it looks like they are reinforcing it several times. There's no point in reinforcing a horse bridle like that."

I let my imagination run wild for bit and suggested, "Maybe it's some sort of giant golem that just walks up to the zombie pigmen and explodes."

"Maybe, but if that is true, what did they mean earlier when they said it was a weapon they couldn't control?" asked Emma.

"Yeah, golems tend to be rather docile unless provoked. I wouldn't think a golem would ever get out-of-control," said Biff.

"Plus, the Ender King told us that it could discriminate between zombie pigmen and villagers, so the villagers could survive this attack. It must be rather smart. Golems might be loyal, but they are not smart," said Emma.

At that moment I watched the two scientists opening boxes. They removed what appeared to be blocks of material of some kind, though they remained wrapped in cloth so I could not discern what type of materials they were. The only thing I knew was that these items were cube shaped. I pointed at the blocks being unpacked and said, "Looks like they're going to craft something. I guess ... hurrr ... it's a multipart weapon?"

Biff and Emma shrugged their shoulders. "Maybe."

The ender soldiers had erected a small tent. The scientists were working inside the tent assembling whatever this weapon was. The Ender King and ender general went into the tent a couple of times to check on the progress. Each time they emerged, they seemed satisfied with what was happening.

Aurelius, having completed his debrief with the ender general, returned to talk with the three of us. "How's it going, Aurelius?" I asked.

"Okay, I guess. The ender general was shocked at the size of the invasion force. The amount of zombie pigmen lurking in the valley down there is a tiny fraction of the number that invaded a few weeks ago."

Emma shook her head and said, "Whoa! That sounds like almost every zombie pigman in the Nether must have been here."

Aurelius scratched his foot against the dirt. "Could've been. The ender general thinks maybe there were zombie pigman spawners brought to the island to generate a giant army in a short period of time."

"Diabolical," said Biff.

We were interrupted in our conversation when the Ender King announced, "The weapon is ready. We will now carry it as close to the valley as possible. The weapon has been programmed to kill everything it sees except for villagers and endermen." The Ender King paused dramatically. "Let's hope it works like my scientists say it will."

Several ender soldiers quickly tore down the tent and I anxiously looked, hoping to get a glimpse of this mysterious weapon. But I was disappointed. The weapon itself had been encased in a wooden box from which polls extended on either side. Four ender soldiers stood at the front of the box holding the polls and another four ender soldiers held the polls jutting from the rear of the box. They lifted the box off the ground and began walking toward the valley.

I guess I would have to wait to see what this weapon was until we got there.

Day 44 – One Hour Later

We had slowly and cautiously approached the valley. A few of the ender soldiers teleported ahead a short distance at a time to look for the enemy. If none were spotted, we would move to that position. There was no talking, no complaining, nothing but forward movement during that hour.

"Why don't you just teleport the weapon to the valley and be done with it?" I asked.

"Can't do it," explained one of the scientists. "The weapon is too dangerous and may incorrectly activate during teleportation."

When we had gotten as close to the valley as anyone dared, we could just smell a hint but putrefied bacon, the savory stink of the zombie pigmen. Biff held his nose and whispered, "That is nasty."

Emma, Aurelius, and I nodded our heads in agreement.

The Ender King walked over to the two scientists and said something to them. I couldn't hear it but it must've been something like, "Release the weapon."

The two scientists opened the door on the side of the box which had now been placed on the ground. They walked inside. They were in there for a couple of minutes doing something before they emerged, carrying a rope. The scientists handed the rope to the Ender King.

The King cleared his throat to get our attention and then addressed us very quietly. "When I pull that string, the weapon will come out. If everything goes according to plan, it will not attack us. Do not be frightened when it comes out and do not move to attack it. If it senses you are a threat, it may override its programming. After it emerges, it will begin a search and destroy mission to kill everything in its path except for villagers and endermen."

The King walked back toward the ender general. Then the King looked at everyone and said, "Find a rock to get behind. A big one."

The King didn't have to ask twice. I practically dove behind a large rock to my right, but then I peeked my head out so that I would be able to see what this fabulous weapon was. Emma, Biff, and Aurelius were also behind nearby rocks, straining to get a look at this weapon when it emerged.

The Ender King himself ducked behind a rock and then yanked on the rope. The sides of the box fell away and I saw stacked there four blocks of soul sand and three wither skeleton skulls!

Oh! My! Notch!

A second tug on the rope and all the items came together. There was a swirling of wind, some sparks, and then in front of me floated a wither!

"Netherrack," I swore under my breath.

The wither paused for a few moments while it gained full power and health. Once it was at full strength, it soared into the air before swooping down upon us, looking for something to kill.

It was then that I noticed the harness I had seen earlier was now around the wither. I could see some redstone circuits glowing in the harness. This must have been what kept the wither from killing all of us.

The wither circled us, saw nothing he was permitted to kill, and howled in frustration. One of the ender scientists then approached the wither very cautiously and pointed in the direction of the valley with a tiny black finger and said, "Your prey is that way." The wither howled and then zoomed away toward the valley.

After the initial shock wore off, I said, "Wait a minute! I thought withers did not attack zombie pigmen? What kind of nonsense is this?"

One of the ender scientists approached and snorted his contempt for me. "We have created a harness to control the wither. It will attack what we say and it will ignore what we say."

Nice shorts, bro.

"Really? The Ender King did not sound so confident it would work a little while ago," I said defiantly. "What if it ends up killing the villagers instead?!?"

The scientist snorted again. "It will work. We are scientists!"

Emma had been watching this exchange and intervened. "I am a scientist too, but I would not unleash something so dangerous and untested upon the world!"

"You dumb villager, we have tested it," said the scornful scientist.

The Ender King could not take any more of this. "Dr. Camino. Stop insulting the children. You have admitted to me the risks, and I have made the military decision to deploy the weapon."

Dr. Camino's blood was still riled up. "But, Your Highness, I shouldn't have to –."

"Silence!" commanded the King. "Go stand with your colleagues and get ready to march. We need to get to that valley as soon as possible to recapture the wither once it completes its task. Or, to destroy it if your harness fails to control it."

Dr. Camino did not like being yelled at, I could see it in his eyes. He clenched and unclenched his tiny black fists three times before he wordlessly obeyed the King.

The King stared after Dr. Camino for a long moment before turning back toward us. "Come. Let us see the results of our deeds."

Day 44 – Continued

As the wither zoomed off toward the Valley to complete its task of killing all the nether mobs, we quickly followed in pursuit. Soon, we started hearing wither explosions and the screams that followed. We could hear villagers screaming with fear and zombie pigmen screaming with agony.

I looked over at Emma who was running next to me and said, "It sounds terrible. I hope the targeting system on that wither works like Dr. Camino said it would."

She nodded her head. "If it doesn't, there will be no one left."

Biff was running just behind us. He said, "Do you think that harness can really control the wither?"

I turned around as I kept running. "I don't know. We'll know in a few minutes when we get to the valley."

The endermen had been teleporting short distances to keep up with us as we ran. I looked over at the Ender King who had just materialized next to me and said, "Hey! Why can't you teleport us too?"

"I don't know. It seems like you were enjoying running."

I slapped my head but kept running. "Never mind, it sounds like we are almost there."

We arrived in the valley and ran past the herd of cows. No one was guarding them. We saw puffs of smoke rising from the forest of chorus fruit. We all drew our swords, just in case. We saw the wither rise up from among the trees and then descend again, followed by a massive explosion soon thereafter.

As we slowly approached the killing field, the explosions stopped. As the sound of the violence died down, I heard the sobbing of villagers. They were still alive!

We rushed forward and saw that it was true. Dozens of villagers were huddled together in a mass. Dozens of drops from dead zombie pigmen surrounded them and huge portions of the ground had been blown away by the wither explosions. But it didn't look like any villagers had been harmed.

I looked over at the ender scientist. "This was amazing! Good job."

Dr. Camino looked at me with contempt and said, "Of course it worked. I am the smartest person in all of the End."

I rolled my eyes. What an arrogant fool! I'm just trying to give the guy a complement and still he has to build himself up even bigger.

The Ender King walked over to the scientist and clapped him on the back with his hand. "Great job, Dr. Camino. Now, how do we stop the wither?"

Dr. Camino reached into his inventory and pulled out a small redstone device with a lever on it. "I just flip this lever and the wither will come to me like a dog. Then we'll put him in a box and store him away for later."

Somehow, I didn't think it was going to be that easy. But I had doubted the scientist earlier when he said the wither could discriminate between different mobs because of the harness. *Maybe you really could control it like a dog?*

The scientist walked in front of all of us and looked at the wither and said, "Wither. Come here." He then flipped the switch on the redstone device. The redstone device glowed red but nothing happened.

The wither just hovered in the air staring at the scientist.

The scientist looked at the redstone device and smacked it against his leg a couple times as if that would fix any weak connection inside of it. Then he flipped a lever again. Again the wither stared at him.

I saw sweat forming on the scientist's forehead. He said nervously, "Um, it doesn't appear to be working as planned. But that's okay, the harness should control the wither. We can just attach a leash to it and it will come along."

Again, I didn't think this was very likely to work. And, now that the remote control didn't function like the scientist had hoped, I was feeling more confident in my lack of confidence.

The ender scientist motioned to a couple of soldiers who brought him a long leash. The scientist took it and walked toward the wither. The wither did not move. The scientist approached the wither and reached up to hook the leash onto a metallic portion of the harness.

Just as the end of the leash clicked into place, the wither howled and shrieked with anger and then exploded. In the aftermath, Dr. Camino had been vaporized, passing on to the great respawning area in the sky. The wither hovered and stared at us with menace.

I looked over at the Ender King. "What are we going to do now? We can't just leave this thing here."

"Agreed. I really don't want to fight a wither right now, but it looks like that might be our only option."

Aurelius looked over at the King. "What kind of arrogant scientists do you have over on the main island? Why would anyone think they could control a wither?"

The King looked at Aurelius and I could see in his eyes that he wanted to scold him, but he was more diplomatic than that. "There are many who would like to destroy us, as your people have found out. Sometimes in trying to develop a better weapon, you fail."

Aurelius nodded his head with sad understanding.

Then the King looked at the ender general and gave him a nod. The ender general turned around to face his men and said, "Prepare to attack. I want ten archers at a distance shooting at the wither. When the wither is distracted, I want the rest of you to teleported and chop at it with swords. We will keep this up until we kill it."

As the endermen got into position, I remembered I had the rainbow colored ropes made of Rainbow Creeper skin in my inventory. I thought for a moment and then wondered if it was worth the risk. But I thought I would try. "King, I think I can do this without any fighting."

The King looked at me like I was insane. "What you mean?"

"Just hold your men back for a few seconds. I want to try something."

Emma reached out her hand and grabbed my wrist. "Jimmy. Are you insane? Don't go near the wither."

"I have to try something. If I don't, I'll always wonder."

"Don't be stupid, Jimmy," said Biff.

Aurelius nodded his head in agreement. "Yeah, man, you are cuckoo."

"I'm going," I said as I pulled the rainbow colored ropes out of my inventory and dashed toward the wither. The wither remained hovering in the air staring at me with menace. I held one end of the rope in each hand and jumped at the wither.

The wither shot a skull at me, but I ducked my head and it exploded on the ground nearby. The concussion from the explosion shook me, but did not change my trajectory. I hit the wither's central head. I wrapped the rope around the wither's central face and suddenly it became calm. It floated down to the ground and sat there, its three heads looking at us calmly. And then much to my surprise, the wither shuddered twice and then returned to its constituent parts: four blocks of soul sand and three wither skeleton skulls. The pieces fell apart and the wither was no more.

An audible gasp went through everyone watching, partly because I was so stupid to do what I had done but mainly because the rainbow colored ropes had defeated the wither so easily.

The Ender King teleported immediately to my side and said, "How did you know that would work?"

"I didn't. I just thought that if they could restrain Herobrine, they would probably work on a wither too."

Aurelius approached, looked at the rainbow colored ropes, and said, "What are those, exactly?"

"They say it is a rope made from the skin of the Rainbow Creeper."

Aurelius' his eyes went wide. "Our people speak of the Rainbow Creeper."

Now my eyes went wide. "What are you talking about?" We continued our conversation with our eyes wide and unblinking, like maniacs.

"My people believe that the Rainbow Creeper is what gave us the ability to think. The ability to have free will."

"That doesn't make any sense," said Biff. "Wouldn't free will have been created at the same time Notch created all of Minecraft?"

Aurelius shrugged his shoulders. "I didn't study much philosophy or religious history in school, I only know the legend. Our people say that is where free will came from. Before the Rainbow Creeper, we were just automatons."

This was getting crazy. Plus, my eyes were starting to dry out because they were still wide. I narrowed them.

The more I heard about the Rainbow Creeper from different sources, the more confused I become about what it truly was. The only thing I knew was that its skin was able to perform various powerful actions. In the form of rope, it appeared that it could restrain anything. In the form of tiny little pebbles, it could cause explosions. If its skin was this powerful, what could the rest of it do? What was it thinking? What else could it control?

Meanwhile, the ender soldiers gathered the pieces of the wither and put them back into storage. They teleported back to the end gate and returned the wither weapon to wherever the Ender King had it stored. The remaining soldiers along with the King, the general, Aurelius, Emma, Biff, and me, approached the freed villagers.

I walked up to one of them and said, "How did you get here?"

He explained that he had been kidnapped in his home village by some zombie pigmen who had been lurking in a nearby alley. He said there is a similar story for everyone here. They were all trapped and brought here to harvest chorus fruit and flowers.

I nodded my head. "Have you seen Clayton Dretsky or Spike?"

He shook his head. "But, I've heard their names. Some of the guards were talking about them. Apparently they control everything."

"Apparently so," I muttered.

The King climbed up on a rock and said, "Villagers, I will have several of my men ferry you back to the End and then transport you to the Overworld. We should be able to return you to your home villages in short order."

The villagers let out a cheer of joy and thanksgiving.

The King assigned five ender soldiers to handle this task. The rest of us headed for the end city to free Claire.

Day 44 – Moments Later

We made our way to the end city as quickly as we could. Teleporting as much distance as possible each time. Within about two minutes, we had arrived at the base of the end city.

It surprised me that our trip was so easy. Although we had defeated the zombie pigmen who were guarding the enslaved villagers, I expected there to be other obstacles in our path. There was nothing. No more zombie pigmen, no blazes, no strays, nothing.

I looked up at the immense end city, with the end ship beginning to sail away from its top level. I looked over at the King and said, "How do we get up there?"

The King smiled confidently. "We can just teleport up to the ship. We will have to stop a few times inside the city, but we should get there fairly quickly."

I smiled. This had been remarkably easy. When the King had sent us over to this island without any endermen to assist us, I was extremely worried. But now, everything seemed well in hand.

But then it happened.

It started to rain. Hard.

I looked up into the black cloudless sky in the End. I shielded my eyes with one of my hands and said, "I didn't know it rained in the End?"

I looked over at the endermen who were screaming in pain as the rain hit them.

"What is it King?" I asked in confusion.

The Ender King was talking through teeth clenched with pain. "The rain. It burns. That's why we live somewhere it doesn't rain." The King paused and braced himself against several more drops of rain before saying, "We can't stay with you, Jimmy. You will have to handle this yourself."

I was destroyed. This must have been Entity 303 or Spike's doing. There's no way it could have rained in the End without some sort of magical intervention.

Emma walked over to the King said, "Can't you just teleport inside the end city? It's probably not raining in there."

The King nodded his head. "Good idea." And then he teleported into the city. But he was back a few seconds later. "The roof is gone. The water is coming down inside the city like a waterfall."

At that moment the ender general teleported next to the King and said, "The men are losing health rapidly, Your Highness. If we don't get out of here in the next thirty seconds, we will all be dead."

The King understood. He looked over at us and said, "I'm sorry. But you're on your own." The King then looked over at his general and said, "Give the order. We evacuate now."

Before he teleported away, the Ender King said to me, "When the rain stops or when you rescue Claire, summon me again using the redstone device."

"Sorry guys. I have to go with the King. I don't want to die either," said Aurelius.

We nodded our heads with understanding as we watched Aurelius walk to the King's side and then teleport away.

I had a suspicion the rain would stop once they left, the objective of driving the endermen away having been accomplished, but it did not. It kept raining. The downpour was torrential. It was unlike anything I'd ever seen. Rivers began to form on the end stone, wearing away the stone into shallow canyons. It was something quite extraordinary to behold.

"Let's get inside the city," said Biff.

Emma and I followed Biff into the city. And ... we were immediately attacked by two shulkers.

The shulkers opened their shells and spat slow-moving bullets directly at us.

"Get a shield and block them!" Emma shouted.

We fought off a few of the bullets before Emma was hit with one. She levitated up into the sky but was able to grab onto a piece of stone jutting out from the wall of the end city. Fortunately, she wasn't too high in the air when the levitation effect wore off. Nevertheless, she slammed to the ground with a THUMP.

By then, Biff and I had defeated the two shulkers who had attacked us. Their shells fell to the ground.

When Emma recovered from her fall and stood up, she rubbed her shoulder and said, "Ouch. Maybe I should've tried to land on a higher floor?" As she continued to rub her shoulder, she picked up the shulker shells. "I'm going to make a shulker box. I heard they are really good for storing things."

"Really?" asked Biff. "Maybe I should make one for storing my emeralds."

"No time to talk about your greedy desires, guys," I said. "We need to get up there and save Claire."

So, finally, we were on our way up the end city. It was about ten stories high. We had to fight about a dozen shulkers on the way up. When we were almost to the top, I was hit with a bullet and received the levitation effect. As I was floating up into the rainy sky, I reached for a stone outcropping on the wall of the end city to keep myself from floating into oblivion.

I thought I had it, but the rain made the rock wet and I could not get a grasp on it!

Biff and Emma screamed, "Jimmy! No!"

I began to float higher and higher. I was trying to drift in a direction where I would at least land on something fairly high up once the levitation effect wore off, rather than falling all the way down to the ground, a fall which would likely kill me. But I could not control my drift and I drifted beyond the edge of the end city and floated high above the solid ground.

Realizing my precarious situation, I started screaming like a little baby, "Help! Help! I'm going to die!"

As Biff fought the shulkers and kept their bullets away from Emma, she acted quickly. She pulled out a bow and arrow and tied a rope to the end of the arrow's shaft. She aimed the arrow toward me and yelled, "Grab this when it comes by."

She loosed the arrow and it shot straight at my head. Somehow, I managed to grab the rope as it passed by me! Emma held the other end of the rope and tied it to a stone outcropping, just as my levitation effect wore off.

I fell down, faster and faster. It felt like my stomach was coming up through my mouth. But I held onto the rope. As I fell, the rope landed on the top edge of the end city. I saw the rope stretch tight as I passed the top of the end city and continued hurtling toward the ground, but because Emma had tied it off, I only fell about 10 feet past the top of the roof before slamming into the side of the building.

"Ooof."

Biff, having defeated the last of the shulkers, ran to the side of the building and looked over. He saw me there hanging on to the rope for dear life. "Hang on, Jimmy! I will pull you up."

When I had slammed into the side of the building, I bashed my head a little bit. I was feeling dizzy. I wasn't sure I could hold onto the rope much longer. I could feel Biff starting to pull me up. I felt as though I were floating. Drifting in the air. I hoped I wasn't actually falling to the ground. To my death. But then a hand grabbed one of my hands and pulled me over the edge of the wall back into the end city.

Emma was kneeling beside me and shaking my shoulders. "Jimmy! Jimmy? Are you okay?"

I rubbed my head with my right hand for a moment before I responded. I was starting to become more lucid. I said, "I think so. That was a close one."

"Yes it was," said Emma as she hugged me.

Biff tapped his foot impatiently while Emma hugged me and then after a few seconds said, "Shouldn't we be trying to get on the end ship. It seems like it's sailing away from the city."

I stood up and even though I felt dizzy, I willed myself to walk toward the edge of the end city where I could see the end ship sailing away. I looked at both of them. "I hope one of you brought ender pearls."

Day 44 – Continued

"What do you mean?" asked Biff.

I pointed at the ship sailing slowly away. "How else can we get out there? We have to teleport."

Emma was digging around in her inventory and managed to locate two ender pearls. She held them out so we could see them and said, "Just need one more."

Biff and I dug around in our inventories and Biff managed to find an ender pearl. I didn't have any. Stupid.

Emma handed me one of her ender pearls and said, "Make it count."

Biff held his ender pearl in his hand and said, "So, I need to throw it into the ship right? That's how I get out there?"

Emma nodded her head. "Yep. I'll go first." Emma stood close to the edge of the end city and was pulling her arm back, about to throw her ender pearl when she said, "I'll never make it that far. Let's build a little pier out there so we can get closer."

Emma placed blocks at the edge of the end city until she had made a pier about ten blocks long. The end ship continued to sail away very slowly, but she had gotten probably eight blocks closer. She stood on the end of the pier, pulled her arm back, and launched the ender pearl at the ship. We all saw it land inside the ship and then Emma disappeared. A second later, she was in the ship waving to us. "Your turn!" she called.

"I'll go next," said Biff. He walked to the end of the pier and aimed his ender pearl. I saw his lips moving like he was saying a quick prayer to Notch. Then he pulled his arm back and threw the ender pearl.

I watched as it arced into the sky and began falling. I looked back and forth between the ship and the pearl and came to a terrible conclusion: I didn't think it was going to make it. I watched as the ender pearl slowly came down from its apex and then hit the rail of the end ship. The pearl then bounced up in the air for a moment and then fell inside of the ship. Biff disappeared and materialized on the ship in the back of the ship.

Biff yelled at me, "Make the pier a little longer! I almost missed."

I agreed that was a good idea, so I added five blocks to the end of the pier. I stood there, looking down from such a great height at the ground. I felt a little woozy and then looked back at the end ship. Emma stood there, waiting for me. "Hurry up," said Emma. "We can't search the ship while you are still over there."

I put the Ender Pearl in my left hand and wiped the wetness from my right hand, the rain was still falling steadily. I transferred the ender pearl back into my right hand, cocked my arm behind my head, aimed, and threw it at the ship.

At that precise moment, a huge gust of wind came up. Before that, there had been no wind. Just a torrent of water falling straight down from a cloudless sky.

The ender pearl drifted away and then the next thing I knew, I was in midair. The Ender Pearl must have reached its full range and then teleported me into midair. I heard Emma and Biff scream in terror. I was falling towards the ground. If I hit from this height, I would surely die. I was filled with rage. I knew that wind was caused by my enemies, by the power of Entity 303 or Spike.

To die like this?

To be defeated like this?

After all I'd gone through, I wasn't going to allow it to happen. I was filled with such rage that my eyes turned red and then a deep purple. I looked up at the end ship falling away from me but it wasn't falling away from me I was falling away from it. I was only moments from impacting the ground. My vision turned the world a deep purple and my anger filled my soul. I was about to die.

And then, I hit the ground.

But ... it wasn't the ground. It was the deck of the ship! Somehow I had teleported and escaped death. Emma and Biff stood staring at me, completely amazed.

"Jimmy? Jimmy? Are you okay?" asked Biff.

I sat up and rubbed my head. "I think so. Did … did … hurrr … did I just teleport?"

"I think so," said Emma.

I looked at her in shock. "How could I have done that? I am not an enderman!" That's when I remembered. The world seemed purple right before I teleported. Like I was looking through purple eyeballs. Like I had momentarily **become** an enderman.

"There must be some other explanation," I said, not wanting to believe it.

"I don't know, Jimmy. You never had evoking powers until you were in the Nether yesterday. It was when you thought you were going to die that the powers came out. The same thing happened here. You should be dead. Yet, you managed to save yourself by teleporting."

I was dumbfounded. I felt the rain falling on my face. Normally rain felt cleansing. But not this rain. It felt evil. In fact, I was detecting massively bad vibes emanating from each individual raindrop.

I stood up and blinked the water out of my eyes a few times. "We'll figure it out later. Let's go find Claire."

Day 44 – Continued Yet Again

We quickly searched the deck of the ship, finding nothing except a shulker which we killed very quickly. The rain continued to fall.

I looked at Biff and Emma and said, "She must be trapped in the hold of the ship. Maybe in the treasure room."

Biff had a determined look on his face and said, "Let's go save my cousin."

We descended into the first level of the ship. As we entered the room at the bottom of the stairs, another shulker began his attack. We barely managed to dodge the bullets before killing it. There was a chest in the corner. It was unlocked. There was not much inside of it. We turned the corner into another room and found a brewing stand with some health potions. I took them and put into my inventory. At the rate I was going, I would need them.

"Well, she's not here. I guess we need to go down another level," said Emma.

"I will lead the way," said Biff.

We descended the stairs and entered the next level. We saw a large box made of obsidian. It was large enough that a person could have been inside. There was a strange tube leading up from the top of the box. Perhaps for air. I looked around the room but didn't see any obvious traps or lurking enemies.

"Claire! Claire! Are you in here?" asked Biff.

We heard mumbling coming from the end of the pipe leading out of the obsidian box. We could not make out the words, but it did sound like girl's voice. It must've been Claire!

Biff quickly pulled out a diamond pickaxe from his inventory and began mining the obsidian. As he did, I pulled my diamond pickaxe out of my inventory and was about to start mining too when I noticed another shulker in a corner of the room. Somehow we hadn't seen it when we had first entered.

I could've sworn I checked the whole room.

I put away my diamond pickaxe and pulled out my diamond sword, ready to do battle with the shulker. As its shell rose to allow it to shoot at me, I saw it was no normal shulker.

It was Spike!

Spike leapt out of the shulker shell and started hacking at me with his two-handed sword attack. I managed to block his first two strikes but then Spike hit me in the chest plate of my diamond armor. Fortunately, the armor softened the blow, but I took several hearts of damage.

Emma pulled out her bow and managed to shoot Spike in the back with an arrow. He reached back and viciously yanked the arrow from his body, laughing like an insane maniac.

Biff continued hacking at the obsidian box, hoping to free his cousin before Spike could stop him.

While Spike was distracted by the arrow in his back, I managed to land a blow with my sword to his arm. But his armor kept him from being too severely injured.

Spike continued to laugh and slashed at me again with both of his swords. This time I took a heavy but glancing blow to the head. I lost several more hearts of damage and felt dizzy. Emma managed to hit Spike with two arrows in the meanwhile. One in the leg; one in the arm. This forced Spike to drop one of his swords and back away for a moment. Emma landed two more arrows, one in his chest plate and one in the front of his leg.

Spike howled in anger. "You won't get Claire! We won't allow it!"

We?!? Was Entity 303 or Clayton near?

While Spike was telling us what we could and couldn't do, I managed to grab one of my health potions and drink it. My health restored, I stood up and reached into my inventory and pulled out a potion of slowness. I tossed it Spike and hit him. It had the desired effect.

I closed on him with my sword and began hacking at him. His lack of speed made him unable to defend against my blows. Emma put away her bow and arrow, and switched to a diamond sword. She was slashing at Spike's legs while I was slashing at his chest and head. We were doing severe damage to Spike. It was only a matter of time before we killed him.

But, as I was pulling my sword back for what I thought might be the final blow, Spike vanished. I looked up to the heavens and screamed, "No!"

A moment later I heard Biff say, "She's here! She's here!"

I ran over to the obsidian box and saw that Claire was indeed inside it, her arms and legs tied together. But not with rainbow colored rope, just normal rope.

I pulled out my diamond pickaxe and helped Biff finish picking enough of the obsidian so that we could get her out. This took a few more moments but we finally lifted her out she looked at us. "Biff? Jimmy?"

Biff hugged his cousin and said, "Yes, Claire. You're safe now."

Claire smiled. "Untie me. I've been tied up for so long." Biff reached down and untied her wrists and then kneeled and untied her feet. She flexed her hands and rotated her ankles a few times to get the blood flow back into her extremities.

She smiled. She looked over at Emma and exchanged a smile with her as well.

"Claire, did they do anything to you? Are you okay?" Emma asked.

Claire rubbed her head and said, "I don't know. I just remember being at the surf contest and then waking up inside this box. Entity 303 visited me once. He didn't say anything. He just looked at me for a while and then went away. Spike came every day and dropped off food for me. But that was it."

"It was very frightening to see you possessed at the surf contest. Your eyes turned red and you vanished with Spike into thin air," I said.

Claire nodded her head. She paused for a moment and glanced down at the floor. When she looked up, her eyes were a bright, bloody red. "Like this?"

It was at that terrible moment I realized I had forgotten to bring the potion of sanity!!! The Ender King still had it. And now, Spike had possessed Claire again. All this work, all this death, for nothing. Spike would have her again.

Biff fell to his knees and began to cry. "No! Claire, no!"

"You stupid boy," said Claire in a deep, menacing voice that was not her own. "You think you can defeat us? You think you can defeat Spike? You think you can defeat the legions of Entity 303?"

Wait. Legions?

I had only one chance. I could tell that Claire was, at that moment, possessed by Spike's spirit. I knew she was good inside. I had felt good vibes coming from her at the moment we saved her. She did not want to be a part of Spike's evil plan. She did not want Entity 303 to succeed. And besides, she was a priestess for the Rainbow Creeper. We needed her on our side.

As she was berating Biff, I managed to sneak up behind her and wrap the rainbow-colored rope around her waist.

Claire began to thrash and screamed in her own voice. "No! No!"

She kept thrashing but I held onto the rope as tightly as I could. "Emma, help me. Pull her down."

Claire's voice switched from her own to a more guttural voice. The voice of Spike. "No! You cannot do this. You are not permitted!"

Emma managed to force Claire to the ground while I tied the rainbow-colored rope around her wrists and then around her ankles. When she was secured, she thrashed a few more times before going limp and passing out.

We stood there in shock for more than a minute. Then, Claire's eyelids began to flutter and when she opened her eyes. They were back to normal. "What? What happened?"

Day 44 – 10 Minutes Later

After we explained to Claire what happened, she was distraught. "Will I ever escape the clutches of Spike? Can we ever be free of him or Entity 303?"

"You will be," I said with determination. "The head monk of the Rainbow Creeper gave me a potion of sanity. I forgot to bring it. Once I throw it on you, you will be free of Spike's control forever."

Claire looked at me startled. "You've met the head monk?"

"Yes, but she is kind of an annoying old woman, truth be told," I said.

Claire looked at me like I had just committed the worst crime in the history of Minecraft. "How dare you?!? She is a great leader."

I shrugged. "Well, she hasn't given us any bad advice yet, so that's something."

"How will you get the potion of sanity?" asked Claire.

"The Ender King has it. We just need to get you to him, or vice versa."

Claire nodded her head. "Leave me tied up until then. I don't want Spike to be able to possess me."

And, just like that, the rain stopped as suddenly as it had begun. I didn't know if it was temporary or permanent so I quickly pulled out a redstone communicator to summon the Ender King. After I pressed the button, the Ender King appeared within ten seconds. He had a sword drawn and was ready to fight. The ender general and several soldiers materialized an instant later. They looked around and saw that Claire was free and everything was fine.

The King immediately walked over to me and handed me the potion of sanity. "When I realized you had forgotten this, I feared the worst."

I took the potion. "Thank you."

I walked up to Claire and held the potion in front of her. "Sorry, but I have to throw this on you."

She nodded her head and closed her eyes. I threw the potion on her. For a moment nothing happened and then her eyes opened wide as if in a state of ultimate shock. She then screamed hysterically, like someone who discovered everything they've ever known and everything they've ever loved has been taken away from them in an instant. The screaming was horrific. I can only imagine what might have brought it on. Everyone on the deck of the ship stood back and watched Claire with fear on their faces.

After thirty seconds, it was all over. Claire had passed out again. I cautiously approached and untied the rainbow-colored ropes. Then we waited.

It took about five minutes for Claire to regain consciousness. She sat up with a start, obviously still in the throes of whatever had made her scream. She looked around furtively, like a trapped mouse. Then she put her face in her hands and cried. Emma walked over to her and knelt down next to her and put an arm around her. She didn't say anything.

Claire sobbed for about five minutes while we stood guard, hoping we would be left alone. Fearing Spike might still return.

When she finished sobbing, Claire stood up, wiped the tears from her face, and looked at us. "I have something terrible to tell you."

We didn't say anything. The King nodded his head indicating he was ready to hear it.

Claire took a deep breath and then said, "Entity 303 is ... hurrr ... is ... my father."

Day 44 – Mind Blown

As this short sentence came out of Claire's mouth, I think my head may have exploded. There was a ringing in my ears and everything went fuzzy. I may have passed out and stood back up. I may have floated into the air and come back down. I honestly have no idea.

When I regained my senses, I looked around. Everyone else appeared to be having similar feelings as I did. Two endermen kept teleporting a foot to the left or a foot to the right, back and forth like they were caught in some kind of weird loop. I saw Biff vomit over the railing of the ship. A shulker attached to the bottom of the ship shot a bullet at the vomit glob, and it levitated back up so we could all see how nasty it was, until the levitation effect finally wore off and the barf fell to the ground.

I looked at Claire and asked with a trembling voice, "What do you mean? How is that even possible? How can Entity 303 be your father? Anyone's father?"

Claire pulled her hair. "The potion of sanity. When you threw it on me, I understood the truth about all things for just a brief moment."

That's what the head monk had said. I remembered. I guess sometimes the truth is not what we want to know.

Claire continued, "I saw that Entity 303 had taken the form of a villager and moved into Capitol City. He met my mother and married her. It was all part of his plan.... Then three children spawned in their household. The first was Spike, the second Clayton, and lastly me. He revealed himself to Spike first, corrupting his mind and making him into an evil slave. Clayton came next. Spike did the dirty work there. I don't think Clayton knows Entity 303 is our father. And me...?" Her voice trailed off.

"And you?" I asked, not wanting to hear the answer, but knowing I had to.

I saw a tear fall from Claire's right eye. "And me? I was just a little sister. I didn't know anything about it. Until recently. You know the rest. My mom was a believer in the Rainbow Creeper. She took me to the meetings. To the worship services. Why would Entity

303 have chosen her? What is his plan? Does he want access to the Rainbow Creeper?"

The possibilities had my head spinning. I could not think about it right now. This was too much.

"I don't know the answers either, Claire," said the Ender King with a concerned voice. "But I know we need to get ready for anything. To *be* ready for anything. But before that, we need to get out of here. We need to get you back to the End."

The Ender King's words reminded me of something. "But the head monk," I began, "she said we would learn where Notch was when we freed Claire. Has anyone heard anything? Seen anything?"

Everyone shook his or her head in the negative.

I sighed. "The head monk has been right so far. I can't imagine she was wrong on this one," I said as I walked along the side of the ship, looking for any sort of clue. A note. Something scratched into the side of the ship. A chest we had missed.

Anything.

As I approached the bow of the ship, I thought I heard breathing. Slow, deep breathing, like something large nearby was breathing. I slowly walked toward the sound. I saw nothing that could have been so large that it could make a breathing sound like that ... but then ... I saw it. The head of a dragon on the prow of the ship!

I quickly built a cobblestone platform so I could get out to the dragon's head. Everyone looked at me like I was crazy.

"Be careful, Jimmy," said Emma.

I walked up to the dragon's head and saw that it was indeed breathing. I knelt down close to it and its eyes turned and looked at me. I looked back.

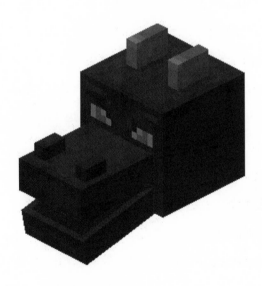

Oh my Notch! Now what?

"Hurrr, did you want to tell me something?" I asked, feeling scared and stupid all at the same time.

The dragon took a few more deep breaths and then opened its mouth and said, "You shall find Notch in the Update Aquatic in a monument of his own making." And with that, the dragon's mouth closed. His breathing stopped, and his eyes turned stony, staring straight ahead.

In a daze, I walked back into the bow of the ship. I told everyone what the dragon had said.

"But there hasn't been an Update Aquatic!" said Emma. "Notch did not finish it before he was kidnapped."

Or did he?

Biff looked at the Ender King and implored him, "Do you know what this means, Ender King? Could the Update Aquatic have been implemented already? Could it be out there somewhere that we just don't know about?"

The Ender King shook his head sadly. "I'm not aware of any changes to any of the dimensions of Minecraft. But then again, I didn't think it could rain in the End either."

I took a deep breath and said the King, "Let's get back to your Palace. We can speculate there. There has to be an answer. I'm sure we can figure it out." I paused for a moment. I had much less certainty in my mind than the words coming from my lips might have implied. "At least, I hope we can."

As the Ender King was preparing to teleport back to the main End island, Emma said breathlessly, "Hold on a second! We never got the elytra!"

How could I have forgotten about the mythical elytra? It's not like anything else had been happening....

I watched as Emma ran down into the ship's treasure room and then returned shortly thereafter with the magical pair of wings. She held them out and we all looked at them, amazed.

"Why don't you put them on and glide down to the ground?" I suggested.

Emma smiled, but shook her head. "I'm going to save these for a special occasion." She tucked the elytra into her inventory.

"Is everyone ready now?" asked the Ender King impatiently.

We were ready.

Some nodded their heads.

Others said, "Yes, Your Highness."

And so, we teleported back to the Ender King's Palace, to determine our next moves.

End of Book 10

A Note from Dr. Block

I hope you enjoyed this collection of books 6-10 of the *Diary of a Surfer Villager Series*. **Would you mind leaving a review** on your favorite online bookstore or review site to let me know what you thought? I would really appreciate it. And, after you leave a review, be sure to pick up a copy of *Surfer Villager 11* to find out what happens next!